Stealing Nasreen

Stealing Nasreen

a novel by

Farzana Doctor

Inanna Poetry & Fiction Series

INANNA Publications and Education Inc.
Toronto, Canada

Canada Council **Conseil des Arts**
for the Arts **du Canada**

The publisher gratefully acknowledges the support of the Canada Council for the Arts for its publishing program.

Library and Archives Canada Cataloguing in Publication

Doctor, Farzana
        Stealing nasreen : a novel / by Farzana Doctor

(Inanna poetry and fiction series)
ISBN 978-0-9782233-0-4

        I. Title. II. Series.

PS8607.O35S74 2007   C813'.6   C2007-902490-4

Cover design by Valerie Fullard
Interior design by Luciana Ricciutelli
Printed and bound in Canada

Inanna Publications and Education Inc.
210 Founders College, York University
4700 Keele Street
Toronto, Ontario, Canada M3J 1P3
Telephone: (416) 736-5356 Fax (416) 736-5765
Email: inanna@yorku.ca Website: www.yorku.ca/inanna

For Judith,
the first to call me "writer."

Chapter 1

SHAFFIQ SCRATCHES THE STUBBLE on his chin and pushes his cleaning cart sluggishly down the long hallway. It is just seven p.m., only the beginning of his shift. He rounds a corner, and then stops for a moment to retrieve a Walkman from his bag. He slips the earphones over his head and allows the *Greatest Hits of Bollywood II* to saturate the silence around him.

He listens for his favourite song, number two on Side A: *Dum Maro Dum*. Ah, here it is. He closes his eyes, imagining the black-haired, fair-skinned songstress trilling out her high-pitched longing. He sways to the tune, taking his cleaning cart as his dance partner. He opens his eyes and once again sees the bland institutional walls around him. He sighs.

He hates working the night shift. He is bitter that he is working in darkness and sleeping through the afternoon sun. He misses the world's regular rhythms. Right now, he should be sitting at home with his family, eating his *daal* and rice, watching *Who Wants To Be a Millionaire?* Somewhere deep in his heart he believes that this must be a sacrilege of some kind, a crime against nature, even.

He empties the garbage bin in the Vice President's office. Stuck to the bottom are the two halves of a woman's photograph. Shaffiq holds the pieces together, admiring the puzzle she makes. He decides that he likes her eyes and that she is a good-looking white woman. He pockets the torn photo and considers its possibilities. Why did the torn-up woman end up in the Vice-President's garbage? Is he cheating on his wife, that silver-haired lady in the framed portrait on his desk? Carrying on with his cleaning, he imagines love affairs as he scrubs toilets, conflicts and ruined lives while mopping floors, and heartbreaking betrayals when emptying garbage cans. This is the kind of drama he catches on *Maury* at three-thirty. He wonders, not for the first time, if his thinking has become more melodramatic since moving to Canada.

He has made a habit of studying the clues left behind by the daytime workers: the half-eaten lunches, candy bar wrappers, the stains on carpets. He notices if some maverick has snuck a smoke in the bathroom, discarding the butt in the sink, even though the signs clearly says "Smoking prohibited – penalty $2000." He looks at the beginnings of notes and memos that get crumpled up in mid-sentence. He uses all these clues to construct stories about the people who work here. His sleuthing helps pass the time and relieves the monotony of his work.

He'll bring the photo home and show it to Salma. She'll get a laugh out of it. Then he'll store it away in his top drawer along with the other bits of clues and curiosities he has picked up at work: a going-away card for Louise who retired (which unfortunately had very few well-wishes), a crumpled bowtie he found at the top of a recycling bin, and Mr. Sneider's discarded Atavan prescription. He doesn't like to throw these things away.

Upstairs, Nasreen says good-bye to her last client of the day. She stretches her arms over her head, arching her long back and then sits down heavily at her desk to write her notes. This task prolongs her workday by twenty minutes, but she prefers to complete her reports before going home rather than leaving them for the next day. She gathers together all her client files and arranges them alphabetically in a steel cabinet. She collects the stray pens and pencils on her desk and corrals them into their places, sliding open drawers and shutting them again efficiently. Her eyes linger a moment on a gold box on top of her desk, its lustre and fine details pleasing her. She moves it slightly, centering its position. Satisfied with the state of her desk, she switches off her computer and desk lamp. In the half-light of her office, the gold box shines, beckoning her. She reaches for it, opens the lid slightly and then snaps it shut again. She grabs her coat and bag and hastily steps out into the empty corridor.

Shaffiq stops his cart in front of the washrooms near the building's rear exit. He takes off his Walkman and selects his cleaning supplies. There are three different bottles of identical-looking aquamarine fluid that he must spray, pour, and wipe over everything. The solvents cause his stomach to rumble, his lunch and bile coming up for an instant, before being swallowed down again.

He hears footsteps coming down the corridor. Checking his watch, he sees that it is just past nine o'clock. Who is here this late? Usually, just as he arrives for his shift, the last bunch of daytime workers are rushing to the back doors, eager for the sane, cool air outside.

Except her. He has seen her many times since he started working here three months ago. She has always stood out to him. Not only because she works so late, but because she doesn't seem anxious to leave this place. And, of course he recognizes Home in this woman. She has those features so like the women in his family: the round-oval face with the strong, but not too large nose; the full lips; the dark almond eyes that will grow creases in their corners the more she laughs. She has long black hair that almost reaches her bottom, so much like his mother's. Indeed, she does remind him of his mother. Only, this girl is blessed with height; he estimates that she must be what, five-four, five-five?

Despite her familiarity, there is also something vaguely foreign about her. It is in the way she walks with that busy, hurried tightness in the hips. There is also that disinterested, closed look in her eyes. Shaffiq guesses that maybe she has lived here longer than he, and perhaps has become more Canadian too. He wonders if his daughters will become like this one day, possessing the faces of their elders but the expressions and strides of strangers.

Recently, he has tried to be friendly to her, to say hello, to look directly into her dark eyes the way people do in Canada. A few nights ago, while mopping near the back door, he said to her, "Hello, hello! How are you tonight?" At first he wondered if he was being too forward, if she took offence at the question. Her eyes darted between his face and the back door as though she were afraid of him. She answered him with, a curt "I'm fine thank you," her tone telling him that she was not scared, but irritated, and so he lowered his eyes to the grey linoleum and continued his cleaning.

Tonight, he decides to try again. As he bends down to empty a garbage can, he sees her polished black boots approaching, her presence filling the long hallway. Straightening slightly, he looks over his shoulder and beams at her with a broad gap-toothed grin.

"Hello, hello! How are you? What is your name? I see you often here." She continues walking but slows her pace a little. She settles her gaze on him for just a moment.

"Nas. Actually, it's really Nasreen." She picks up her pace and is out the doors before he can tell her that his name is Shaffiq. Before he can tell her that he comes from India and has been here for over two years. That he got this job in July, almost three months ago, after looking for so long. That he isn't really a janitor. He doesn't know why, but he wants to tell her all this and more. Like how he looked for work everyday until he felt a kind of helplessness and humiliation he has never felt before. Like how useless he felt while his wife and children left every morning and returned each afternoon to him sitting on the couch. He doesn't say any of this. A gust of cold air let in by her departure chills him. After a moment, he shrugs off Nasreen's bad manners and finishes the bathroom. So now he knows her name, at least. He chooses to see this as progress.

Nasreen pulls her long coat around her, shivering in the cold, the janitor's sweet smell of patchouli still lingering in her nostrils. She likes the scent and wonders for a moment if it is his cologne, but then registers the smell as incense. He must burn a lot of it at home, she thinks. She sniffs the cuff of her own coat and smells damp wool.

The streetcar lumbers up to her stop and she races across the street, dodging a man on a bicycle. She boards the streetcar and heads toward the back where there are a few empty seats. She feels the fabric of the seat before sitting down (you never know who has emptied their bladder at the back of a streetcar) and then settles herself behind a man on a cell phone, talking too loudly to someone.

"Well, we just passed Beverley, no, now we are at Huron," the man says. "Do you want me to meet you at Bathurst, or should I walk the three blocks over?" Nasreen bristles and moves to another seat further back to get away from the cell phone tour guide.

Now, in a quieter seat, she reviews her day, trying to remember the stream of clients she saw. How many? She lists them off in her mind. First there was the women's anxiety group, or WAG for short. Then there was Josie, Angela, Miranda, and Cora, back to back in the late afternoon. That's six hours of counseling, she calculates, pressing her throbbing temples.

It was Miranda who really wore out Nasreen today. At least she was cooperative, and Nasreen appreciates that in a client, especially when she is tired. And she has felt tired for a long time now. Overtired. Maybe burned out, even. I have to start going back to the gym, she thinks. Get myself in shape.

At Palmerston, the streetcar jerks to an abrupt stop, interrupting Nasreen's thoughts. She sits up in her seat, and along with the other passengers, cranes her neck left and right to see the source of the trip's disruption. A middle-aged man staggers across the street slowly, wearing only a pair of boxers and a red Santa hat. He's yelling something, his muscled arms raised in some kind of victorious salute to himself. A woman in an SUV pulls up beside the streetcar and begins honking at the man. The other streetcar passengers, who at first were quiet, perhaps unsure how to assess the situation, begin chuckling and talking amongst themselves about the seemingly crazy or intoxicated man blocking the road.

The woman in the seat ahead of her has opened the window wide, leaning her head out to get a better look at the spectacle. Nasreen pulls her wool coat around her against the chill of the autumn evening. She wants to admonish the passengers-turned-audience, wants to tell them to keep quiet, to shut their windows. She has seen this scantily-clad Santa near the entrance of the hospital before and she feels protective of him, wishes she could stop his humiliating performance.

Eventually, the man stumbles across the road and clears the way. The streetcar lumbers forward, and Nasreen turns in her seat to see the man talking animatedly to pedestrians on the sidewalk. Each gives him a wide berth as they pass by him.

She turns back around in her seat, and rubs her neck. There is a familiar strain there, an ache that travels from her jawbone to her shoulder. As she massages the tension there, her mind shifts back to Miranda.

"When I was a kid, my father and I would practically do acrobatics to drag my mother out of bed. That went on for years until she finally got diagnosed with depression," Miranda told her, taking in a deep breath, her pink cheeks filling with air. "After being medicated, she started to feel better and began to take part in family stuff again. We were all really relieved about that. Then two years ago, a day before my birthday, she went out and stepped in front of a casino tour bus," Miranda explained, with little emotion.

Nasreen sometimes marvels at the ease with which some of her clients are able to reveal shameful secrets, intimate details, and harrowing stories. Nasreen nodded at Miranda and tried to look empathetic, the two Therapist Skills she relies on most when she can't think of anything to say. She wondered how she would bring Miranda back to the task at hand. She still had the rest of the intake forms to fill out.

A group of East Asian girls gets on the streetcar, giggling loudly and

Nasreen watches them settle into nearby seats. They wear the funky orange tones and shiny synthetics that Nasreen recognizes as teeny-bopper club wear. She feels boxed in by their warm cheery bodies. She shifts her hips and tote bag to make more room for herself and the girl beside her interprets this to be as an invitation to take even more space. Nasreen studies the girl's amber plastic skirt and then looks out the window, steering her mind back to Miranda.

"I guess I started drinking when I was fifteen or sixteen. I began nipping into the basement bar. Nothing serious. Anyway, I didn't start to drink heavily until two years ago, after she killed herself."

"I see," Nasreen said, knowing that this response was not quite adequate.

After Miranda left, Nasreen locked her office door and struggled to pull open the bottom drawer of her steel filing cabinet. The old, stiff drawer resisted and so she crouched down, putting all her weight into the effort. Finally it jerked open, hurling her backwards onto her ass. Undeterred, she steadied herself on her haunches and searched through some loose papers and books. Underneath she found the three chocolate bars she had hidden there. She hesitated for a moment, giving cursory attention to resisting them. Then she grabbed them all, kicked the drawer shut and mindlessly ingested them while contemplating the case note for Miranda's visit.

"How do I summarize the pain of a whole life and a mother's suicide?" She wondered.

"What?" The teenager in plastic asks her. Nasreen orients herself back to the present, on the streetcar, among the girls. Did she say that out loud? Nasreen looks at the girl's black-lined eyes. Embarrassed, she pulls herself up, sees that they have reached Dovercourt. She pushes past the girl and moves toward the back door. It's OK, she tells herself, my stop is just two blocks away. I could use the exercise anyway. She rings the bell and steps off onto the cracked sidewalk, plodding briskly across College and then down Donald Street to her apartment. As she climbs the steps to the door, she hears the recognizable mewing of Id, who waits noisily for her dinner. Damn, Nasreen thinks, I forgot to fill his bowl this morning.

Having cleaned half his floors, Shaffiq pushes his cart to a patient waiting area. He walks around the chairs and table, stooping to collect countless coffee cups from tables and overflowing garbage receptacles.

He has never seen so many of them in his life. But then, it was never his job to hunt, gather, and then throw them out before. He finds the white cups everywhere, in lounges, in staff rooms, in waiting areas, in offices. He hates the smell of coffee, being a man true to his heritage, a tea drinker. Even in India the coffee is not this bitter, acrid liquid. Rather, there is cafelatte, thick and creamy and sweet. In the waiting room he stacks the magazines and wipes down the tables. He looks around to inspect the room, and decides that the vacuuming can wait another day. According to his supervisor, he is supposed to vacuum daily in the high traffic areas, but who can tell the difference? He wheels his cart toward the offices.

Sometimes, while cleaning offices, he glances over desks, reading scrawled case-notes about depression, or anxiety, or family problems. He knows that these notes are confidential and that he shouldn't be reading them, but he can't help himself. He has even opened patient files left on desks, caressing their cardboard covers before reading their mysteries inside. Sometimes the entries are rather dull: "John came to the appointment suitably attired. He states his mood was low all month, and shoplifted once this week." Sometimes the notes are stranger and more interesting to him: "Allison says that she hears voices while traveling on the TTC. She reports feeling afraid to travel by subway, but not by bus." He wonders about these Canadian people and why they seem to have so many problems. Such complicated problems. He has never heard of these things back home. Yes, of course some of the men in his family sometimes drank a little, and once in a while he heard about people's marital problems. But hearing voices? Fears of transit? Depression? What do these white people have to feel depressed about anyway? After all, he and his family have been through so much and they are not going around depressed and drinking and shoplifting.

He wonders what a counsellor would write about him. "Shaffiq is a nosy man who hates his job, and came to the interview dressed in janitor's clothes." Or, "Shaffiq has a florid imagination and thinks jealous thoughts about people who work from nine to five." He laughs out loud at his own joke.

He lets himself into one of the offices, scans the room and empties a garbage can containing a half-eaten (tuna?) sandwich, a coffee cup (no big surprise) and some plastic wrap. Nothing so interesting. Looking around, he sees that the plants are dry and wilted. On the desk is a muddle of paper, pens, and folders. Back home, he had a little cubicle, which he kept scrupulously tidy and organized. If he had had the privilege of such a nice, big office, surely it would have been better kept than this. He turns off the light, shuts the door, and pushes his cart further down the hallway.

Nasreen doesn't go to bed until after *Springer*. She likes the late night, loves to stay up into the darkness, and although the TV is raging about lesbians who have cheated on their boyfriends and girlfriends, she considers this her quiet time. When the phone rings, she thinks she might ignore it, but then senses that something could be wrong. She mutes the TV and answers it after the fourth ring.

"Hello?"

"Nasreen, Oh good, it's your father. You're home."

"What's up, Dad? You're usually in bed by now."

"Yes, but I just had to tell you my news. I called earlier and left you a message. Didn't you get it?"

"I forgot to check my messages today," Nasreen lies. She listened to all her messages earlier, but skipped over his.

"Well, today I won a trip for two to any destination of my choice! Can you believe it? Anywhere in the world! It was from a contest I entered online!" Nasreen's father retired last year and has started using words like "online." Before his retirement, he barely knew how to use a typewriter. Now with the whole day for leisure, his favourite pastime has become entering contests and trying to get "free stuff" on the "net."

"Oh, that's great Dad. Where are you gonna go?"

"Well of course I'm going Home. You know we haven't visited since a few years before your mom died. I want to see everyone again. Why don't you come with me?"

"Really? A trip to India? Well, I uh…," she stammers. This she wasn't expecting.

"Everyone will want to see you too. We'll have a great time," he says enthusiastically.

"Gee Dad, but –"

"And we don't get to spend much time together these days. You haven't come to visit me for awhile. This would be a nice time for us to be together too."

"Oh I don't know. When were you going to go? I don't know if I can take time off work," Nasreen says, tiredly.

"But it is a free trip! Surely you can plan to take time off. You work so hard. You really should take some time off. Don't you want to go to India?" he asks, in a tone that sounds like a plea to her.

"Let me think about it. Why don't I call you tomorrow after I've checked out my vacation time?"

"Fine, fine. Think about it then. I hope you come with me. Who else could I ask otherwise? You know, since you mother died, I haven't taken any vacations because I didn't want to go alone." Nasreen feels a familiar pain in her sternum that her therapist aptly labelled Daughter Guilt.

"Well, thanks for asking me, Dad. I'll call you tomorrow, OK?"

"Goodnight, then. Sleep well, Nasreen."

"Goodnight." She hears his sigh just before she hangs up the phone.

She stares at the silent TV, wondering what she should do. Two women who don't look like lesbians to her are swinging at each other while three beefy bouncers try to separate them. The audience goes wild.

She considers her father's proposal. After all, she has been thinking about taking a vacation, just not with her father, and not India. The last family trip was not much fun for her. She was treated like a twelve-year-old by her relatives who seemed to want to feed her all the time. She got sick a lot. She couldn't understand anything anyone said to her and then felt embarrassed when her cousins laughed at her for not knowing Gujarati. There were endless visits to family she didn't know and more eating to do. She felt bullied by the persistent questions: "What are you up to now?" "When are you getting married?" "Are you looking for a boy in India?" Often she felt like she was being scoped out as someone's nephew's potential bride.

Nasreen turns off the TV and heads to bed. She rolls herself into the down quilt and dark blue sheets her friends bought for her last year on her thirtieth birthday. Id joins her, curling up on the pillow next to her, the side that has been vacant since the break-up. Before long, Nasreen is asleep and dreaming about swimming in the Indian Ocean with her mother and father. She is wearing an orange *salwar kameez*, the thin *dupatta* floating up around her body. The sun is warm on her face. Her mother does the butterfly stroke, splashing away from her while her father treads water nearby. She feels light and calm. She floats over to some steep wooden steps and climbs them. As she emerges from the water she realizes she is now naked and that big, ugly, brown bugs are stuck like leeches to her skin. She tries frantically to pull them off her arms, legs, and stomach. She shouts for help, but her mother has drifted out with the tide and her father is nowhere to be seen.

At four-thirty-five in the morning, Shaffiq boards the twenty-four hour bus that will deliver him to his home, his bed, his sleeping family. Shaffiq counts his blessings that he only has to walk twenty minutes to get to Ossington where an all-night bus passes every fifteen minutes. He feels bad for his co-worker Ravi who has to spend an hour in a coffee shop waiting for the subway to start running each morning.

There is only one other passenger on the bus, a young disheveled man who sleeps uncomfortably, his head bumping against the cold window whenever the driver presses on the accelerator. Shaffiq passes him, smelling the alcohol reeking from the man's pores. He mutters a judgmental *"chaa"* under his breath, guessing that the man is probably on his way home after too much boozing. But then Shaffiq has a moment of sympathy for the man and begins to worry that maybe he will miss his stop, or that he has already slept well past his destination and will awake on the wrong side of town. Shaffiq looks around and notices that they are almost at St. Clair. He has just eight more stops to go and he knows this because counting stops is the only way that he has managed to stay awake on these pre-dawn rides. Should he wake the man? But what if he hasn't missed his stop and Shaffiq has interfered unnecessarily?

A block away from his apartment building, Shaffiq rings the bell and the young man stirs. Cautiously, Shaffiq averts his gaze. Men don't like to be stared at in their sleep. He finds his way to the back door and down the steps of the bus.

His building's dimly lit lobby is deserted at this hour. He checks the mailbox, hoping for a blue air mail envelope from his ma, but the box is empty and he remembers that Salma already picked up the mail yesterday. He sometimes forgets the many small tasks of the day that pass him by while he sleeps. He taps the elevator "up" button and watches it slowly descend from the eighteenth floor, the indicator lights blinking teasingly at him. He resists an urge to yell "Why is this elevator always stuck at the top floor at five-o-five every morning?" Finally, the doors open and the old elevator carries him upwards, wheezing with the effort. At the fifth floor he steps out, turns right and walks what feels like an eternity to his door. He digs into his pocket for his keys and soundlessly turns the lock. He leaves his coat, shoes, and bag in the small foyer and tiptoes through the quiet apartment to his bedroom. In the dark he slips off his clothes and slithers gently into bed. Despite his slow and careful movements, Salma turns over and says,

"Hello, Shaffiq."

"Go back to sleep, Salma dear."

"Wait," she says groggily, her voice thick with sleep, "first tell me what strange thing you picked up and brought home today." Then, turning onto her stomach, she resumes her snoring. He strokes her head gently, willing her back to the depths of her dreaming. He scans her round, relaxed body tangled in the sheets. There is a quickening in his groin, a memory of warm pleasures.

Chapter 2

BEING A WOMAN ON the verge of burn-out, Nasreen loves Fridays. But it's not because she enjoys the weekend so much. In fact, she finds the prospect of two days at home in her empty apartment depressing. The real reason Fridays are special to a burn-out case is because there is a one-in-three chance that clients will cancel their appointments. This free time at the end of the week has given Nasreen and her colleagues the opportunity to calculate the odds and sometimes they gather in the hallways as they wait for no-shows and make nickel wagers, betting on whether their two-thirties or three-forty-fives will turn up. They've developed conjectures and hypotheses for the phenomenon. Nasreen thinks that the high truancy rate is due to the fact that Fridays are too close to the weekend for the extra burden that therapy demands. Her co-worker, Michael, agrees with her and thinks that all therapists should have Fridays off.

Nasreen, however, doesn't mind seeing her own therapist on a Friday afternoon. In fact, Fridays are when she feels most able to let go of other people's problems and focus on her own life for a change. Not that she has been to therapy for awhile. She checks her calendar and estimates that she has not seen her therapist in over a month. She canceled her last two appointments because she just didn't feel like going.

As expected, two of Nasreen's clients have canceled today. Rather than step out into the hallway to talk with her coworkers, she uses the time to make phone calls. First she dials her supervisor, Wendy Noseworthy, also known as Nosywendy, a woman who gave up her two-decade-long career doing psychotherapy to become an administrator. Nasreen and her colleagues believe that Nosywendy likes to practice her now rusty therapy skills on all the fourth floor therapists during their supervision meetings and has taken a particularly keen interest in Nasreen since her mother died. She has a way of stopping Nasreen in the hallway and enquiring, "So, how are you *doing*?" the last word always tinged with a kind of desperate longing to be involved in someone else's emotional life. Nasreen dodges her most days, wanting to avoid any impromptu hallway psychoanalysis.

But today, Nasreen needs her supervisor to authorize a month-long vacation. She's decided to go to India with her father as long as she can negotiate two weeks of beach time and tourism for herself. She made the decision that morning when she woke up with a splitting headache. As she attempted to extinguish it with an extra-strength painkiller and a cup of coffee, she visualized herself on a beach in Goa and knew that she should take her father up on his offer.

She picks up the phone and asks Nosywendy for the time off. Nasreen cites the importance of returning to her long-lost homeland. She adds to her case her recent break-up and the situation of her poor, lonely, widowed father, who really needs her company. In short, she uses all her persuasive powers and Nosywendy readily agrees, as Nasreen predicted. "Go take good care of yourself, I know this has been a difficult time for you. And your father," she adds. "How have you been doing lately? You've had so much loss lately. I'm so sorry about your break-up with Connie. Grief is not an easy thing Nas," Nosywendy says, with an empathetic sigh. Nasreen feels somewhat charitable towards her supervisor right then, so she offers her just a little more fodder, telling her about how she just completed the Anger Stage in her grieving process. Then, she excuses herself, fibbing about a client who has just arrived.

Her next phone call is to her father.

"Dad, I can go on that trip. I just spoke with my boss," she says, glad to be delivering him some good news.

"Nasreen you won't regret this, thank you, thank you! We are going to have a great time!" Nasreen thinks she hears relief in his giddy laughter. They set the date for December third. In just over two months. They will stay four weeks.

Later that day, Nasreen meets with two non-truant clients. Abby has just moved in with her boyfriend and has been having panic attacks all week. Joyce is a long-time client who thinks it is time to quit therapy. Nasreen catches her mind wandering to India during both sessions. She imagines herself on a Goan beach, the sun soaking deeply into her pores, feels herself breathing in the scent of salt water and suntan lotion. She wonders if she should buy a new bathing suit, if she's gained too much weight for the one she owns.

At four o'clock, she writes her note about Joyce, and then checks her day planner. She sees that she is clear for the rest of the afternoon and phones Asha, who picks up on the first ring.

"House of Lust and Fallen Women, Proprietress Asha speaking."

"Hi Ash. Aren't you ever afraid that it might be your mother calling?"

"Oh my god. It can't be Nas. The long-lost stranger is back! No, my mother only ever calls after six or on weekends to traumatize me. She's the frugal type. How are you doing?"

"I'm OK. Sorry for not calling for a while. I've sort of been hibernating. I guess I've been busy too."

"Have you heard from Connie lately?"

"No," Nasreen says, forcing herself to inhale and then exhale before answering her friend's query. "I asked her to stop calling me two weeks ago. It's too hard talking to her." She fiddles with the gold box on her desk and opens it clumsily with her free hand.

"I was wondering when you were going to place a moratorium on her. I'm so glad you're no longer speaking to her. I think this whole thing about lesbians always trying to be best friends with their exes is really messy."

"I don't even know if we'll end up being acquaintances, let alone best friends." She rifles through the stack of photos in the box and pulls out the one she has been looking for.

"Maybe that's for the best. Good for you for telling her not to call."

"Yeah, I think it was a smart thing. I no longer cringe when I hear the phone ringing. She's been good – she hasn't called me since I told her not to. That's one good thing you could say about her, I guess. When she's gone, she's really gone." She studies the photo of herself and Connie, taken on a vacation to New York City.

"Did I ever tell you that she was no good for you?"

"A few times." She scrutinizes herself in the photo. I looked thinner then, she thinks.

"I guess I'm not the subtle type –"

"No, not exactly. And I should have listened to you ages ago. But, hey, I didn't call you to talk about old news." She replaces the photo in the box and slams it shut. "Here's something more interesting. I may be crazy, but I agreed to go to India with my Dad. He won a free trip for two."

"Wow, really? I wish I was going somewhere for free. And you know I wish –"

"That you had my father. Yeah I know."

"I'll trade you mine any day. How'd he win the tickets?"

"He entered a contest on some Internet site."

"For real? That's amazing. And he's taking you?"

"Who else would he take?"

"He could take me if he wanted."

"I should suggest that to him, get myself off the hook. But really, he's been rather antisocial lately. Most of the time, it's just him and his computer in that big house. And, of course, he calls me all the time."

"You don't sound very happy to be going."

"Well, he's been so, I don't know, needy the last while. I hope I have a good time with him. I think I really need a holiday. I mean a real one. Not one taking care of my father."

"Poor Bashir Uncle. I guess he must be lonely. But I'm sure the two of you will have a good time. It'll be a good distraction for you both. I love going to India. Think about all the great shopping and food and…"

"And meddling Aunties and pollution and poverty. And I don't speak Gujarati, like you."

"You're sounding quite the Indophobe. Hey, but you know I'm just learning to speak Gujarati. Did I tell you about my class? Why don't you come with me? Mrs. Paperwala, the teacher, is werry charming, and such a lawelly cook too," Asha falls into a bad Indian accent, "Really, she's great. Just twenty bucks for a two-hour class and she never lets me leave without a fresh *parantha*."

"Gujarati classes? I don't know, Asha –"

"Come on, it will be fun. I never see you any more. We can practice together."

"Well, it would help if I could communicate better…"

"Great. Maybe she'll give us a discount if there are two of us. Geez, I sound like my mother. *Chalo*, Mrs. Paperwala, I'm bringing you extra student. Give us good price, *yaar*. I'll pick you up next Monday at your work? I have to go. I'll be late for my Rhetoric and Meaning class. Bye."

"OK. Bye."

Nasreen hangs up, feeling a bit stunned. She wonders how she is so easily talked into things, so effortlessly swayed to join in with another's agenda; first her father's trip to India and now Asha's Gujarati classes. But Nasreen also feels a sense of excitement and energy, a rush of possibilities that has been absent for some time. How long? She rests her face in her hands, her elbows leaning against her desk. She picks up her pen and writes in her day-planner: *Asha, 6:00 p.m., Monday*. Who knows, maybe she will become fluent in Gujarati. Maybe the trip to India will be fun. Maybe her father will get so cheered up he'll stop leaning on her so much. Maybe she'll meet a nice woman there and live happily ever after. She catches herself laughing out loud.

She is on a roll and so she dials Mona's number. After four rings, the machine picks up and the recording begins with Mona's deadpan voice delivering a joke. These ones are new. "What's the only good kind of Tory? A suppository!" "Have you heard the one about the Liberal Member of Parliament with a big heart? Yeah he bought it last week with your tax dollars!" There is a beep and Nasreen says, "Hi Mona, it's Nas, sorry it's taken me so long to return your call –" There is an electronic squeal as the receiver is picked up. "Hello? Nas, is that you?"

"Yeah, I'm finally calling people back. What are you doing home?"

"I took today off to use up some of my overtime. Our big funding proposal was due yesterday. I sent it in just under the wire." Mona is known for being one of the best fundraisers in the nonprofit sector. "All I've been doing lately is working. Like you, I've heard."

"I suppose I have been working late to avoid my empty apartment. Well, I shouldn't say empty. There is Id, my steadfast and loyal feline companion."

"The best kind there is, eh?" she laughs. "But you should have called me. I would have been there in a flash."

"You know how I am. Sometimes I need to be alone to work things out."

"Yeah, I do know. You don't take your own advice. Don't you always tell everyone to talk about their feelings? You're like a gardener who lets her own yard get weedy. Are you still seeing your therapist, at least?"

"Well, sort of. I had to cancel the last couple of times."

"Uh huh. Well, I'm glad that you're finally emerging from your isolation tank. Let's go out and celebrate that." Mona suggests dinner and then clubbing. Nasreen hesitates but agrees before she has a chance to turn down Mona's invitation. Perhaps it will be good to get out, she thinks. It's as though something unclasps in her mind, allowing fresh air to whoosh through its inner chambers. She packs up her things and decides to leave work a few minutes early.

The phone rings at two p.m., shaking Shaffiq from his deep sleep. Still horizontal, he reaches for the phone and looks at the red numbers on his digital clock, trying to make sense of them. He hears the enthusiastic voice of his Housekeeping supervisor, James.

"Hey how are you Shaffiq? I hope I'm not calling at a bad time. I'm looking for someone to go in a few hours early to cover for Ravi. He's sick. Think you can make it in for five?" Shaffiq wants to say no, wants to return to his slumber, but realizes it is probably too late for that.

"Yeah, okay. I will be getting overtime, right?" He considers The Girls' University Fund that he and Salma started two weeks ago and calculates that the extra pay will allow for a nice deposit into it. So far the balance is a meager forty dollars, a small sum for sure, but at least it is a start, isn't it? They celebrated their ability to start the fund by taking the children to Gerrard Street. They had *bhel puris* and *chaana bhatura* and later he had an extra big *paan* that he chewed for almost an hour. He estimates that if they continue to save at this rate, they may be able to help each child through their first year of university. Maybe two years if things go well.

By four-forty-five he is ready to start his five o'clock shift. Tonight he will be cleaning his usual areas as well as covering Ravi's two floors. He wheels the cleaning cart to the elevator, passing employees leaving for the weekend, their shift ending as his begins. He presses the elevator button and waits. As the doors open a group of teenagers unload, laughing and shoving each other out of the elevator. Shaffiq thinks it is curious that all their pants are so big that they drag across the floor, bagging at their rear ends, making the boys walk with an exaggerated swagger. Maybe that's the point, Shaffiq muses. The last of them vacate the elevator, and then she steps out. Nasreen.

"Nasreen, hello! How are you?"

"Just fine, thanks." She maneuvers herself gracefully around and past his cart.

"You are from India, no?" He is breathless, searching his head for any words, any topic to make conversation, to keep her there even for a moment.

"Yes." She starts down the corridor, but then hesitates, slowing her steps. She looks over her shoulder at him. "Well, I was born here. But my

parents are from Bombay, um, well, I guess it is called Mumbai, now."
She smiles, her white teeth flashing bright between cherry-red lips. Then
she quickens her pace and is gone.

As he gets on the elevator, he sees that every floor button is lit up, the
result of the swaggering-loose-pant-fitting-youth prank. Hooligans. No
respect. But his mind is busy with something else. From which floor did
she get off? Bombay. Her parents are from Bombay. Of course she was
born here. No wonder she is so western looking. But today she seemed
a little friendlier, letting out a few words before the rush-rush away.

After stopping at the second and the third floors, he finally reaches
the fourth. He pushes his cart down the hallway to the first bathroom,
opens the door and begins the ritual of spray, wipe, spray, flush, spray,
scrub. By seven p.m., Shaffiq is finished with the washrooms and heads
toward the offices to begin vacuuming. He reads the name plate on the
door of the first office he gets to, "Randolph Volitis." Shaffiq likes to say
names out loud, and guess their origins. This game is more difficult here
in Canada compared to in India, where he was quite adept at hearing a
person's name and then placing their religion, state, language. He could
accurately guess if a person was Muslim, maybe even identify whether
they were Sunni or Shia.

Of course, religion caused problems for him. No pay raises, no promo-
tions for the minority man in India. But those subtleties don't seem to
matter here, Shaffiq thinks. Here they mix us up, think we all look the
same. A few times his supervisor has called him Ravi and then apologized
profusely for the mistake.

Whatever Randolph's origins, he certainly is a tidy sort. Randolph
Volitis, Shaffiq says, sounding out the strange name, still unable to guess
the man's ethnicity. He finds nothing out of place, no client files open on
the desk to peruse, nothing of interest even in the garbage bin. He pulls
the vacuum out of the office, turns off the lights and moves down the
hallway to a room with nine blue chairs in an almost perfect circle. On
his training day, his supervisor called this room a group therapy room
and Shaffiq guesses that this is where classes of some sort take place. He
doesn't like vacuuming here; there is too much furniture to move and
the mounted cameras and blinking red lights on the ceiling microphones
make him nervous. Shaffiq ensures he never does anything unusual when
cleaning these rooms and he doesn't make eye contact with the cameras
either. He empties the garbage can and is meticulous about cleaning in
the corners just in case he is being spied on.

Shaffiq checks his watch and decides that it is time for a break. He stops in a waiting area, pulls out his plastic thermos and pours a cup of hot *chai*. He inhales the fragrant steam escaping the thermos. Salma packed him some snacks, but he will save those for later. Yesterday, she told him that *chai* is sold in the coffee shops for $3.75 a cup.

"No, it's not true!" He laughed. He couldn't believe it.

"Shaffiq, I think they find Indian things exotic. Imagine, paying so much for a cup of tea!"

"Maybe we should go into business! We could make a killing selling ordinary Indian things and marketing them as exotic."

"Perhaps we could sell small bags of salt and call it Gandhi Holy Salt. What do you think, Shaffiq?"

"Or maybe tiny bottles of vegetable oil. We could stick on labels that say Karmic Elixir!"

He takes out the Walkman and sits back to rest. Sipping the warm liquid, he surveys the waiting area and the long hallway ahead of him. Except for the fact that this floor is two above his usual areas, it seems indistinguishable from those below. The walls are painted the identical listless grey and the floors are all of the same used-up yellow. Even the smells match up: cleaning solvents and coffee. He checks his watch and sees that he is still entitled to nine more minutes of his break. He stands up, stretches and scans the magazines piled messily on the tables. He picks up a thick glossy one with a picture of a laughing blonde woman on the cover and reads through the headlines: *Winter Fashion Guide, How to Look Hot in the Cold; Easy Holiday Entertaining Ideas; Arranged Marriages, One Woman's Agony.* He flips the magazine open to the last story and reads about an Indian woman who was forced to marry a man she did not love. She soon became suicidal and eventually tried to slit her wrists. Shaffiq closes the magazine. He doesn't want to read anymore and his break is almost over anyway.

Shaffiq and Salma came from opposite sides of Bombay. They had never met before their first formal meeting, but they belonged to the same religious community. Later, their mothers realized that they had been classmates years before at the St. Theresa Convent Girls School. Shaffiq and Salma were not an obvious match, but his mother was no longer being picky. By this point, Shaffiq was thirty-one and had been introduced to twelve prospective brides already. He had come to think of these arranged meetings as embarrassing and unsuccessful shopping escapades; he would start out full of hope but always went home empty-handed and unsatisfied. His mother chided him for being too fussy and difficult and he knew that he would eventually have to choose one of the women, marry her, and have children. But he just knew that not one of the twelve potentials was the one for him. How did he know? He had never before been in love, never had a previous relationship. He had kissed only two girls before, and one of those had been his own cousin-sister. But as he made awkward conversation with each of the twelve nervous women while their chaperones looked on, he had a strong sense that each of them was not to be his Mrs. Paperwala.

Salma was the thirteenth to be presented to him in her family's sitting room. Shaffiq's mother wondered if the girl was too old already and besides that, she had heard distressing gossip about Salma's mental instability and independent streak. But she was desperate and more than willing to overlook these rumours to give the girl a try. At least she was pretty and came from a good family, unlike a few of the ugly-puglies she had previously introduced to his son.

The adult children sat stiffly across from one other, a plate of *pakoras* the neutral territory between them.

"Salma has just made these fresh," said her mother, doing her best to be positive, "taste them. Already she is so good at cookery." Salma smirked at her mother's lie. It was true that she was a good cook, but her mother had fried the snacks herself that morning.

He dutifully took one and responded, "Oh yes, very nice. And such good chutney too." Her mother smiled approvingly at him. He remembers that Salma wore a yellow *shalwaar kameez* and a hard, almost stubborn expression. Beneath this, he thought he saw sadness in her long-lashed eyes. He liked the way her hair hung unconventionally loose around her shoulders, like a thin woolen shawl, making her look simultaneously tartish and chaste.

The pair made strained conversation about the recent rainy season and then their mothers left the room sharing matching looks of hopelessness for their unbetrothed children. Despite his discomfort, something about Salma interested Shaffiq. After they were left alone, he leaned in closer.

"So how many times have you done this? Me, myself, this is the thirteenth time! I sat down yesterday and counted them up. Twelve meetings like this before today! Can you believe it? My poor ma is getting fed up." Salma looked up at him, blinking hard. She frowned, and then began counting under her breath and on her fingers.

"What's wrong, did I say something wrong? I guess I'm not exactly doing a good job of selling myself as an eligible –"

"Shhh. Hold on a second." Shaffiq watched her as she continued to count. "Sorry, how many?"

"Pardon me?" Shaffiq was growing increasingly unconfident with this girl. Unsure of what to say, he instead stuffed a *pakora* in his mouth.

"How many times did you say you've done this? How many girls have you met?" She was now perched at the edge of her seat, her face just a few, indecorous inches away from his.

"Twelve," he responded obediently, surprised at the urgency in her voice.

"Bloody hell," she whispered, "me too." She sat back in her seat and they both looked down at the *pakoras* and contemplated the coincidence.

Then, she started to talk. She told him that she was a Standard Five teacher and loved her work and independence. She admitted to Shaffiq that she had not wanted to be married and had intentionally acted rudely with previous suitors. Still, there had been a few proposals, each one turned down. She told him that as each year had passed, she noticed her rebellion growing wishy-washy and felt herself giving in more readily to her parents' urgings. Perhaps she would try to settle down with someone, but he had to be the right person, she said, with a stubborn air. Shaffiq listened to her speak for many more minutes, noticing that their mothers were looking in periodically, his own shooting him alternating looks of concern and approval. He listened carefully to Salma, knowing that he needed to remember everything she had told him. He studied her dark eyes, her full lips, the small birth marks dotting their way down from her temple to her chin. He noticed how her hair seemed to tickle her neck just before she brushed it away and down her back. When she stopped speaking, he said, "Thirteen is now my lucky number."

Within a year of that meeting they were married.

So does he believe in arranged marriages then? He's not sure. Hadn't things worked out well for him? And don't these Canadians have too many divorces even though they have so-called love marriages? He throws the magazine down in a huff and walks away.

He turns on the floor polisher and pushes the heavy rumbling machine down the deserted hallway. As he approaches the first office on the left he looks up to read the metal name plate on the door: Nasreen Bastawala. He gasps at the familiar name, the tell-tale surname suffix that conjures up the salesmen, the merchants, the businessmen who constitute his own clan. Nasreen Bastawala, he says aloud. Nasreen Bastawala, I knew you were one of us.

Chapter 3

NASREEN SUMMONS UP HER courage, arranges a last-minute appointment with her hairdresser, and searches her closet for something worthwhile to wear.

Each time she has been ripe from a break-up, her friends have prescribed a night of clubbing, a lesbian household remedy. And so she complies, hoping that this time it will deliver some relief for her condition.

Her hairdresser is a young guy named Stephane who works in a collectively-run salon on Queen Street near Trinity Bellwoods. On each visit, he sports a different coif, often in experimental colours. His last hairdo was a spiky magenta creation that made him look like a purple porcupine. This afternoon, he surprises her with a less inspired look: a Blue Jays cap over what looks like a brush cut. He takes her to the back and washes her hair, massaging warm half-circles into her scalp, while she sighs gratefully under his strong, soapy fingers.

"So, what would you like me to do?" He asks, toweling her head maternally.

"I don't know. I just want something ... different," She peeks up at his face looking down at hers, "I suppose that is a bit of a cliché in your business. I must say that each time I'm here."

"Honey, a hairdresser is just like a bartender. Or maybe like a therapist. I hear everything. So tell me, what's the occasion? No, let me guess. Your man walk out on you?"

Nasreen is somewhat taken aback by his flippancy. "Actually, I asked *her* to leave a couple of months ago."

"And what did she do to deserve that?" Stephane pulls a comb gently through tangled hair.

"Well, for starters she cheated on me with her best friend," Nasreen says coolly, wondering how this detail could so easily roll off her tongue. A week ago, the mere mention of Connie put her either into a rage, or made her cry until her eyes were red and puffy.

"Uggh, the best friend. How tasteless. It all makes sense then. You came to the right place. A haircut will fix you right up."

"Well, it can't hurt, I guess. Good to cut off the dead ends, you know what I mean?"

"Girl, do I. I did the same just last month. Dumped his ass, then shaved my head. Got rid of it all so something new could take root. You like my new look? Sorta butch, eh?" She smiles at his joke. "But how about I just give you a trim? A little layering in here," he says pointing to the back of her head, "and maybe a touch shorter than usual. But I refuse to cut it all off. You have such beautiful hair."

Nasreen rises from the chair feeling lighter after her salon confessions. She tips Stephane well and even allows him to sell her a bottle of stupidly expensive hair gel.

She meets Mona for a late dinner at a little Greek restaurant on Church Street. They get a window seat so she and Mona can watch people while they dig into their souvlaki platters. Although it's a cool night, the street is packed with dressed-up men walking arm-in-arm, looking as though they are on their way to some important, stylish party. A few women pass by on the sidewalk too, some noticing her gaze and responding with their own direct or furtive glances.

Later, they go dancing at Tango. Despite the chill of the autumn night, the air inside is humid and saturated with that familiar blend of smoke and beer that sticks to skin and hair until scrubbed clean the next day. Mona and Nasreen scan the collective gyrating on the dance floor, recognizing and waving to people they know. Mona notices her first.

"Well, if it isn't our favourite gal pal over there." Mona yells hot breath into Nasreen's ear.

Nasreen spots her too. The contents of her stomach tip sideways, and she holds onto Mona's arm for support. She watches Connie slow dance with a woman with long blonde hair. Blonde on blonde, Nasreen observes. At least they match, she thinks, bitterly. In the dim light, Nasreen sees Connie's left hand holding tightly onto a thin waist, her thumb sinking into bare midriff. The woman dancing with Connie wears a short skirt and a tiny halter top. Connie's right hand slides down the woman's bare thigh and Nasreen wonders what has become of Laura, Connie's best friend, the first Other Woman.

"Are you OK, do you want to go? We can probably still get the cover charge back –"

"No, I expected she'd be here. I mean, there is only one good dyke bar on Church and this is her favourite. I'll be fine. I need to stay. I can't keep trying to avoid her, can I? I'm going to have a good time tonight and just ignore her." "Maybe you should try to act normal, like maybe go talk to her later. Be casual," Mona advises.

"Nah, I like our communication breakdown."

"Who's that she's with? That's not the skank she was cheating with, is it? I don't recognize her."

"No, it's not Laura. I don't know who that woman is. Never seen her before."

"Nas, I am so glad you kicked her out," Mona says, and Nasreen feels the weight of her friend's sympathetic brown eyes on her.

"Yeah," Nasreen says, turning away."Let's get a drink."

At the bar, Nasreen surreptitiously looks over at Connie and her dance partner, watching their pelvises grind to the beat of a *bangra* song. Mona mocks some of the off-rhythm moves of the dancers and Nasreen nods smugly. Despite Mona's best efforts to distract Nasreen with gossip, jokes, and cutting remarks about women's outfits, Nasreen's eyes find their way back to Connie and her thin femme date. The music changes and Connie looks up and notices Nasreen's gaze. It takes them both a moment to look away.

Later, the DJ spins an old Prince record and Mona jumps up and pulls Nasreen to the dance floor. They take care to stay at the edge of the parquet border, far from Connie, but by the middle of the song, Connie has migrated across the dance floor to Nasreen's side.

"I haven't seen you around for awhile," she says, her expression friendly.

"Yeah." Nasreen sways to the music awkwardly and looks for Mona, who, with eyes closed, is engrossed in herself and her dancing.

"How have you been?" Connie's touch is like melted chocolate on Nasreen's arm, her sweet damp fingers wrapping Nasreen's elbow, her thumb pressing into the soft skin of her inner arm. A heat rises up and through Nasreen's pores. She pulls her arm free.

"Look, Connie, I'm not interested in talking, OK?" Nasreen's pulse quickens, "Go back to your little girlfriend over there." She instantly wishes that she could take her words back, wishes she could feign indifference. Connie looks over at her date. Nasreen unsuccessfully tries to get Mona's attention, but Mona dances, as though in a trance, singing along with *Little Red Corvette*.

"But I've really wanted to talk to you. Don't you think it's time we had coffee, discussed it, you know … had some closure or something?" Nasreen notes Connie's awkward use of psychobabble.

"Baby you're much too fast," Mona sings, out of tune.

"As far as I'm concerned, Connie, I have closure. I didn't need to talk to you to achieve that." Connie looks at her, quizzically. "Perhaps you should talk to someone else if you need help," she hisses. "Maybe you should see a therapist and figure out why the hell you're such a fuck-up." Nasreen's words come out like sharp stones. She watches as they hit Connie and make their mark, reddening her face. Connie turns away and strides out of the bar, her date running after her.

A warm wind of calm rises through Nasreen, starting in her groin and moving up to her skull. I won, she thinks. I chased her away.

"What'd she say to you? I saw her coming over but wasn't sure if I should step in, you know, interfere…" Mona says, her eyes darting between Nasreen and the door through which Connie just exited. Nasreen is surprised that Mona did not hear the argument. In her mind the music stopped, time slowed down, and she yelled so loud that everyone in the bar would have paused to witness her victory. But as the rest of Tango's patrons continue to vibrate as one collective rhythm, oblivious to the battle that has just transpired, Nasreen's triumph withers. She orders another drink.

Shaffiq finishes all of the other offices on the fourth floor before cleaning Nasreen's. Wanting to ensure that he is completely alone, he circles the dull grey hallways once more, stepping carefully over the yellowing linoleum. Sure enough, not a soul is to be found in the clinic this late on a Friday night. He slides his master key into the lock and takes a deep breath before entering Nasreen's dark office.

He stands at the door, surveying the room. He wants to get a wide-angle look first and then focus on the details. Like the other offices, hers is the usual rectangle with a small vertical-blinded window. Facing into the wall, there is an old wooden desk, and a newish looking computer. A flashing green light winks at him from its monitor.

There are three blue chairs, spaced more or less in a triangle. At the back wall is an old beaten-up filing cabinet. A plastic plant sits on the window's ledge. He studies the leaflets and flyers tacked haphazardly to the bulletin board over her desk: advertisements for women's therapy groups, self-defense classes, a list of women's shelters. So she must be a psychologist then, he considers. A women's psychologist. She definitely is not one of the administrators, who have different sorts of work spaces, with spreadsheets and charts and dry erase white boards. In those offices there are no seats in circles, or triangles, or any other shape. Rather, a generous, cushioned chair usually holds court from behind an imposing desk while lesser chairs sit patiently and submissively before it. He knows those kinds of offices; his bosses in Bombay had them.

He finds Nasreen's metal garbage can and empties it into the bag attached to his cart. Inside it is a carry-out container with a lonely tomato and a few bits of wilted lettuce. She is a salad eater, then. He puts down the garbage can and picks up her recycling bin, which is half-filled with the classified section of a newspaper and some empty water bottles. Below all of this are a few pieces of paper. He shuts his eyes and reaches in to randomly extract one of them. He unfolds it and reads the scrawled red handwriting: "Bombay, Air India Flight 360, December 3, 17:40 (5:40 p.m.)." He tucks the paper into his pants pocket.

He scans the the top of the desk. There are neat stacks of memos, blank forms, a few binders and a gold lacquered box at the far edge of the desk. It's the kind of box easily found in Indian craft shops, with gold paint and raised swirling designs. He opens it gingerly, holds his breath, closes his eyes, and waits for a moment to take in the possibilities that it might hold. He has a feeling about this box. He opens his eyes again and inside is a photo of Nasreen, holding hands with another woman. It looks like a sunny day by the way the light shines on their hair. They look like opposites to Shaffiq: one blonde and thin, the other dark and round. He focuses on the hands clasped together. Brown and white fingers interlaced. Not the way friends hold hands back home as they stroll through the streets, he thinks. No, this is different. It is all in the eyes. He takes a second look at Nasreen's brown eyes looking at the other woman and recognizes it. He sees love in her face, but not just that. He sees adoration. He sees devotion.

He arrives home to Salma awake in bed.

"What's wrong, why are you awake? It's still early Salma, go to sleep," he says, noticing the dark under her eyes.

"Oh I couldn't sleep. I woke up and couldn't fall back again so I thought I would wait up for you. I thought we could talk a little while."

"OK. What do you want to talk about?" he says, cautiously, sitting down beside her, the mattress slumping under his weight.

"I don't know. Nothing really. Just talk. Sometimes I miss seeing you. Since you've had this job you are either coming or going or sleeping." She shifts down a little, onto one elbow. He watches her eyes carefully. "I don't like it this way, Shaffiq." She releases a long sigh. He searches his mind for something to say.

"But what can I do, Salma? We've talked about this many times now. This is how it is. At least now I have a job. I wish I didn't have to work the night shift. But what can I do?" He feels his back stiffen, the fatigued muscles roping around him defensively. He watches her lie down onto her back, her heavy breasts settling down on her chest. His tone softens, "And tonight I earned extra. Maybe I'll put another twenty-five into The Girls' University Fund." He calculates, "hey that will bring us up to sixty-five dollars."

"I don't know Shaffiq. I don't know what's wrong with me. I just feel so –" her chest heaves and she begins to cry, the tears sliding down her cheeks and onto the pillowcase. He scrambles down beside her. He has learned how she needs to be comforted. Only tonight, he wishes he didn't have to. What he'd like to do is to wrap himself in Salma's warm blankets, and close his eyes.

"Oh Salma, what is it? Don't cry."

"I'm just being silly, I guess. Sometimes I feel so … so lonely. Sometimes I wish we were back home. Not here. Like we made a huge mistake." He reaches for a tissue from the side table and wipes her face. He hands her another. She blows her nose.

"I know. I know. But this is home. This is home now. Don't worry Salma, it just will take time. Don't cry … they say all new immigrants feel this way. Remember that newcomers' pamphlets they gave us when we first arrived? It said that there would be hard times. We'll be okay. You'll see." She puts her head into his lap. She stops crying after a while. Shaffiq relaxes.

"I miss Bombay. I miss teaching, I miss the students. I miss my brothers and even my mother," she says sniffing. Shaffiq rubs her back. "I don't like working in at Blue Dove Dry Cleaners, Shaffiq. I have no real friends here. Sometimes I wish we could just pack up and go back. And the children. You know Saleema is really having a hard time adjusting, and it has been two years already."

"But they will adjust, Salma, and so will we. You'll see, things will be fine."

"Do you really believe that, Shaffiq? I mean, aren't you just a little tired of this? You can't find work in your field, you see what is happening with the girls, how they are changing."

"Well yes, I do see the girls becoming more like the Canadian children, but that's to be expected, isn't it? And we can have some control over what they are exposed to, I think," Shaffiq says, stiffening. His mind travels to the photo of Nasreen and the blonde girl. He shakes the thought away. "Salma, we just have to be patient and persistent. I'm going to start looking for a better job soon and once we're more settled, perhaps in a few years, you can go back to university to take those courses you need. And you just got your accreditation." He smiles at her and she wipes her face, then blows her nose again.

"Yes, it's so stupid. I am a fully trained teacher, but to even be considered for a job I need more courses."

"Yes, it is stupid. But just wait, in time, once we are more settled, we will be able to afford it."

"All right, all right. I've had enough crying for now. So, what strange thing did you pick up today?" She says with a forced smile. He reaches into his pocket and takes out a small scrap of paper. She reads the red letters and numbers.

"I suppose I've been feeling a little like you, Salma. See, it's part of an itinerary, I think, someone going to India. I saw it and it looked like a good luck charm. It was in one of the counsellor's offices."

"Shaffiq, you didn't just take this from someone's desk? You need to be careful. These people here, they will think –"

"No, no, it was in the garbage. You know how I am. I always look before I throw away." He smiles down at her. She is still studying the scrap of paper.

"This is a woman's writing, I can tell. Look at the way she loops the top of the 'd'," she says, participating in the sleuthing game she knows he loves.

"Yes, you may be right," he says. He is not sure why, but he doesn't want to tell her about the paper's exact origins right now. He will talk about Nasreen Bastawala another day. "I need to sleep now. I worked eleven hours today, or yesterday, or whatever day I worked." She passes the paper back to him and he puts it in his bureau drawer, tucking it away with the rest of his special finds. Salma watches him as he removes his clothes and gets into bed. She snuggles in beside him. He listens as her breathing calms and deepens. Then, lying awake, he ponders Nasreen, the gold box, and the woman with her in the photo.

Half-asleep, Nasreen turns over and reaches across the bed for Connie. She feels around for the warmth of her lover and instead touches velvety fur. She opens one eye and sees Id staring at her.

"Oh god, I'm so pathetic, Id." Id meows and she takes this as feline agreement. Nasreen rolls onto her back and stares at the ceiling, tears filling her eyes.

She used to love waking up beside Connie, her body heavy and warm, like the damp heat of a hot water bottle. Nasreen would nestle in close and wait for Connie to stir. She used to believe that she would wake up next to her for the rest of her life. And hadn't Connie felt the same way?

Now, Nasreen feels foolish. She sits up and Id moves onto her lap, settling in for some morning petting.

"Even you make me out to be a sucker. You're only here for the food and the odd bit of affection and because you can't go anywhere. I'm sure if you were an outdoor cat, you'd have disappeared by now too." Id purrs louder, his kitty-motor warming up.

There is not much of Connie left in this room. She moved in with very little and left with the same. She did not even take the crockery set they bought together, which Nasreen was glad for. Connie owed her at least this much. According to Nasreen's grief logic, since Connie broke her heart, the dishes should be left behind.

Nasreen swings her legs out of bed, relocating Id to the floor, and opens the drapes. Raindrops dot the window and grey clouds threaten more rain. She consults the clock and remembers that she made plans to see her father for lunch. Why had she agreed to meet him so early? She heads to the shower and checks the cartoon cat calendar hanging above the toilet. The fat felines smirk at her, and the writing beneath indicates that this is breast examination day. Under the steam of the hot water, she raises her left arm and palpates her breast with her right hand. Under the armpit, around the aureole, and down to her ribs. Then the other side. She is never sure if she is doing it correctly and is unable to tell normal breast tissue from cancer. She gives up the self-exam and begins the more satisfying routine of soaping up with some expensive raspberry body wash.

Nasreen stands on the westbound platform at Exhibition station, waiting for the GO Train. When she was a teenager, she travelled in the opposite direction every chance she got. She and her friends would take the subway to Queen Street where they would check out the second-hand clothing stores that used to predominate before the fashion chains took over. She loved going downtown and imagined herself living there after high school, a cool Torontonian, free from the conforming pressures of suburbia. However, when she finished grade thirteen, her father convinced her to stay at home and commute to her classes.

"*Beti*, you'll be leaving home soon enough. Stay a few years more at home. We can save a lot of money not paying residence fees." He even bought her a used Honda Civic, which has long since broken down, for the commute to York. At the time, the car seemed like a good trade off for staying in Mississauga.

While in university, she was again lured back to Queen Street, but not for the fashion. Instead, she and her friends headed to the Boom Boom Room, a bar that hosted a dyke night on Saturdays. The bar's gloomy interior and dance floor was full of every kind of lesbian: leather dykes, stone butches, high femmes, S/M lesbians, and more run of the mill women like her. She used to be both scared and titillated by the women at the bar. She and her friends would dance late into the night and she met a couple of her first girlfriends there.

She managed to keep her love life secret from her parents until her third year of university, when Muriam Bandukwala saw her kissing Rita Mirelli on Yonge Street. Rita and Nasreen didn't date for very long, but their short fling had far reaching consequences for Nasreen. Muriam Bandukwala set the community phone tree into action, telling the news to a third cousin in Idaho, who called Nasreen's aunt in Rhode Island, who then phoned her mother in Mississauga two days later. The result was a serious, dining-room family meeting where her mother asked embarrassing questions while her father paced in the hallway like an angry lion. Phrases like "this must be a phase" and "you will be unhappy in the long run" streamed from her mother's mouth while her father wanted to know which "bad influence" had "corrupted" his daughter.

Over the years, their disdain for her sexual orientation turned into worry, then an uncomfortable tolerance. Connie was the first girlfriend they managed to welcome wholeheartedly into their home, a gesture of acceptance Nasreen had never expected from them.

The train is ten minutes late and when she arrives at Clarkson her father's silver Passat is already parked in the "kiss and ride" laneway. When she was a kid, he had always been tardy, leaving her waiting in school and recreation centre parking lots after swimming or dance lessons, always the last parent to to drive up. But these days, he is almost always early.

"Hi Dad, were you waiting long?" She leans over to kiss him on the cheek. There is more grey in his thick hair than when she last saw him.

"Nasreen, hello. I've been here about twenty minutes or so. But that's alright, I've been listening to the radio. I guess the train is running late today."

"As usual."

"Where are your bags? Not staying over?"

"Nah, I should get back this evening, I have to meet some friends," she says, fibbing, avoiding his eyes. "Thanks for coming to get me."

"*Arré*, what is this thanks? You are my daughter, of course I would come and get you. But are you thinking about getting a car sometime soon? You earn well now, don't you? Wouldn't you like one? I can surf around on the net and do some research for you if you –"

"No, Dad, not now. Maybe I will one day, but I don't really need one in the city. I don't have parking anyway. Where are we going for lunch? Home or out?" Nasreen hopes they will go out. Neutral territory.

"I made some rice and a salad. I thought we could have that with the mutton curry I got from Mrs. Khairullah. You should order from her, you know. She makes good food and I know you don't get much time to cook. I could get some for you and then you could pick it up when you come over next," he says, checking his mirror before pulling out of the parking lot.

"Well I have been cooking more, I think I'll be all right." Another small lie spontaneously pops out of her mouth. She did cook more often when she was with Connie. She finds it hard to feel motivated to cook for herself now. "Besides, Mrs. Khairullah uses too much oil in her cooking."

"She's cut down on the oil lately. All of us have been urging her to change. All us Indian men have coronary problems, you know. We all have to be careful," he says, solemnly. He turns onto the familiar tree-lined street. Nasreen notices the houses have remained more or less the same. On one side are sprawling bungalows and on the other are simple two-storey family homes.

"Yes, I guess you all have to take care of your hearts." They drive up the black-tarred slope of the three-bedroom family home that now houses just one. Nasreen looks at her mother's roses still in bloom and the ivy grown thick around the side of the house. Bashir gets out and pulls open the garage door, cursing the broken automatic opener that he is always talking about getting fixed.

"Have to get that fixed," Bashir says, landing heavily on the seat and once again buckling up for the final three metres into the garage.

Inside, Nasreen breathes in familiar smells. The air holds memories of thousands of meals cooked here, hints of cumin mixed expertly with tumeric, coriander, and chili. People say that Indian cooking has a way of coating the walls and seeping into the foundation, rendering an Indian home unsellable by even the best real estate agent. But Nasreen loves the heavy aromas of home. Just beneath the spices is another familiar scent, subtle now, but still present: Fleur de Jardin, her mother's perfume. She sniffs the air hungrily, taking in her mother's faint presence. Nasreen scans the foyer and then the living room as she had done each time she has visited her father since her mother died two years ago, feeling both irritated and glad that nothing has changed. All the furniture, knick-knacks and carpets were her mother's choices and purchases and remain where she would have placed them, unaltered, unmoved since her death. Meanwhile, her father occupies the residence almost like a tenant, his landlady away on some kind of extended vacation.

"The food should be ready in maybe fifteen minutes." Her father twists a knob and the burner under the mutton turns red. He disappears into the den and Nasreen peeks under pot lids appraising the warming food. She opens the fridge, looking for something to drink, just like she used to when she was a teenager, standing in the door far to long, letting the cold escape. Between thoughts of apple vs. orange, she hears a whisper of her mother's voice nagging her to stop wasting electricity and so she quickly chooses the orange juice, shuts the door and pours out two glasses.

Bashir returns, a pile of photos and some sheets of paper in his hand. He sets the photos to the side and passes her the papers.

"See? This is our itinerary. I did it nicely all colour-coded. Did I tell you I bought a new colour printer?" Nasreen shakes her head.

"The dates are in purple and the cities are in blue. I listed some other things on this page, places I thought we could go after visiting everyone. They are in green. I want to show you around a little. See here, I want to go to Surat for a few days." She looks blankly at him. He raises his slightly greying eyebrows in moderate alarm. "You remember, this is where we are from. Your great grandmother was born there before they all moved to Bombay." She nods, looking further down his extensive list. "Maybe your *Nani* will want to come with us. She still keeps in touch with some of the family there and I think your *Mamaji* even owns a little house there." Nasreen tries to remember her mother's brother. She hasn't seen him since her last visit to India.

"You mean Mamaji Murtuza?"

"Yes, yes," he says impatiently. "After that, we can go to see some of my family who has settled in Ahmedabad. I think it will be good. You'll find it interesting."

"But Dad, all this family visiting? You know that bores me to death."

"Don't you want to meet the family?" She detects the slight rise at the end of his sentence. Family. He says the word like he would say God, Humanity, Trudeau. "OK, well take these as suggestions only then. You think about where you want to go too and then we can come up with a plan," he says, placating her.

"I really just want a holiday. I need a holiday. We can go to some of those places, but I'm going to want to do more than just hang out with people I don't know, who I am supposed to visit just because they are family. I'd like some time at a beach. I hear Goa is really great." She looks up at him to see his crestfallen expression. He had been excited just a moment ago. "Anyway Dad, we still have a couple of months to plan this trip."

They eat lunch and make conversation about her work, the new computer programs he bought recently, and people they both know who have recently married, had children, or died. He gets up to clear the table and passes her some photos.

"I have been meaning to give you those pictures," he stirs the leftover mutton, taps the spoon against the side of the pot. "I didn't know if you wanted them. They are from the last time you and Connie visited. By the way, do you see her at all anymore?" He stretches to reach a high cupboard and takes out a plastic container. Nasreen passes him the two dirty plates, then the cutlery. She studies her distorted image in a serving spoon's shiny surface.

"No, not really. Well, I saw her last night while I was out with Mona, but we didn't really talk to each other." She hears the fridge door open, then close.

"Mona, how is she? Is she doing well?" She nods at him and he continues, "You know, I don't really understand. Maybe it is not for me to know everything, but you never told me what happened. I thought that you and Connie were serious about each other," his face is strained, and she thinks that he is likely trying to choose his words carefully. "Although I like her very much – she is a nice girl – it's just that I wasn't really sure if this kind of thing could be permanent, and –"

"It could have been permanent," Nasreen blurts out, her voice louder than she wants it to sound. "I thought that it would be. Anyway, the reason we broke up is pretty much the same as why any heterosexual couple breaks up." She feels her face flushing, "we didn't break up because we were two women."

"OK, OK, that's not what I meant. I just didn't know if she would be, you know, committed to you, like in a marriage." He slides his hands into the big lobster-paw oven mitts he and her mother bought a few summers ago in Halifax. He lifts the mutton pot off the stove.

"Well it turned out she wasn't committed," she feels her voice squeaking, her throat drying up. Nasreen picks up a photo from the top of the stack. She and Connie stand together, not smiling, their eyes red from her father's flash. It had not been a good time for them. They argued a lot back then and she remembers they'd had a huge fight on the way over to her father's house that day. Connie threatened to abandon Nasreen at the Port Credit stop while the other GO train passengers looked on, curious, interested in the entertainment they were providing. In the end, they both calmed down, Connie stayed on the train and Nasreen was relieved. She wouldn't have known how to explain Connie's absence to her father. That was just a few weeks before they broke up. Nasreen recalls that on the way back home, they argued again, that time about how Connie was never at home. Connie defended herself with excuses about work deadlines that Nasreen believed, more or less.

"I thought she was committed. She said she was. I couldn't believe that she would cheat and lie and then leave me." Tears drip down her face. She looks up at Bashir, "I never thought she would leave me. I was prepared to work it out, even after she told me she was cheating. The truth is she left me, packed up everything in a couple of hours and moved out the next day. You know, I told everyone that I threw her out. I just couldn't believe she'd ever leave, Dad." Bashir puts his arms around his daughter, holds her tightly, not sure what to say, but pretty sure that he should not let her go just yet. He mumbles into her ear, "I know, I know.

It will be OK."

And does he know? Does he have any real understanding of what his lesbian daughter is going through? How does he cross the vast expanse of his middle-aged Indian experience to join with hers? Bashir holds his daughter as he did when she was a small child. When she fell off her bicycle after he took off the training wheels. Or when she wasn't invited to a classmate's birthday party when she was ten. He could ease those pains with a few caresses and kind words. Those were easy wounds to heal.

He feels her heart beating against his chest and thinks about his own fractured core. He does know. He knows what it means to be left. He knows what it means when a promise of a life together is broken. When marriage vows are torn to shreds by the lying, lecherous powers of disease. He knows betrayal. As his daughter cries hot tears on his neck, he rubs her back with his lobster oven-mitted hands while shouldering his own grief. "There, there, don't cry now," is all that he manages to say.

Chapter 4

SHAFFIQ WAKES EARLY TO Salma fishing through their closet, the clink-clink of the wire hangers knocking each other. Half-asleep, his brain groggily works to identify the sounds. He opens one sticky eye and sees Salma pull out a blue *ridah* still wrapped in Blue Dove Dry Cleaner's thin plastic. Salma takes liberties to have many of their clothes cleaned while her supervisor is away and now half the closet is filled with the soft plastic-sheathed clothing. He watches as she holds the full-length garment out in front of her, studying it at arms-length. She rips the plastic away and it swishes softly to the floor.

"Why are you taking that out?" Shaffiq mumbles in his just-awake voice.

"Oh, you are up. Sorry to wake you. It's still early. Go back to sleep."

"It's OK. It's Saturday right? I don't have to work today. Why are you taking out your *ridah*?"

"Asima Aunty asked me to go for prayers with her this week. I thought I'd go this time." Asima has become a little more religious and conservative each of the thirty years she has lived in Canada. Salma and Shaffiq have often made fun of her, joking about how she is more Indian than their family in Bombay. It is as though she has crystallized her memory of life in the '70s and tried to recreate it in the present. She is always urging Salma to go to the mosque with her, to "keep up the old ways."

Shaffiq stretches and yawns. "Is it a special occasion or something? No. Eid isn't for another couple of months."

"I thought I'd go and maybe meet some of the other women. I need to make some friends, Shaffiq."

"But at the *masjid*? What do you have in common with those *ridah* ladies? I thought you hated wearing that thing."

"Well, we'll see. I'm going to keep an open mind. Maybe it is good for the girls if they go, too. And this *ridah* isn't so bad. Just like a long dress, no?"

"A long hooded shroud that covers over your pretty hair and everything else." He leers at her from the bed.

"Well, then you should be glad that I'm wearing it. This way I only share my beauty with you," she says, smiling down at him. "Isn't that what you men want? Hmm?"

"I have an idea. Why don't you take all your clothes off, put on that "long dress" and then come to bed with me?" His sacrilegious eyes flash mischief.

"*Arré?*" she says, rubbing a small stain near the *ridah*'s hem, "and mess up this *ridah* before going to mosque? I can only sneak so many free dry cleanings, Shaffiq," she says, walking out of the bedroom. Shaffiq sighs, checks the clock, and decides to go back to sleep.

He wakes later to Shireen's expectant six-year-old eyes upon him.

"What are you doing?"

"Watching you sleep. When are you going to get up? It's lunchtime already. I've been up since seven waiting to play with you. Mummy said me and Memsahib could come in now."

"Really, she did?" She nods seriously, clutching her doll in front of her. Memsahib's glassy eyes stare back at him vacantly. "What game are we going to play? Have you planned it all out, or shall I go back to sleep for a while so you have a chance to organize yourself first?" He pulls the covers up in mock going-back-to-sleep.

"No, no, Daddy!" She says lunging on top of him, "I do have it all organized. First I thought we would play going to tea with Memsahib and then we could take her out for a walk in her stroller." She waves the limp rag doll in front of him, "See, she says that you should get up right now so we can have tea."

"OK, Memsahib. Give me a few minutes to brush my teeth first. I'm sure we would not want to submit Shireen to my terrible sleepy breath, or shall we forgo the tooth brushing for now," he breathes into the doll's face and Shireen backs away theatrically.

"Fine, first go brush your teeth and then meet me in the tea shop." She points in the direction of the living room, "it's that way."

"This way?" He points to the bathroom, his brow knitting in confusion.

"No, that way!" Her finger jabs the air.

"Oh, this way?" He asks, pointing out the window.

"No, Daddy! Thaaat way," she shrieks.

"OK, OK. See you later then," he laughs, his hands up in surrender.

As Shaffiq heads to the bathroom, he thinks about how Shireen's doll got her name. Shireen has been an assertive, almost bossy child from the start and he and Salma would call her the "*memsahib*" when they were alternately amused with or irritated by her demands. "The *memsahib* is not behaving," Salma would mutter. Or Shaffiq would say, "I can't seem to get the *memsahib* to eat today." Curiously, Shireen passed the name on to her favourite doll.

Saleema, three years older, is a different sort of girl altogether. While Shireen usually has her doll in her arms, Saleema is often found with a book in hand. Halfway through the journey to Canada, she read through all the primary readers Salma had packed for her. In order to help her occupy herself through the remaining ten hours on the plane, Shaffiq had to convince her that reading books twice is more fun than reading them just once and to his relief, she believed him. Now, a bright nine-year-old, she reads even faster than before. On the way to the bathroom, Shaffiq looks into the girls' room and sees Saleema there, engrossed in Harry Potter's latest adventures.

Shaffiq emerges from the bathroom and sits down to his morning cup of dolly-tea. He arranges his bony legs cross-ways on the carpet in front of Shireen's tea set and declares loudly, "such nice hot tea! Slurp, slurp, ah, so nice!"

"Daddy, no, not yet," squeals Shireen, "You are so silly! I haven't even poured it out yet!" She carefully tips the plastic pot over his miniature cup, then adds pretend milk and sugar. "There. Now be careful, it's hot. Make sure you foo it first." Shaffiq smiles obediently and looks up to see Salma watching the make-believe from the kitchen. She smiles at him then points to her own mug and raises a questioning eyebrow. He nods to her gratefully.

"Gulp, gulp, gulp, oh yes, that's much better. That first cup was very weak, almost like air! This one is the real thing." Shireen nods, pleased as a grandmother. "Now that I've had a cup of your tea, maybe now I will try some from Mumma's pot?" Shireen frowns slightly, but then waves her hand, conferring permission. He reaches up as Salma passes down a mug to him. "Ah, this one is nice too, but I think if there were to be a competition, Shireen's just might win." Shireen giggles and hugs him, almost spilling the hot liquid all over his striped pajamas. Saleema walks into the living room and her little sister seizes the window of opportunity, "Saleeeema, come on now, have your tea. You haven't had one cup even and I made this special pot," she carries the cup over to her sister.

"Yeah, OK, very nice imaginary tea. It tastes so good, yet strangely imaginary," she says sarcastically, half-heartedly sipping from the tiny cup. Shireen sticks her tongue out and Saleema impatiently smacks the side of Shireen's head.

"Mumma, Daddy, she hit me! Saleema hit me and she spilt the tea on the carpet." She runs behind her father and clings to his arm.

"Stop it you two," Salma's tone is stern and the girls go quiet.

"I don't know why you have to hit, Saleema. Be civilized. If you wanted Shireen to not bother you, then tell her, don't hit her. Use your mouth, not you hands," Shaffiq lectures his eldest daughter. She sniffs as though threatening to cry but then he sees her rolling her eyes just before they disappear behind her book. He doesn't understand what's wrong with Saleema. Ever since they moved to Canada, his sweet and quiet child has been swatting, swiping, and grabbing at her younger sister. And now this eye-rolling! Shaffiq slurps down his irritation along with the rest of his real tea.

"OK, the tea party is over. I have to go take my bath."

"Fine, Memsahib and I will finish our tea and then we can all go for our walk when you are ready," she says, her eyes following him into the bathroom. "Right Daddy?"

Nasreen spends the trip home from Mississauga meditating on photos and gnawing through an Oh Henry and a Coffee Crisp she bought from the station vending machine. She spreads the glossy images across her lap, trying to keep them from slipping off her thighs, while the train rocks unsteadily. She gazes at Connie and herself, a couple just about to come undone. They look unhappy, their eyes glassy and devil-red from being shocked by Bashir's flashbulb. She fingers her ex-girlfriend's slender figure, and feels a dull pain in her chest.

At Mimico, a harried looking woman and her preschooler board and settle themselves in the seats across from her. The little boy cranes his head forward, attracted by the sweet smelling chocolate. He tries to steal a glance at the glossy snapshots and so Nasreen gathers them together and stuffs the last of the chocolate into her mouth. She looks out the smudged window the rest of the trip home, avoiding his young, curious eyes.

Entering her apartment, all Nasreen can think of is how hungry she is even though her stomach is full. She paces through the apartment while Id watches her. She checks her messages. There is just one from her father, "*Beti*, it's your father. Thanks for coming over. I had a nice time ... look, try not to think about all the sad things so much. Things will be better with time." And after an awkward pause, "OK, bye bye now." She hears a beep, and stands at the machine, her finger hovering over the delete button. She changes her mind and saves the message.

She heads to the kitchen, opening cupboards and then banging them closed again, looking for something to munch on. Then, she forces herself to sit down on the couch, trying to hold herself together by keeping still. It doesn't work. She goes back to the kitchen, rummages the cupboards like an angry raccoon and eats a few vanilla sandwich cookies while a bag of popcorn sputters in the microwave.

She knows about the psychology of these things, has studied and written about them in fact. *The Incidence of Eating Disorders Among South Asian Girls in Canada*, her fraudulently objective Master's thesis, received high marks and praise from her professors. She understands that the persistent thoughts of food and her frequent visits to the fridge and pantry to retrieve one sweet thing, then one salty thing – the calorie-reduced cookies followed by the olives, followed by the frozen yogurt and then the low-fat popcorn – must mean something. She sinks into the couch, her fingers salty from artificial butter flavour and thinks, OK, what do you feel Nasreen, what is it that you need? Her chest aches and her parched throat holds back the tears she is not interested in shedding. *What do you feel, godammit!*

She gets up and paces the living room. She heads toward a bookcase and extracts a photo album labeled Fall 1998 to – . It sits on the shelf beside Summer 1996 to Summer 1998. And Fall 1995 to Spring 1996. She flips through the cellophane-covered pages, looking at a photo of her father, smiling, balding, an arm around her mother. They stand together in front of the house, wearing matching red windbreakers, holding each other against the cool winds of autumn. They seem to be sharing a joke. A few pages away she and her mother are outside, shoveling snow during the biggest snowfall in the history of Ontario, the year that the mayor of Toronto called in the army to clear the snow. In the next photo, she and her father pose in front of the plastic Christmas tree they have pulled out of the basement and resurrected every year since Nasreen was small. In another photo, her mother, father, Connie and Nasreen sit formally around the dinner table, waiting for the automatic timer on Connie's camera to hurry up and take the picture. Nasreen remembers that she and Connie had just started dating earlier that year. They felt so optimistic and stupid with love that they rushed to introduce one another to their families. Both sets of parents were polite and cautious at first, but the couple's devotion seemed infectious, drawing the elders into their children's enthusiasm for one another.

Nasreen continues her tour through the year and arrives at a photo of her mother perched on the side of her hospital bed. She wears a floral print housecoat over a standard-issue hospital gown. She is having a good day. It must be her birthday because she is posed with a gift in her lap.

"Come on, hurry up and take the photo, Nasreen, your mother is getting tired." There was a click and a flash that momentarily illuminated the grey room.

"Thank you *Beti*," Zainab said wearily, "I'm okay Bashir. What's this present you two have given me? You already gave me a gift each. This is too much. Why one more?"

"Open it and see, Mom." Zainab carefully peeled back the cellotape, removing the wrapping paper without ripping it.

"Just go ahead and rip it, Mom."

"Has your mother ever wasted one iota of anything in her life?" Bashir said, a proud smile stretching over his weary face.

"Nope, and why would she start now?" Nasreen laughed, and then saw her father's expression change, realizing her faux pas. The family had carefully avoided discussions about Zainab's impending death. Nasreen wished she could take the words back. Zainab, oblivious to the new tension in the room, continued her slow, focused, unwrapping.

"Oh, it's beautiful," Zainab whispered, holding the framed photograph two feet away from her, squinting her eyes, "Nasreen, get me my glasses, will you? They are in the drawer over there," she said, pointing across the bed. "Yes, there." Eyeglasses in place, she smiled at the family photo in front of her.

"It was Dad's idea."

"We took those pictures over a year ago but never got around to displaying them properly. I thought you'd like one for your nightstand."

"What a lovely thought. Thank you both. I'll keep it right here, so that I can see it while I'm resting."

"You want to try some cake, Mom?"

"No, I don't think I'll be able to keep it down." With a grunt, she swung her legs onto the bed. "Nasreen, why don't you wrap it up and take it home to share with Connie?" Nasreen wondered how to tell her mother she had to leave, never knew how to end her hospital visits, feeling simultaneously like staying there twenty-four hours and escaping at her first chance. She picked up her bag and looked at her father.

"I'll drop Nasreen off at the station and come back again in a couple of hours, then."

"I'll be back soon, OK Mom? Maybe not this week, but the weekend for sure." Zainab nodded and Nasreen embraced her mother, trying to hide her wet eyes.

There are no more photos after that. Nasreen takes out the paper label from within its plastic sheath and fills in the date: Fall 2000.

Chapter 5

SALMA OPENS THE DOOR of Asima Aunty's Saab and gathering up her *ridah*, she carefully leans out of the car to avoid getting her hemline wet. She hurries to catch up to Asima, who is already at the opposite end of the large parking lot. She is not Salma's favourite relative, but she is her only family in Toronto, the one who hosted the Paperwala family for three weeks until they found their own place. She taught them the intricacies of getting a phone number, a bank account, the mysteries of the subway system. She knew things that Salma didn't, like that you don't have pay each time you transfer from one bus to another, that aluminum is pronounced aLUminum here and not aluMINium, that mittens are warmer than gloves. Salma gratefully accepts her help. She needs it.

Since coming to Canada, Salma has felt moorless, unsure of herself, a kind of uncertainty that she hasn't been able to shake. Asima Aunty, on the other hand, always appears convinced of things and Salma enjoys the vicarious feeling of security she feels in her presence.

Finally just two steps behind her, Salma follows Asima Aunty up the long cement walk to the mosque. Salma looks up at the imposing white structure, recently erected by the local community on a large parcel of land just off the highway in north Toronto. She watches her stop every few steps to greet the other congregants who reciprocate with their respectful *salaams*. She introduces most of these to Salma, who nods and smiles before they move on to the next person. Once out of earshot, Asima's commentary to Salma is more acidic, muttering under her breath warnings such as "stay away from that one, she is a filthy back-stabber" or "there are rumours that her daughter is going out with a Canadian boy." Asima continues her tirade, "but what to do? This seems to be the way things are going. I'll do my best to not have that happen to my Sherie." Salma frowns, considering Asima Aunty's cheeky sixteen-year-old daughter. Just last week Sherie confided to Salma that she has a new boyfriend her mother knows nothing about. And he is not Muslim or Indian in the least.

At the top of the steps, Asima Aunty stands back while Salma pulls the heavy door aside for her. Asima takes a sweeping look inside and announces, "there looks to be a poor turnout today. It seems that some people think that they are good Muslims if they appear for Eid and the big occasions. What about the other days?" Salma remains quiet. Her own unholy family has not been to mosque since last Eid. "I really think that people need to return to their communities, the traditions. Just look at how children behave these days. I am so glad that you have joined me today, Salma. Just give it a chance. Soon you will want to be here as often as you can too," Asima adds.

"Well, we'll see Asima Aunty. I don't have that much time, with my job and the girls –"

"Really this is such a haven from the crazy North American way of life! I wish Quaid would come here sometimes with me. You know he works too hard and never feels peace." Uncle Quaid, Asima's husband, effectively evades Asima and her calls to prayer through his stubborn workaholism. Salma doesn't blame him. She found those first few weeks at Asima's house difficult; Aunty Asima is not an easy woman to live with.

They make their way to the right side of the hall where the women sit, segregated from the men by a thick, dusty sheet rigged up by wire from the ceiling. Asima makes a point to remind Salma that theirs is a progressive mosque. "Yes, the women are separated from the men, as is instructed, but not behind them. Side by side is how we pray. This way we all get to see everything. Now that is equality, Salma." Salma gazes at the shadows cast by the men on the other side of the divider.

They continue to the front of the hall. Although they've arrived after many others, there is a small clearing left open at the very front where Asima's friends have congregated.

"See, we saved a place for you, Asima," titters a small woman wearing a pale yellow *ridah*. "And look you brought Salma! How nice. I haven't seen you here for some time."

"You remember Ben Nishreen, don't you Salma? And this is Taslima and Farida." She points to the other two women seated nearby, who smile agreeably up at her from the floor. Salma takes each woman's damp hand in her own and smiles pleasantly back. She looks around, admiring the sea of soft peaches, corals, pinks, light greens, and yellows sluicing around her. She sits down and the women shift, their *ridahs* rustling as they create more space for her.

Across the cloth divide that segregates the congregation by gender, Bashir listens to the *imam* lecture. He strains to follow the words, understanding more or less what is said. His Gujarati feels rather rusty and he wonders why the holy men seem only to be able to speak in the most academic of ways. He shifts his position on the floor, tucks his left leg under his right. He looks around and wonders if everyone else is following the high language. Who else here is getting lost, bored, uncomfortable? Almost in answer, he hears giggling on the other side of the heavy drape. Bashir smiles, turns his head to listen. The sound is so familiar to him, he would recognize it anywhere.

Zainab. Such a unique laugh she had. Her laughter was infectious, the sound of a light delightful squeal. Some other men around him look over at the divider with irritation. Bashir hopes that the girl loses control again; he wants to hear that sound once more. Soon she is laughing again, this time more quietly. He hears urgent whispers and shushing sounds.

Zainab? Do you remember, like I do? Do you remember how you loved to laugh? Your laughter would take you over and sometimes you laughed out loud in the worst possible places. Like here even! And do you remember, Zainab, that time back when Nasreen was younger, we all went out to see a movie, a very sad one about a woman who had cancer. What was it called? Oh yes, Terms of Endearment. *At some point in the film, Zainab, you made a silly comment about something and then before long you and I were in the middle of a long, loud laughing fit. Others around us started to notice and Nasreen tried to quiet us. So embarrassed she was.*

Bashir listens for the laughter again, envisioning his wife just across the curtain, fantasizing that she will meet him on the front steps when the prayers end. He permits himself the luxury of longing for her. He smiles and sighs and then his reverie is over when he recalls that they stopped coming to mosque when Zainab was diagnosed with cancer. She lost interest in prayers when she became sick, giving up her faith at a time when others might have renewed theirs and so they both stayed home.

So, Zainab, what do you think about my return to the mosque? How different we are from each other, really. Do you think me silly for coming back after my test results? Do you think me a fool for retreating back to religion? I hope you are not still angry with God. I suppose you wouldn't be anymore, right? From where you are? Suffering and anger and hate are all supposed to be gone once you leave this earth, right?

Salma listens to the *imam* talking about the importance of maintaining the fast during Ramadan. She finds his words compelling and wonders what Shaffiq would think if she fasted this year.

Salma feels a soft tapping on her left shoulder.

"You should come visit us sometime, Salma. You live in the west end, right? We're not too far from you," whispers Farida. She smiles and Salma notices that one of Farida's front teeth is badly stained, "My youngest daughter is ten. You have a daughter that age, too, no?"

"Yes, Saleema is nine," Salma says too loudly. Asima Aunty shushes her. She lowers her voice, "That's nice of you. I don't know too many people here."

"Your husband is an accountant?"

"Well, yes. But he works in a hospital now."

"How great. Being an accountant at a hospital is a good position."

"Well, actually –"Asima Aunty shushes them both again.

"I'll get your number from Asima, later," Farida whispers as she turns back to the *imam*.

Bashir's reverie is interrupted by movement around him. More than a hundred brown men of various heights and girths, lift themselves to their feet and begin to move out of the hall. He follows the crowd, joining the awkward shuffle of pious men whose legs and feet have gone numb from sitting cross-legged. In the hallway they form new lines with the women to reclaim shoes and coats. A few feet ahead of him Bashir sees a woman wearing a light blue *ridah* who smells like spring flowers. He lingers behind her, taking in her familiar scent, following his memory. From this angle, she could be his Zainab, she is just the right height and weight. And look! She even fidgets like Zainab while she waits for her shoes. The blue-swathed woman turns and he sees that her soft brown face and dark eyes are not his Zainab's. His eyes water as he looks away from her and he is relieved when she finally collects her belongings and steps away from the line. He collects his loafers and windbreaker and leaves the mosque. The thickness of grief settles in around him and is the passenger that accompanies him on his drive home.

Back in the parking lot, Salma stands beside the car and pulls her *ridah* off.

"*Arré,* Salma, you should not remove your ridah until you are inside the car. It doesn't look good." Salma obediently hurries into the car and closes the door. "So, did you like it, Salma? Will you join me again?"

"Yes, call me when you are coming next." I have nothing better to do, Salma thinks. And it wasn't so bad, was it? "Farida and some of the women talked with me and invited us over to their homes."

"Great. I'm glad to hear it. You know I've been worried about you, all alone in your apartment out there. You must meet more people."

"Asima Aunty, it's not that bad. I do go out and work and I'm teaching Gujarati to one student now. And I have a nice neighbour, who has children the same age as Saleema and Shireen. She's very nice and watches the children sometimes."

"Is she Indian or Canadian?"

"She's from Jamaica."

"You should be a little careful, Salma. Here, at the *masjid*, you can be sure you will meet mostly quality people. But you know, the area you live in," she hesitates and then continues, "I know it is what you can afford right now, but it is not what you'd call a good area."

"Well, my neighbour and her children are very nice."

"Just be careful what kind of influences the children are under. You never know. Anyway. Why don't we go home and eat? Hopefully my Sherie has fed the kids already."

"Yes, it is getting late. We should get back." Asima's daughter is not always the most willing babysitter and often forgets details like giving the children dinner.

"Good. That will give me chance to give you another *ridah*. I noticed you wear that same one every time," Asima says, appraising the folded *ridah* in Salma's lap, "When we were in India last winter I picked up a few extras. I'll give you one of those."

"Oh, that's quite alright, Asima Aunty. I mean, I don't go to the mosque that often. I only really need one. We're really not that devout."

"But if you are going to join me more often you don't want people to always see you in the same *ridah* each time, do you?" Asima's expertly-plucked eyebrows arch quizzically. "Really, it's no trouble, Salma. I have so many. I'd like to give you one."

After dinner, Asima takes Salma upstairs to her walk-in closet and unzips an old plastic blanket bag. She unpacks a selection of *ridahs* in a variety of colours, most with sequins, bows, and multiple layers of ruffles. Salma chooses a cream-coloured one with just a little lace around the neck.

"Salma, you're choosing such a plain one?"

"Yes, it is more my style than these others," she says, trying to be diplomatic. Satisfied enough with Salma's choice, Asima hands Salma the *ridah*, and turns her attention to folding and packing up the rest into the zippered blanket bag. Meanwhile, Salma looks around the bedroom, enviously noticing the matching oak furniture, the armoire, dresser, bed, and side tables. Asima bought this set to replace the older one she gave to Salma when they first arrived in Canada. A colourful painting hanging above Asima's bed catches Salma's eye.

"Asima is that new? It's so beautiful," Salma says, admiring the painting of an ancient *raja* surrounded by his servants.

"Yes, Quaid bought it during our last trip. I think that's his ultimate fantasy. He'd like to be a king in his court, you know?" she scoffs.

"Good thing you keep him in line, Asima Aunty." Salma says, joking back.

"You know, if you'd like, we have another one sort of like this in the basement. It's not as pretty, but still nice. As usual, we bought too much in India and we don't really have any space left for it all."

"Really? We could use a bit more decoration in our place. It's a shame that we couldn't bring some of our nice things from India. I never thought I would miss that stuff when I was packing up."

"It's only when you leave India that you realize how much you long for it. Perhaps Quaid and I will retire there one day," she says wistfully. "But take the painting. Quaid won't mind. He won't even notice that it is gone. Come, let's go downstairs and see what the children are up to."

Later, Asima directs Salma to the painting in storage downstairs. She descends the steps to the cool basement, where there is enough furniture, old clothing and food to fill a second house. She pauses to look at the clutter: the labeled, green garbage bags filled for charity; the shelves of boxed and canned goods lining the walls; the useless possessions. She wonders, is this what living in Canada does to a person: causing one to buy and collect so many things that a large basement is required to store everything? She wonders if she, too, will become a hoarder one day.

Salma easily finds the painting beside the stairwell. She clicks on a nearby light and studies it carefully. A *raani* reclines on a dais. She is on some kind of terrace overlooking well-manicured gardens and there is a blue lake or pond off in the distance. She wears a regal blue sari trimmed in gold. Her blouse is red and encircling her neck are multiple bands of gold. She has smooth, unblemished skin and thick black hair befitting a queen. Salma can't quite make out if she is old or young, but there is something about her expression that makes her appear arrogant, or perhaps shrewd. She drinks from a small gold goblet and not far from her stands a young female servant, waiting to refill her cup. The servant is also beautiful, perhaps more beautiful than the queen, but her eyes are slightly averted to demonstrate submission to her mistress. She wears a gauzy green blouse. The queen gazes at the servant, smiling indulgently. Salma smiles to herself, feeling as though she has found hidden treasure. She grips the painting's edges tightly, not wanting to smear the glass with her fingers, and carefully carries it upstairs.

"Ah, you found it. How do you like it?"

"It's lovely, Aunty Asima. The colours are so rich. Are you sure that Quaid won't want to keep it? It almost looks like it should go with the one upstairs. Shouldn't the *raja* have his *raani*?"

"That's what Quaid said too. But the wall is not big enough for them both and I prefer the other one. Keep it," she says, looking for a bag large enough to contain it, "I'll have Sherie drop you and the children at the subway." She encases the painting in a heavy-duty green garbage bag and hands it back to Salma.

At home, after she had tucked the girls in for the night, Salma searched the kitchen drawers looking for picture hooks large enough for the new painting. Of course, there weren't any to be found, for the Paperwalas didn't have any artwork or wallhangings that would require such hardware. Sighing, she placed the painting at the back of the closet, taking care to stand it at an angle so that it would not fall over and be damaged when one of her children went looking for a pair of *chappals* or boots. She wanted to keep her new painting safe.

Chapter 6

BY MONDAY AFTERNOON, SHAFFIQ feels somewhat rested. Two days of sleeping in darkness, playing dolls with Shireen, talking to Saleema about fantasy book plots, and lying on the couch with Salma, leave him feeling almost ready to return to work. He heads to the Institute early again to cover for Ravi, who is still sick. Shaffiq considers calling Ravi at home, to check on his bachelor friend, but decides to wait until tomorrow. At five o'clock he is in the elevator, on his way to the fourth floor. James, his supervisor, approaches in the hallway. He is younger than Shaffiq, and maybe better looking, with a confident walk. Shaffiq eyes his supervisor's bulging biceps enviously as he approaches and ponders the fact that he has never had a single bulging muscle in his life.

"Shaffiq," James pronounces his name so it rhymes with 'reek', all the soft lilting nuances disappearing from it, "thanks for covering Ravi. Just do what you can with his areas; I don't expect you to spend as much time there as you do you own floors. Clean up any visible messes and the garbage and recycling. Ravi can do the rest when he's back."

"Thanks. That will save me some time. Tonight at least." Why didn't he tell me that last week, Shaffiq grumbles to himself. Missing the tenor of his employee's gripe, James beams a happy grin Shaffiq's way.

"And speaking of saving time, we just got in a brand new machine for cleaning the floors. Top of the line. You'll need to be trained on it. Come see me at the beginning of your shift tomorrow and I'll walk you through it."

"OK then, I'll see you tomorrow. A new machine, how great!" Shaffiq tries to sound chipper and allows a wide smile to overtake his face, hoping that he is not overdoing it. He would not want the man to think he was mocking him. James returns the smile and Shaffiq watches him stroll down the hallway, stopping once to inspect something on the floor. He watches James rub away the offending mark with his fingernail and then walk on. How lucky the man is, so at home in this place, Shaffiq thinks. This latest cleaning machine is probably like a new toy for him.

James reminds Shaffiq of Ashok, his supervisor in Bombay. Ashok was a middle manager in the Government of Maharashtra, a young lackey with no real power but desperately content to take whatever scraps of authority he was given. He started at Shaffiq's division more than six years after Shaffiq, but advanced much faster up the civil service ladder even with his obvious lack of accounting aptitude. Shaffiq's progess was much more difficult, full of broken rungs and slippery steps. When he complained bitterly to his friends and Salma about his young boss, they commiserated that the government was no place for a Muslim, and that there would be few new prospects for him there.

Shaffiq upends a blue recycling box into a clear plastic bag. He watches the white pages fall, forming haphazard piles at the bottom. Then he empties another bin, and then another until the bag is full, and ready to cinched and taken to the basement. As he lifts the bag onto his cart, he glimpses something familiar through the plastic, a translucent window into his past. Heart pounding, he retrieves the paper, flattens out its creases, his accountant's mind recognizing the tidy horizontal and vertical lines of the crumpled budget sheet. Scanning the columns agitatedly, he discerns that there is a significant error in the calculations: the actuals are three percent over budgeted estimates.

"What are you doing?" The voice is cautious, but stern. Shaffiq turns to the woman in the business suit standing behind him, looking at him warily.

"Sorry, I was just noticing this as I emptied your recycling bin." Shaffiq is not used to interacting with the people he cleans up after. He holds his breath, and thinks of something to say, "I couldn't help myself, you see there is a calculation error here that overestimates the deficit significantly and –"

"What, there is?" she says, looking confused, taking the page and scanning the line his fingertip is pointing to. Shaffiq takes a moment to study the crows' feet around her grey eyes, the wisps of red hair escaping from her hair clip. "Oh, I see. On this line, "she says.

"I'm sorry if I was looking at something I shouldn't have."

"Yes, these are confidential budget sheets. I'm not sure that cleaning staff should be scrutinizing them."

"You see I am not really a janitor. Well I am here, but back in Bombay I did this kind of thing in my job –"

"Oh, well, I suppose I should thank you for noticing my mistake. But please, for future reference, you really shouldn't be –" She frowns, not able to hide her irritation.

"You see I am an accountant," Shaffiq adds, wanting her to understand. That's what I really am. I guess my eyes were just drawn to what used to be so familiar to me."

"I see," she says, with a frozen smile that tells Shaffiq that she doesn't, that it would take a leap of understanding to see beyond his janitor's uniform, and listen beyond his Bombayite accent. She takes the paper from his hands and walks across the hall to her office, closing the door firmly behind her.

He wouldn't have wanted to take the spreadsheet home with him anyway.

Miranda is back in Nasreen's office for her second appointment. Her short, ice-blond hair, clutched into a tight ponytail, stretches her forehead back, making her look wide-eyed to Nasreen. She sits forward in her chair, her crisp black trousered legs crossed over and around themselves in a half slip knot, in a manner that only really skinny women can manage. She holds a typewritten list of questions in front of her and is advancing through them while Nasreen follows along, holding an identical sheet on her lap. Nasreen fingers the expensive stationary, her eyes moving back and forth between its contents and Miranda's pointed expression. In the preceding twenty-five minutes, they have run through half of the questions already. Nasreen's interpretations of them so far are: do you think I'm nuts; how exactly are you going to help me; and are you really qualified to do this job, because I'm not really so sure of it, you look so young. Nasreen has come to expect these kinds of questions from her more assertive clients and is quite good at hearing the fear flowing beneath the words; after a few years on the job, she no longer takes the questions personally. She almost expected them from Miranda, and here they are, arriving promptly at session two.

"Would you mind if I interrupted you here? I have something I wanted to ask you." Nothing ventured, nothing gained, thinks Nasreen. A tingly sensation moves through her now, the electricity of clarity, intuition. She is on her game today, undistracted, and focused for a change.

"Fine," Miranda says, a hint of irritation in her voice.

"Many of my clients take some time to trust me and themselves in this therapy process, which is very normal. Are you worried that you cannot trust what is going to happen here?" Nasreen asks, trying to regain control of the session.

"Trust, how do you mean?" Miranda tucks some mutinous stray blond hairs behind her ear.

"Well, it could be a mistrust of both what could happen and what may not happen," Nasreen says in her best Therapist voice. Miranda continues to look confused, and chews on the edge of her thumb. Nasreen notices a torn nail and cuticle. "Therapy is about exploring who you are and why you behave in the ways that you do. It is also about trying to create changes that are important to you. The answers you come up with can be interesting or upsetting or exciting, or scary or all of those feelings put together." Nasreen adds. She is almost enjoying herself.

"My last therapy experience was definitely not trustworthy," Miranda laughs nervously. "Some of my worst fears about myself were brought to light. I think I came here to try to disprove all of that." She picks up the strap on her briefcase, winds it first around her thumb and then her wrist.

"Do you mean that you have a problem with alcohol?" Nasreen straightens in her seat. She feels herself readying for something.

"Not exactly. I know I have a problem with alcohol," she says defensively. "What I suppose I have to talk about is my mother. I think she's the reason for the drinking. You must hear a lot of that here. Doesn't everyone blame their mothers for everything?" she says, with a sarcastic tone.

Nasreen watches as the leather strap cuts off the blood in Miranda's hand. "So what can you predict will happen for you if you start talking about her?" she asks, her tone gentler now.

"I'll want to leave." She releases the strap and looks down, surprised at the red welts left on her pale wrist. "And I'll want to blame you. I'll want to believe that you are the wrong therapist for me. Too young, not understanding enough, too different," Miranda coughs, "you know, from a different culture, all that. I've used that excuse before you know." Nasreen nods at the familiar sentiment.

"So what are we going to do about that?" Nasreen sits back in her chair. "How can we keep track of all of that so that it doesn't interfere with what you need to do here?"

"I suppose I'll have to try trusting you," Miranda mutters while watching Nasreen's face carefully.

"Take your time with that. And yourself? Will you need to trust yourself?"

"And myself." A stream of hot breath leaks out of Miranda's mouth and rushes at Nasreen, rustling the expensive stationary in her hand. Nasreen looks down at the typewritten words, hoping Miranda will come back for her next session.

Nasreen had never thought she'd become a psychologist, didn't even know what one was until she reached university and took a first year elective that piqued her interest. If you'd asked her what she wanted to be when she was a child, she would have told you that she would be a dancer. Perhaps like so many children who grew up watching too much television, she held in high esteem entertainers of all kinds. From the age of eight, she took a number of classes: tap and jazz, guitar, singing, ballet, drama. There was a different class for every season, and by the time the weather changed, she became disappointed and bored with each one. In the spring of her ninth year, her mother enrolled her in a ballet class to help her to develop more grace, and Nasreen soon decided that it was her favourite dance form despite its toe-crunching moves. By the summer, she was thoroughly fascinated with, and religious about, her twice-a-week classes. She loved the pink tights and satin shoes and hoped to one day to wear a stiff tutu and skirt like the older dancers who performed on television at Christmastime. She also loved her teacher, Miss Harlingen, who was thin and tall and wore her platinum blond hair in a tight bun pinned high on her head, like a small crown. She was the prettiest woman Nasreen had ever seen in all of her nine years. Even prettier than her mother.

Her parents encouraged her to continue taking the classes because they sensed her obvious pleasure and like other parents of only-children, they very much wanted to make their daughter happy. They dropped her off and picked her up each Monday and Thursday, sometimes staying to watch the class behind a window from the hallway. They complimented her on her pliés and pointes. They bought expensive seats at performances in Toronto and gifted her with books and posters about Karen Kain. But they drew the line when Nasreen confessed her dream of being a professional dancer; they made it clear to her that this would not be a good career path for her, not a serious endeavour, but a nice hobby. They suggested that a girl like her could be anything she wanted in this day and age. She could be a doctor or lawyer or the Prime Minister. But Nasreen knew they were wrong. She would be a dancer, even if they didn't think that she could. She would keep trying, working harder, and eventually she would dance in a theatre like the girls in the Nutcracker. She'd show them. She dreamed of going to the special ballet school in Toronto that Miss Harlingen talked about. She adopted the toe-to-heel walk of ballet stars and in each class she watched for her teacher's approval, tried harder to match her steps with the others.

It didn't work. In time, she came to understand that she was not the class favourite. She frowned when her teacher told her to hold in her stomach and patted her round rump in an attempt to straighten her stance. Nasreen knew that Miss Harlingen only did that to the plump girls. She never gave these instructions to the skinny dancers who she placed in the front row of the hall.

One day, at the end of the spring that marked Nasreen's second year of classes with Miss Harlingen, the top eight students were chosen to perform in the end-of-year recital. Nasreen waited, holding her breath, her stomach held in and her buttocks clenched as she stood as tall as she could, while one by one the names of other students were announced. She concentrated on Miss Harlingen's voice, trying to get noticed. Surely there was some mistake. Miss Harlingen smiled at the remaining three girls and told them to try again next year. Nasreen looked over to the parents' window to see if her mother had witnessed her humiliation but she hadn't, being too short to see past the small group of mothers crowded around the window. Nasreen stepped off the dance floor, toe-to-heel, toe-to-heel, and told her mother that she had a stomach-ache and wanted to go home.

In her bedroom, she stripped off her sweaty tights and leotard and tossed them in a black and pink heap at the back of her closet. She stood on her bed and studied herself in her dresser mirror, holding in her gut, feeling disgusted and ashamed. She exhaled, clutching her stomach fat between her fingers, pulling it out as far as it could stretch. Then she turned around and did the same with her hips, her buttocks and thighs, craning her neck to view the results. She was revolted by her reflection and in her ten-year-old wisdom, resolved to go on a diet that day. She was way too fat to be a dancer.

She made up an excuse to miss her Monday night class and then another for Thursday evening. Her father grew worried about her sudden disinterest in what had become her favourite activity. By the third missed ballet class, her mother complained, "Nasreen, these classes cost money, you know, and we have paid Mrs. Harlingen until the end of the next month already."

When it came time to register for summer activities, Nasreen decided to follow her mother's urgings to take Gujarati classes on Monday nights at the Mississauga Community Centre. On the way there one night, her mother suggested that her daughter take a ballet class once a week on another day.

"Come on, Nasreen, why not keep up your ballet skills. You've already learned so much. Don't you want to be in the Nutcracker anymore?" she teased, while they waited at a red light.

"Those classes are stupid. And they're boring. And anyway, I won't ever get picked to have a part like that. They don't pick girls like me."

"What do you mean? What's wrong with you?" The light changed then and Nasreen could feel the car lurch forward as her mother pressed on the accelerator too hard.

"My stomach is too big and my bum is too fat. If Miss Harlingen didn't pick me for the recital, then that means I won't get picked to be in the Nutcracker."

"Did she tell you that? You are not fat, Nasreen." Her mother looked like she was going to get angry, or maybe cry. She pulled into the community centre parking lot.

"No. But I know because I didn't get picked and the skinny girls did. But I don't care," she said, sullenly, "dancing is stupid anyway." Nasreen stepped out of the car and into the warm summer evening, stomping ungracefully heel-to-toe, heel-to toe, across the parking lot to the big doors. When she looked back, her mother was still there, parked but with the engine running, watching her pensively.

On the fourth floor, Shaffiq passes Nasreen's slightly ajar door, and he hears her voice, "OK, Asha, just give me two minutes. I just have to turn off my computer and pee and then I'll be at the front doors." Shaffiq moves further down the hallway and opens the door next to hers. He empties the garbage, barely noticing its contents. Then he hears a door slamming. He pokes his head into the hallway to see Nasreen striding away hurriedly. Before he can think what to say, she is gone, out of reach.

He opens her door next and steps inside. The desk is cluttered with files and papers. He picks up the garbage can and then sees the gold box again. He hesitates a moment, then reaches for its glittery cover.

"Oh sorry, I forgot something," Nasreen says.

"No problem, just emptied the garbage."

"Thanks. Bye," she leaves as quickly as she arrived.

Heart pounding, Shaffiq curses himself for almost being caught, for being so sloppy in his curiosity for the second time that evening. He hurriedly leaves the office, almost tripping over her garbage can on the way out. He finishes the rest of the corridor quickly, his mind racing at the thought that she may have seen him touch the gold box. At the end of the hallway, he sits down for a moment in a waiting area and replays the encounter with Nasreen Bastawala, remembering her blank expression, the unaccusatory eyes. Finally, he manages to calm himself convinced that no harm was done.

On his way to the elevator, he inspects the floors, looking for what James would discern to be obvious messes. Then he detects something shiny on the yellowing linoleum. He bends down, picks up a small silver teardrop earring. He holds it up to the light and admires its luster and shape. Pity there aren't two of them, he thinks. If there were, he would give them a polish and take them home to Salma. He puts the earring on a shelf in his cleaning cart and continues down the hallway.

"Hey girl, ready for your first Gujarati lesson?" Asha calls out the window as Nasreen approaches the old burgundy hatchback.

"I guess so," she says, opening the car door, "but this isn't my first lesson. Remember? I was forced to take classes when I was ten. I couldn't stand it and eventually my folks gave up and took me out of the class. I remember us reciting the Gujarati alphabet to some folk song. How useful was that?" Nasreen says, buckling up.

"Hey, did you have to take *garba* classes too? There were a whole lot of us uncoordinated girls wearing fancy dress and dancing around with sticks in some Aunty's basement. I'm lucky I didn't take out someone's eye."

"No, but I think we did that at parties a few times. And at the time I thought it was so uncool to be Indian, you know. I didn't like any of those kids. I just wanted to be out running around the neighbourhood with my white friends from school."

"Sounds like the old internalized racism had already hit and sunk in its teeth by then, hmmm?" Asha speeds up as she overtakes a lumbering streetcar.

"That was my treasured surburban girlhood. So what's this Mrs. Paperwala like?"

"She's a real Aunty type, you know, wears the cardigan over her *salwaar kameez*. Hair in a big bun," Asha says, with a knowing smile. Then, as though to correct herself she adds, "But she's not that old, really. She's nice. Used to be a teacher in India. Her daughters are kind of cute. The few times I've been there the little one's been a bit clingy, hanging off me the whole time. I've never seen a husband. I think there must be one, but he hasn't been there when I've been there."

"Well, let's get this over with then."

When Nasreen walks into the small apartment with Asha, all three of the Paperwala females look up simultaneously, transfixed. Shireen stops her imaginary tea-making, her mouth gaping and silent for a precious moment, her eyes focused on Nasreen's tall shiny Barbie-like boots. Saleema, too, is distracted from her reading, closes her Harry Potter book absentmindedly, losing her page. Salma looks a little too long at Nasreen's round eyes, her lipstick-stained lips and soft breasts and notices that Nasreen does not avert her eyes either. Asha watches the interchange for a second, fails to identify what she is sensing, and feels the need to interrupt the strange stillness in the air.

"Mrs. Paperwala, this is my friend Nas. Did you get my message? I told you I was bringing her along to try out a class. Nas, this is Mrs. Paperwala and her daughters Shireen and Saleema."

"Nice to meet you, Mrs. Paperwala. And you too, Shireen and Saleema." She says, smiling at each of them. She surveys the humble apartment. The air is heavy with the familiar smells of deep frying and incense.

"Of course I remember. Welcome Nas. Please, what's with all this formality?" Salma says, her arms opening graciously, "Why not call me Salma?" Asha wonders why she has not heard Mrs. Paperwala's first name before. Shireen scampers forward, takes Nasreen's hand and pulls her toward the low coffee table that is set for tea. She shoves Memsahib in Nasreen's face. She is at a loss for words in front of this new creature but manages to say, "this is my doll." Her voice is small and tinny.

"Oh, that's a nice doll." Nasreen smiles generously at Shireen, crouching down to look at Memsahib. She is not used to children taking a liking to her. She looks up to see Saleema's eyes following her and then retreating furtively behind her book again.

"Why do you have only one earring on? Where is the other one?" Shireen asks, her verbal skills returning. Nasreen probes her naked left earlobe and then the right one, feeling the familiar smooth silver of the earrings her mother had given her on her twenty-eighth birthday, just six months before she died. Nasreen has been wearing them almost daily since. Even in the shower. Shireen climbs onto Nasreen's leg and peers at the side of her face.

"Maybe it fell out when you took off your coat?" Saleema asks, scanning the floor from the living room to the foyer.

"No, I noticed you didn't have it on when you got in the car today," says Asha.

"I guess it must have fallen out. Why didn't you say something in the car, Asha? I wonder where it is. I got these earrings –" Nasreen stops, looks up at Asha, recognizing worry in her friend's eyes, "Oh well, it's nothing. I'm sure I'll find it."

"You can't just wear one. That will look silly."

"Shireen, leave Nas alone. Stop asking so many questions. She is here for a class with Asha. Nas, is that Nasreen for short?" Nasreen nods. "I once had a school friend named Nasreen. She was a lovely girl," she says looking into Nasreen's eyes intently and long enough to make Nasreen's face flush. "Come, let's sit down at the kitchen table and we can go over what Asha and I did last time so you can catch up, Nas," she said, steering her guest away from her precocious child and over to the table.

Salma, Asha and Nasreen review basic Gujarati greetings, the weather in all its incarnations, the numbers one through ten. The students haltingly chant the days of the week forwards and backwards while Saleema observes and Shireen giggles at them.

"Mumma, why don't they know how to say Saturday?"

"Because they have lived here since they were young. Here they didn't learn Gujarati," Salma says patiently.

"But even I know more words than they do."

Nasreen looks at the small girl, feeling a little silly, the familiar shame of not being Indian-enough. "But see, I know it now. *Shanivaar,*" she says, smiling self-consciously at Shireen.

"You two should make sure you practice so you don't forget how to speak," Asha says to the girls, "I wish I had learned when I was younger. It's so much easier to remember this stuff when your brain is young."

"*Ravivaar, somovaar, mangalvaar,*" Shireen singsongs the days of the week as she hops around the kitchen.

"But nobody speaks Gujarati here. It's not important. Why would you two bother learning now?" Saleema asks.

"*Budhvaar, guruvaar, shukravaar, shanivaar.*"

"Saleema, it is good to know the language of your homeland. Asha is right, you should practice with us more." Salma says. Saleema rolls her eyes at her mother and returns to her book. Salma sighs and turns her attention back to her students. "So why are you girls trying to learn Gujarati now?"

"Well, my father just sponsored his mother – my *daadi* – and she's living with my parents now. I thought it would be nice to be able to communicate with her. I'd like to do an oral history of her life before she gets too old," Asha says, sitting tall in the kitchen chair. Salma smiles politely at her and then reaches for Nasreen's arm and holds it a moment.

"And you?" She says, her eyes widening. Nasreen traces the amber patterns in Salma's brown eyes and tells her about the trip to India she and her father are planning. Salma's hand is warm on her arm and she doesn't feel like pulling it away.

"How much time do we have to get you ready before the trip," asks Salma, and then as an afterthought, "and for you to be able to do your interviews with your *daadi?*"

"Well, there's no hurry for me. My *daadi* is living here now and so it's just a question of –"

"Good. Plenty of time. And you Nas?"

"Until December. In about two months."

"Well then, you two girls just keep coming until then and soon enough you will be able to speak to your old *daadi* and you will be able to charm everyone in Bombay."

"Isn't it called Mumbai, now?" Asha corrects.

"Only the young people call it that. And the foreigners. The rest of us still use the old British name – it's hard to break that habit."

"You think I can learn enough to be able to converse by December?" Nasreen asks.

"If you practice in between classes. And we can set up extra classes if you'd like that."

Soon, the lesson is over and after turning down an offer of fresh *paranthas*, the students leave the Paperwala apartment, the weight of three sets of wanting eyes heavy on their backs.

When Shaffiq arrives that morning, the apartment is blissfully quiet, except for a soft snore coming from his daughters' room. He looks in at his children in their bunk beds and watches them a moment, their covers rising and falling with their breathing. Salma has told him that Shireen has begun to snore since coming to Canada. Shaffiq wonders if this is a strange manifestation of immigration angst.

"Shaffiq. Come to bed now." He is surprised to find Salma awake. She smiles at him mischievously, throwing back the covers. She wears a lacy black nightie, a daring wedding present given to her by her teacher friends in Bombay. He has not seen Salma wear it for many years and it still looks very good on her, the translucent black lace stretching tautly over her breasts and hips. The few extra pounds Salma has put on since having the children make her all the more delicious-looking.

"Come Sweetie, I've been waiting for you," she says, her voice sounding sly and inviting.

He wastes no time stripping off his janitor's uniform and then dives into bed beside her. She holds his face tightly and kisses him hard, then rolls on top of him, pinning his arms down over his head. For just a moment, Shaffiq questions whether he has wandered into the wrong apartment, and if this is really his wife. He opens his eyes and looks into his darling's eyes, marveling at his wife's sudden peak of libidinal energy. He allows his brain to stop thinking when her soft warmth washes over him, covering every inch of his body, heating his skin.

At six a.m., while Shaffiq surrenders to sleep, Salma lies wide awake, observing her husband's stubbly face, soft shoulders, and heaving chest. She pulls off the too-tight lingerie and wonders what force took her over just minutes earlier. She and Shaffiq haven't been together like that for some time, but everyone says that things slow down after you have kids. Salma looks at the clock again and decides to get out of bed and start her day.

She pulls on her housecoat and closes the bedroom door quietly. In the kitchen, she fills the kettle, and then leans tiredly against the counter waiting for it to boil. Looking out of the open kitchen door, she surveys the still-dark apartment, noticing that Shaffiq has left the hallway closet door ajar. She tries to slide the closet door shut, but it gets jammed on something, and so she turns on the hallway light and crouches down to inspect it more closely, seeing that the rubber edging of the runner has come undone. Just another thing to fix in this shabby apartment, she grumbles to herself.

As she stands up again, she glimpses the black garbage bag encasing the new painting from Asima Aunty. She had left it there at the back of the closet, out of harm's way, until she could go out and buy some picture hooks. In the days following, she had forgotten all about the painting. Touching one corner of the frame poking out of the garbage bag with her index finger, she feels a brief swell of contentment ride up her body. This will look nice on the livingroom wall, she thinks.

Chapter 7

THE NEXT MONDAY WHEN Asha and Nasreen visit the Paperwala apartment, Salma wears a light *shalwaar kameez*. Her hair is long and loose, a silver clip holding it off her face. She greets the women nervously at the door and Nasreen thinks that she gets a whiff of floral perfume from her as she takes Nasreen's coat. The apartment is tidy and quiet and instead of dolls and toys on the living-room coffee table, there are a few books and other trinkets.

"Good to see you both again. Have you been practicing the phrases? *Khem cho*?" Salma self-consciously brushes some hair off her face.

"*Majama chun*," replies Nasreen, dutifully. "Where are the kids? No wait, I know how to say that."

"*Ha, hun practice karunchoo. Baachaoo kaa che*?" says Asha, stealing Nas's thunder.

"Very good. *Barabar. Boh fine che*. Shireen and Saleema are down the hall at the neighbours tonight. Her kids are the same age so they play there often anyway. I decided it would be better to leave them there for a couple of hours so I could teach without any distractions." She guides them into the kitchen. "Tonight I thought we could focus on some of the conversation you will need to have with your family in India," she says looking at Nasreen. "Of course this should be helpful with your *daadi* as well, Asha." Asha tosses a raised-eyebrow glance at Nasreen, who catches it and blushes.

"That sounds good. I guess that would be a good place to start," Nasreen says. Asha folds her arms across her chest and nods unconvincingly at her teacher.

"So let's pretend I am your cousin and I am seeing you after many years. *Khem cho? Dubri pari gai?* Have you lost weight?" Salma asks. Asha laughs.

"Yeah they always hone in on the weight thing. What's that about?"

"Actually, they usually ask me if I've gained weight, I think. How do you say that?" Nasreen says testily.

"*Jadi thai gai.*"

"Uh huh. That's it. That's the greeting I usually get," Nasreen says.

"But I can't imagine them saying that to you. You are a perfect shape, Nas," says Salma, who looks Nasreen up and down and then flushes slightly. "You would say, "*Nahi, hun barabar chuun.* I am just right!"

As the two students get up to leave, Salma insists that they stay for dinner. "Come on now, I am on my own tonight. The kids are out and my husband is at work. You don't want me to eat alone, do you?" So Nasreen and Asha stay and talk with Salma about her children, her last two years in Canada, and life in India.

"But look! I have been going on and on. What about you two? You live with your families, or are you on your own?"

"I have my own place," Nasreen answers.

"My girlfriend is staying with me until she can find her own place," Asha says, "It just didn't work out for us to live together."

"But isn't it nice to have company, to have a roommate, Asha? Don't you feel lonely, all by yourself?" Salma looks at Nasreen.

"Not really – well, sometimes. But living alone has its benefits," Nasreen says, hoping to sound sure of herself.

"Yeah, I can't wait till I can have my place to myself again," Asha shrugs.

Salma shakes her head slightly. "I can't imagine it. I've always lived with other people. First, it was my parents and brothers, then with my in-laws and now here with my family. Of course it sometimes feels crowded, and believe me I enjoy it when everyone goes out for a little while, but I can't imagine living that way all the time."

"I guess with my work, I need lots of time alone. I talk to people all day," Nasreen adds.

"Oh yes? What do you do?"

"I'm a psychologist."

"Oh, how interesting!" Salma coos. "That must be very fascinating work!"

"Nas, I think we need to get going. I've got a paper that's due tomorrow and I've only just started." Asha rises from the table, placing her dishes onto the counter.

"Yeah, OK. I guess it is getting late," Nasreen says, checking her watch.

"I think our Mrs. Paperwala has taken a liking to you, my dear." Asha says as they wait in the hallway for the elevator to arrive.

"Was that what all your eyebrow arching was about! Oh come on. She's just friendly. And maybe lonely –"

"No, it's more than that. She is extra friendly with you. She's got a crush on you!" Asha says, grinning wickedly.

"Shhh, she might hear," Nasreen says, as the elevator door opens. They crowd themselves onto the already packed elevator. "She's only been here a little while. Maybe she doesn't have many friends and she wants to be our friend," Nasreen says, in a low voice.

"Your friend, more like it. Come on Nas, you know she was flirting. She was completely businesslike, completely teacherly with me the whole time," Asha pronounces, her index finger held up, as though making a final ruling on the subject.

Nasreen looks around to see the other elevator passengers' looks of curiosity. "Let's talk about this later. And I think flirting might be taking it too far," she whispers loudly. The elevator lands with a thump at the ground floor and they step out into the apartment lobby.

"Nas, you are not fat, you are just right," Asha mimics their teacher, holding Nasreen's hand in hers and smiling cinematically. She bats her lashes suggestively and Nasreen pulls her hand away. "Of course, she is right, but it was the way she said it. And I saw you getting uncomfortable with it."

"No I wasn't, come on, it wasn't quite like that." Nasreen leads her friend to the car and waits while Asha unlocks the doors.

"Oh Nas, your work must be sooo fascinating!" Asha gushes. "If that isn't flirting –"

"But she's married –" Nasreen protests.

"Like that ever stopped anyone! I'll remind you that I've bedded a few married women in my time, even recruited one to our side."

"All right. So maybe she is flirting with me. What am I supposed to do about it? And even if she's flirting, is that so bad?" Nasreen asks, trying to hide the smile that has started to creep across her face.

"Well it all depends, I guess."

"On what?"

"If you like her flirting with you or not." Asha laughs and revs the engine.

Chapter 8

THE THIRD NIGHT THAT Shaffiq is called to cover Ravi's floors, he begins to worry about his co-worker. Is he terribly ill? Does he need something? He wonders whether Ravi's ungenerous uncle has been to see him yet.

Ravi is Shaffiq's only friend at the Institute. On his first day there, Ravi observed Shaffiq struggling with the heavy floor polisher and came over to assist him. He bent over the machine, expertly unjammed what was stuck, and held out his hand in greeting. He seemed eager to talk with Shaffiq, and happy to make friends with the only other Indian there. Ravi informed him there were *desis* working on the day shift, but the night positions were mostly filled by Filipinos and Somalis. He filled Shaffiq in on cleaning short-cuts like squirting the toilets with cleanser, letting the chemicals do the cleaning and then coming back to flush it away five minutes later.

Shaffiq considers who might look after his friend should he be ill. He is aware that Ravi is a Delhi-ite who was sponsored by his youngest uncle and his wife a few years back. This uncle allowed Ravi to sleep on his couch for a couple of months but soon grew inhospitable, passing him the classified section of the Toronto Star one morning at breakfast. A few ads were circled in red pen and his uncle got up from the table, wiped his mouth with a napkin, and said, "It's time to find your own place. This apartment is too small for my family as it is." So Ravi found an apartment and left his uncle's home, somewhat disappointed at his uncle's lack of warmth.

Shaffiq does not understand Ravi's uncle's mentality. How could he be so cold to good-natured Ravi, his own nephew? In India, family is family, blood is blood. You are required to help even if you don't want to. It is a duty, an unquestionable obligation. Even Salma's Asima Aunty, not really very closely related, actually Salma's cousin's wife's sister, helped them out the first few weeks here. Shaffiq has heard of Canadian families where the parents charge their adult children rent to live with them. And then, years later, the children put the old people in institutions as though they were mentally ill! Such a terrible set of values, so individualistic and greedy, Shaffiq huffs silently. He hopes that his own children will not treat him badly in his old age.

He decides that he had better call Ravi to see if he needs anything. The phone rings three times and then a woman answers the phone.

"Hello?"

"Hullo? May I please speak with Ravi?" He is about to hang up, thinking that he must have the wrong number. Shaffiq knows that Ravi lives alone in a dingy bachelor apartment in someone's basement. He described the place in great detail during one of their coffee breaks and they both decided that the rental is probably illegal because the ceilings are very low. Luckily, Ravi is a short fellow.

"Just a moment, please." There is a clunk as the phone hits something hard and then the same strange voice returns and says, "I'm sorry, he's still asleep. You want to leave a message?" Shaffiq gives her his name and then the woman hangs up, leaving him wondering who she is. Ravi couldn't have a girlfriend staying over there, could he? Is she Canadian? But why would Ravi keep a secret about something like this?

Shaffiq takes his shower and dresses for work. Well, he needn't worry about Ravi. Someone is taking care of him. And a woman at that! Shaffiq buttons up his shirt and yells over to Salma in the kitchen that they really should invite Ravi over for dinner one night soon.

At work the next day, Shaffiq starts at his usual time and to his relief, Ravi is there, filling his cart with big bottles of aquamarine cleaning fluid. Dark circles frame his eyes but he smiles brightly as Shaffiq approaches.

"Hey Shaffiq, thanks for doing my floors. Had the nastiest flu ever! Couldn't tell if I was coming or going for three whole days." His hand pats his stomach, indicating the source of his discomfort.

"Oh, I didn't mind covering for you – they pay good overtime, but it's good to see you back again. You're feeling better now?" Shaffiq looks at the thin red blood vessels travelling through the whites of Ravi's eyes.

"Oh, yes, as good as new. And I'm happy to be up and about. You can only watch so many soap operas every day before you start to go a little cuckoo, right?" He makes little circles beside his head with his index finger. "If it lasted any longer I'd need to come here as a patient, no?"

"Did you get the message I called? Was that your aunt who picked up the phone? I called yesterday to see how you were and someone took the message –"

"No, my Uncle and Aunty are in India now. He and his whole family went back for a few weeks on vacation. You know it has been ten years since they have been back? Can you imagine waiting so long before seeing your Ma again?" Ravi sighs loudly, with a resignation Shaffiq has never heard before in his friend's voice. "I hope I can go back before that." Shaffiq nods, thinking about his own mother back in India. "Well, better get to work then, earn that bread that will pay for Air India, yes?" Ravi's wears a new strained smile. And then he is gone, whistling down the hallway. Shaffiq finishes stocking his cart. How easily Ravi squirmed out of his question about who answered the phone! What is the devil hiding?

Thoughts about Ravi's uncle's trip to India and the possibility of waiting ten years before going back himself inch forward in Shaffiq's brain, taking the place of Ravi's Mystery Woman. Shaffiq's mind wanders to the familiar place of worry he spends so much time visiting, tallying up the losses to his financial standing: one-third of life savings spent on the flight to Canada; two-thirds wasted on surviving the first two unemployed years; sixty percent of family income spent on housing; just five percent left for savings. There is still so much to build: the Girls' University Fund; a larger apartment and perhaps one day a home of their own; a better career for himself, courses for Salma. Surely India can wait. Will his mother recognize him in ten years time? Will she feel proud of him?

He allows his mind to shift from his financial brooding to nostalgia for his parents' two bedroom flat on Garden Road in Colaba. His parents, Amin and Zahabia, have lived there since Zahabia's father died over twenty-five years ago. In truth, Zahabia owns the flat herself, and she will proudly proclaim it to everyone when her husband is not within earshot. And it is true. Her father never trusted any of his daughters' husbands to be proper breadwinners and so, when he wrote up his final will, he stipulated that any money and property he left behind would stay in his daughters' hands and away from his good-for-nothing sons-in-laws. Zahabia's father turned out to have a keen financial sense and correctly predicted Amin's economic ruin. If anyone would have listened, perhaps Zahabia's father could have even predicted Amin's poor sperm production that resulted in the fluke of just one male son born to the couple.

Amin and Zahabia's fluctuating financial situation soon became something that Shaffiq learned to perceive through his parents' behaviour. When there was adequate money, the couple was relaxed and there was an easy feeling throughout their Garden Road flat. When Amin had once again mismanaged one of his many business ventures, a hard silence developed between the couple and all affection between them would evaporate. Shaffiq never actually heard his parents discuss their finances, but he could sense the status of their bank balance through the emotional temperature of the flat.

What Shaffiq learned from his parents, and especially from his grandfather, was that he needed to take his finances into his own hands, even if this meant using them to clean toilets. Of course, he hadn't known that things would turn out this way; he could not have imagined such hardship when he made the decision to move his family away and out of that flat on Garden Road. Still, it was his grandfather's legacy that made him want to leave when his own career path was blocked by managers who preferred dimwits like Ashok over him. He grew tired of being overlooked and excluded at work. He became angry that he was not considered a good candidate because he did not belong to the correct religion, because he could not offer a big enough bribe. The corruption offended him. He did not want this to be a part of his children's life.

And like so many emigrant hopefuls before him, he filed paperwork to leave India with the wish for a home without communal prejudices. They chose Canada, Australia, and New Zealand. Salma was difficult to convince, but even she eventually relented, mostly at the thought that life would be better and easier for them all. Their friends were certain that their application would not succeed, but somehow their forms passed the Canadian officials' scorecard, even though so many of their similarly qualified peers failed. They saw their astonishing pass as a good omen and soon packed up and said good-bye to their families. They didn't wait for replies from Australia and New Zealand.

"If things don't work in Canada, we can return to the Garden Road flat, can't we?" Salma asked him, a few months after they arrived in Toronto. "It's good to have a fall-back plan for the family," she persisted, when he did not reply right away.

"Salma, look. I don't want to go back there. Not to live, anyway. I'm not living there ever again. We have to move forward, think about the future, think about Canada as our new home now," Shaffiq insisted. He surprised himself with his strong words, his clarity. But this is how he feels. To him, things have to work out in Canada. Full stop. End of story. He doesn't want to return to India except to visit like a tourist. Yes, he will take the children to see India one day and they will look upon the dirty streets, the corruption, and poverty and know that Canada is a better place to live.

But now he is not so sure. The Canada he sees up close today is not as wondrous as the one he had imagined from afar. Maybe for his daughters it will be different and they will have opportunities that he cannot have himself. But he will never tell Salma he has doubts. He has been the immigrant cheerleader in the family while everyone else has pined for home. Hurray for Canada! Hip hip hurray!

Shaffiq pushes the broom ahead of him, gathering the day's dust and dirt in its bristles, and gets a sudden longing to sit in that Garden Road flat for just a moment, to hug his mother, shake hands with his father. To breathe in Coloba's sulphur-laden air, be crowded into a city bus with a hundred Indian men and go to his soul-robbing job just one more time.

Shaffiq observes Nasreen approaching while he tidies a waiting area near the first floor elevators. Instead of skirting away, she heads straight for him this time. For a moment, he panics, his heart beating fast, his brain shooting him accusatory, staccato queries: Did she realize what he was doing in her office last week? Does she suspect his unusual acts of nosiness? Did he leave anything amiss? Is she angry with him?

"Nasreen, hello, how are you today? Working late again? Boy, are you a hard worker!" He feels himself dampen under his armpits. Did he remember to put on deodorant today?

"Sorry to bother you. I was wondering if you found a silver earring last week? I'm not sure if I lost it here or someplace else." Shaffiq remembers that he placed the earring on his cart and then transferred it to his pocket to take home last week. Does she think he is a thief?

"Well, I did find something," he says. He feels around in his pocket but finds nothing. Where is it? "But, let's see. No, it wasn't an earring." He searches his brain for something to tell her, "It was a bracelet. That's right, a little bracelet, and I gave it to security for the lost-and-found box. Sorry. If I see anything like that, I'll keep it for you."

"Thanks, that would be great."

"The janitor who usually does your floor is back now," Shaffiq says coolly, relieved. "If you'd like, I can ask him about it if I see him." There, he thinks, now I am seeming helpful. Far too helpful to be some sneaky immigrant who steals jewellery.

"Sure, please ask him if he's seen anything." Nasreen turns to walk away, but then, looking back at him, she asks, "oh, what's your name? I don't think you ever told me."

"Shaffiq. My name is Shaffiq," he answers eagerly. "I am from Bombay too –"

"Nice to meet you, Shaffiq. And thanks," she says over her shoulder. "Have a nice night." Shaffiq waves at her, his right hand digging deep into his pocket, futilely searching for the silver teardrop. But of course the earring is probably long gone by now; last week's pants must have gone through the washer and dryer and must be hung up in the closet by now. Shaffiq watches Nasreen recede down the hallway, the heels of her shiny boots clicking along on the floors he just washed.

Shaffiq tries to remember what might have made him forget to take the earring out of his pocket and place it in his drawer with the other treasures he's found at the Institute. But of course! Shaffiq smiles to himself, remembering with satisfaction, that special morning Salma greeted him with open arms and fancy lingerie.

When Shaffiq arrives home that evening, Salma is fast asleep and snoring. He quietly removes his clothes and takes them to the bathroom hamper. Before he adds his uniform to the pile, he stuffs his hand down to the bottom of the hamper, feeling around it's wicker bottom. When this yields nothing, he empties the contents onto the bath mat, sifting through the pile of girls' t-shirts and socks. He exhales, excited to see one pair of his khaki janitor pants amongst all the other dirty laundry. He fishes his fingers deep into the pants' pockets and comes up with navy blue lint and a paperclip. But no earring. Perhaps one of the girls or Salma found it? Tired, he gives up the search and slips into bed. It is some time before he is able to fall asleep.

Salma continues to sleep soundly. She is dreaming in colour and detailed slow motion. Shaffiq calls out to her from the top of a tall purple escalator. She stands at the bottom, waving back, relieved to see him there. She scales the moving steps and realizes that the escalator is moving downwards, away from him. She quickens her pace, trying to outstep the escalator and the metal stairs move faster, matching her speed. She wants to give up, wants to get off the escalator, but Shaffiq continues to wave to her from the top, cheering her on. Fatigue is soon upon her and so she steps off the escalator and looks up at Shaffiq. Giant silver teardrops leak from his eyes.

Chapter 9

NASREEN IS A LITTLE early for her appointment. She sits uncomfortably in a plastic chair in the makeshift waiting area just outside her therapist's office listening to the muffled sounds of voices on the other side of the door. She flips through an old issue of *Ms.* magazine, reading a review of a book about breast cancer. She checks her watch, uncrosses her legs and crosses them again. She knows she shouldn't read stuff like this. She has read countless articles about women and cancer, tales of hope and resilience, about new treatments and future cures. Ultimately, these stories bring her back to a familiar one.

Zainab Bastawala was neither a smoker nor a drinker. She exercised regularly, ate carefully. She had a good marriage, and a generally happy life. Her cancer got diagnosed in the winter of 1999 and it swiftly moved through her, leaving neither her nor her family with enough time to adjust to its ugly presence. It lodged in her right breast, claiming the tissue there as its residence, threatening to spread further west and annex whatever flesh lay in its ravenous path. It resisted treatment, defying all efforts to be surgically or chemically killed off, and it extinguished all hope the Bastawala family had for recovery. By the autumn of the next year, it had claimed victory.

Nasreen continues to read the magazine in her lap, unconsciously rubbing her left earlobe, her thumb and index finger massaging the soft flesh. She squeezes the hard centre where the tiny hole resides. She hasn't worn any earrings since she lost her small silver teardrop.

"Happy Birthday, *Beti*. I hope you like them," her mother beamed.

She handed over the small jeweller's box with a slight tremor in her hand caused by the fatigue of a recent round of radiation and chemo-therapy.

"Oh, they're pretty," Nasreen said, showing them to Connie.

"Try them on," Connie said, taking them out of the box. Nasreen did, and she almost never took them off after that.

"They look great. Nice choice, Mrs. Bastawala."

"Connie, come on, call her Zainab," Bashir, said, smiling at his daughter's girlfriend.

"Yes. I don't call you Miss Parker, do I?" Zainab laughed. Connie blushed, and Nasreen felt grateful for her family that day, a family that included Connie.

Nasreen closes *Ms.* and reaches for *Glamour*. She considers what to talk about with her therapist today. Her mother? Connie? She resents Connie for giving her something else to grieve, another loss to process in therapy at eighty dollars an hour. And not only that, but Connie's leaving has been bringing up memories in strange Connie-Mother com-binations all the time these days. First a thought about Connie, then one about her mother, or vice versa. Last night she reflected on how she met Connie just a few months before her mother's diagnosis. She was in bed, enjoying a blissful afterglow in Connie's strong arms when the call came. The answering machine beeped and then her father's voice, slightly higher pitched than usually and breathless, called out from the living room.

"*Beti*, it's your father calling. Can you give us a call? We're just back from the hospital and we have some news to tell you. I'm afraid it is bad news, so please call us –" She had launched herself out of bed and was at the phone before he could finish.

"Hold on Dad. Let me turn the machine off." There was an electronic squeal and then she listened in silence while her father told her about breast cancer, treatment options, prognoses. Later, her mother picked up the extension.

"Listen Bashir, don't scare her. The doctor told us that we still have some time to go before we know everything. I'll start treatment next Monday and then they will have to see where things stand." Her mother seemed her invariably calm self, while her husband and daughter imagined various worst-case scenarios. Nasreen hung up the phone, promising to call back the next day. Connie draped her bathrobe over her naked body and she cried for the first time in Connie's presence that day. Her embrace was Nasreen's only reassurance that night and in the months that followed.

And this is how her relationship with Connie became intractably tied to her mother's death. They moved in together when her mother's chemo treatments started because they were spending so much time together anyway. And, Connie reasoned, Nasreen could borrow her car more easily with it parked right outside the apartment.

They gave each other silver rings, gifts of commitment, a day after the funeral. Nasreen was too numb to question the timing, and was grateful for Connie's steadfast company. It was as though the crises of illness and death and later, grief, became the glue that kept Connie and Nasreen together in a heady attachment. And it was only when those forces absented themselves from the relationship that Connie seemed able to reverse the process, slowly coming home later and later at night, pulling away from Nasreen.

The office door opens, releasing a woman with a pink, tear-streaked face. She glances at Nasreen, and their eyes meet, two strangers acknowledging their shared experience of being at the same therapy office at the same time.

"Bye, Carmen. Hi, Nasreen, come on in."

Nasreen settles herself on the couch, still imprinted with and warm from Carmen's body. She gazes at the long-familiar setting; the couch with its many cushions, the South American rug, the obese-goddess statue by the window. Her therapist wears magenta-coloured denim pants and a thin lavender sweater. Nasreen has become used to her therapist's penchant for wearing many shades of purple.

"You haven't been here for a little while, Nas. What has it been, a month or so?"

"Yeah, sorry for cancelling the last appointment. And I've meant to call to re-schedule but things have been really busy." Nasreen fidgets in her seat. She props a mauve cushion behind her back.

"The last time you were here we were talking about Connie and the dynamics in your relationship." Therapist has a knack for remembering the content from one session to another, thinks Nasreen. Perhaps she just takes good notes. Nasreen both likes and hates this quality in her therapist.

"Oh, yeah, that's right. I was supposed to think about whether she is part of a pattern among my choices in women," Nasreen says, feeling self-conscious.

"And were you able to do some journalling or thinking about that?"

"No I never did get there," avoiding Therapist's eyes.

"And is that why you didn't get here too?" Therapist doesn't waste any time. At least, thinks Nasreen, I get my money's worth. She begins to calculate what she has spent on therapy this year. At eighty dollars per session, and if I've come here an average of twice a month ... she looks up to see Therapist watching her expectantly.

"Sorry, can you say that again? I seem to have wandered off," she says, and Therapist complies, repeating her question.

Chapter 10

SALMA SLUMPS IN THE kitchen chair, preparing for her students' next Gujarati lesson. Their departure last time darkened her mood. Alone in her family's apartment, she felt too warm, closed in, and that gloomy sensation returns now. She opens a window, welcomes in the cool afternoon breeze, and imagines herself growing wings and fleeing this place. She takes herself back to her classroom in Bombay, standing authoritatively in front of her prepubescent students. She is teaching them the proper use of English prepositions, writing out an example on the chalkboard, turning to see engaged expressions of the children's earnest faces.

The sound of Saleema's yelling interrupts her daydream. "Stop bothering me Shireen! You're so stupid! Go play in the living room." The children argue for another minute and then there is a peaceful quiet that Salma chooses to interpret as the conflict's resolution.

How she longs to teach again! For now, she must satisfy herself by being an "Experienced language teacher from India. Gujarati, Hindi, English classes," as her handwritten flyers announce. So far no one has asked her to teach them English.

She found Asha, her very first student, this past summer. She walked along Gerrard Street, posting up her hand-made signs in grocery stores, sari shops, and restaurants. When she was almost finished walking the Little India strip she paused to rest at a sweet shop. She found an unoccupied table and put down her remaining flyers. When she returned to the table with her *chai*, a young woman was standing there, bent over, engrossed in reading one of the flyers. Salma's first impression of Asha was that she resembled a skinny goat, her spiky, scruffy hair standing up across the back of her head, the bumps of her spine showing through her light cotton shirt. Asha inquired about Gujarati classes and the two agreed to call one another later that week to arrange a meeting time. Salma watched Asha as she walked away, thinking to herself how unselfconscious and forward the girl was. If Salma had closed her eyes while Asha spoke to her, she would have assumed that the girl was a white Canadian. The only thing that gave Asha away was her name and brown face.

Salma shuts the window and looks around her dreary living room. She studies the mustard-coloured, second-hand couch, the old coffee table Asima Aunty gave to them, the bare walls. She wonders what her students must think of her home. Could they tell that she was just a mother and wife, a woman who works in a dry cleaners, friendless, futureless?

Somehow, while her students were here, she didn't worry about appearances, and the dullness and insufficiency of the apartment did not seem so stark. And neither did her life. While Nas and Asha were here, she was Teacher Salma, interesting Salma, Salma with knowledge. She felt a little tipsy, even giddy from their attention. No, giddy is not the right word. Tingly. She felt tingly. Salma closes her eyes and remembers the heat that ran through her just a few days ago, sliding down her throat and into her gut like a cup of steaming *masala chai*. And each time Nas leaned in close or held her gaze, the heat crept lower down into her belly, flowing all the way to her groin. With her eyes closed, Salma conjures up that feeling again, squeezing her thighs together, crossing her feet at her ankles. An unnatural, vibrant, unholy sensation.

After a few heartbeats, she uncrosses her legs and stands up, interrupting her body's lustful beckoning. She checks her watch. She should get the children ready to go to Aunty Asima's if they are going to make it out there and to the mosque in time. As she opens the hall closet door to take out the children's good shoes, she spies a glint of metal; the painting Asima gave her. I've got to put that up soon, she thinks. She pulls it out of the closet now, removes its plastic cover and admires the bright colours, the classical scene. She leans it up against the closet's frame and steps back from it, her eyes drawn to something she hadn't noticed before. From this angle, the servant's blouse seems translucent, her dark nipples showing through the sheer fabric. The queen, her eyes glistening, a smirk forming on her face, appears to be leering in the servant's direction. Salma wonders for a moment if the painting is a little bawdy or lewd. *No, it can't be, it's just my silly mind.* She puts the painting back in the closet, and calls her children to get ready to leave. I will hang it soon, to brighten up the room, she thinks to herself.

Salma is unable to focus on the sermon. Perhaps it is that today there is a visiting *imam* from the Emirates with a monotone voice and a strange accent, or maybe it is that her restless mind has more important, or at least more distracting, considerations to weigh. She scolds herself for her lack of attention, looking to the other women who appear to be listening attentively. She shuts her eyes, forcing herself to raise the *imam*'s flat words into meaning. She hears him lethargically begin to list – or perhaps it is the middle of the list, she is not sure – key tenets regarding the sanctity of marriage, and the ways one must fulfil the duties of husband or wife. For some reason, the topic makes her think about domestic chores and more specifically, about the load of laundry she sorted last week.

While she separated the lights from the darks, she found a strange thing in her husband's pants' pockets. Nestled among the used transit transfers and dirty handkerchief was a single teardrop earring that matched exactly her student's lost one. She sat on edge of the bathtub, inspecting the small, shiny earring, marvelling at the coincidence. She has grown accustomed to her husband's little hobby and so at first, the earring amused her and she planned to tell Shaffiq about Nas and her lost earring that same evening, imagining how they would laugh that his sleuthing had actually come to some good. Then, she planned to give it to Nas at the next Gujarati class. How happy that would make her student! She looked so crestfallen when she realized that she had lost it.

And yet Salma has neither spoken to her husband about the earring, nor has she returned it to Nas, but kept it, like a thief, or more accurately, a pick-pocket. She puzzles over her own actions and also her husband's. Why didn't Shaffiq mention the silver teardrop; he tends to covet each of his treasures, storing them away in the top dresser drawer for good luck. Now, with a week gone by, it seems strange that he hasn't asked after it and she wonders if it isn't a little late to raise it with him.

While the *imam* lectures, she wonders if she could still manage to return the earring to Nas without having to consider Shaffiq. Could she somehow leave him out of the transaction, making the teardrop a gift to her student, a gift from she alone? She looks down into her lap, her face hot, feeling a little ashamed and unsure why she would be plotting a secret that doesn't include her husband.

She knows she should bring her focus back to the *imam* and stop thinking about Nas. But thoughts like these are difficult to harness and sometimes must be permitted to run free and so she surrenders to her imagination, inventing a verdant scene in which she presents the teardrop to Nas. She coyly requests Nas to close her eyes, and she complies, her long dark eyelashes fluttering in anticipation. Salma takes Nas's hand, places the teardrop in the centre of her warm palm, and then presses each finger down, one by one, until Nas's hand closes into a tight fist. Then, stepping back, she watches as her favourite student opens her eyes, releases her fingers, and is overcome with joy at Salma's offering.

Chapter 11

SHAFFIQ WALKS AROUND THE fourth floor, equipped with a package of Salma's *samosas*, hoping for Ravi's company. He hears the whir of the floor polisher and circles the wing until he catches up with his friend.

"Ravi! Want to take a break?" He shouts. He holds up the greasy paper bag and mimes eating. Ravi turns off the machine and smiles.

"Which of your wife's goodies did you bring this time?"

"*Samosas*. They're good."

"They are always good. Shaffiq you don't know how lucky you are to have such a good cook for a wife."

"So when are you going to find yourself a wife and start bringing me some of her home cooking?" Shaffiq jokes.

"I don't know if that is going to happen to me anytime soon," Ravi says, a frown forming between his abundant eyebrows.

"What do you mean? Don't you want to get married?"

"*Arré*, things aren't as simple as that. You see, I haven't told you this before, but –" he throws a glance over his shoulder and then, confirming that they are alone, he whispers conspiratorily, "I have a girlfriend."

"Ravi, very good! What's the problem? And why so secretive?" Shaffiq thinks back to the woman who answered Ravi's phone a couple of weeks ago.

"Well, she is not Indian. She is a white girl. Well, an Italian, but Canadian. No, Italian-Canadian," says Ravi, seeming bewildered about his girlfriend's cultural identity. "She's my landlord's daughter. No one else knows about it. Her name is Angie. Short for Angela. Which means –" and his tone becomes wistful – "angel."

"Your landlord's daughter? How has her family not found out? They live upstairs, no?"

"Well, she usually leaves the house saying she is going to visit one of her girlfriends. I hear her through the heat vents. Then she quietly slips downstairs to see me and then I have to close the vents so that they won't hear us upstairs."

"So the two of you sneak around? I can't believe you haven't been caught yet," Shaffiq says, biting into a *samosa* excitedly.

"You know it was easier in the summer because the AC is not really needed in my basement flat. I could close the vents all the time. But now, when I do that, it sometimes gets quite cold down there during her visits. I'll have to buy a space heater, I think, and put that on when she's with me. But I hope they don't start complaining about the extra electricity. They would do that you know. They are cheap types."

"Enough about the heat and the vents! What is this girl like?"

"Well, the family is quite religious. They are Catholics and quite restrictive with her. Almost as bad as back home, Shaffiq. She is not allowed to have boyfriends. She is very nice, very pretty. She has blue eyes, Shaffiq. I never imagined I would have a girlfriend with blue eyes. Just like that Karishma in the movies. Have you seen her recent one? She was so lovely in it ... you know which one I mean, you know the one where she plays a princess –"

"Ravi, won't they throw you out if they find out? How old is this girl?" Shaffiq asks, wondering about his friend's judgment.

"She's eighteen. Almost nineteen. We're careful. But her parents are not the biggest obstacle. We'll work it out with them. At least that's what Angie tells me. You see, her older sister eloped with a black Jewish chap last year and they finally accepted him after her sister got pregnant. Angie thinks that they will come to accept a Hindu in time. It's my mother who will be the big problem. My mother will be very upset if I were to marry a Canadian. It would kill her."

"It's that serious? You're thinking about marriage?"

"I don't know. Yes. Maybe. It has been really nice. And she takes good care of me. You know, when I was sick, she was really good to me. She brought me chicken soup."

Shaffiq nods, visualizing Angie with her blue eyes spooning Ravi broth. "You think it can work out with a Canadian? In the long run? They are so different from us Ravi."

"Well, I didn't think so at first. But love is love, right? Why should it matter about our differences?" Ravi sighs wistfully, like a romantic protagonist in a Bollywood film protesting society's confines. "We can overcome our differences."

"But those are big differences. Don't underestimate them. You're talking culture, and religion on top too."

"That doesn't matter to us. That stuff doesn't matter in Canada. I mean, look at you and me," he says pointing to Shaffiq and then back to himself. "Would we ever have been friends in India? A Hindu tailor and a Muslim accountant?"

"Well, I guess things are a little different over there, but –"

"Then tell me this Shaffiq. If Salma was an Italian with blue eyes, would it matter to you?" Shaffiq hesitates, trying to imagine Salma with blue eyes and paler skin. He frowns and Ravi persists, "Look Shaffiq, it would be nice to settle down with someone. I mean you have Salma and your daughters. I am pretty much alone over here. It would be good to have a wife. And maybe down the road, a houseful of babies."

"Yes, you're right. I hope it works out for you, Ravi. I really do. But remember that having a family is a blessing, but it is also a big responsibility. A big responsibility. You don't know about all that as a bachelor. Marriage has its struggles." Shaffiq sighs heavily.

"What? Is something wrong at home? With the kids?" Ravi places his hand tentatively on his friend's shoulder.

"It's not a big thing. It's nothing really. We're fine." Shaffiq shifts his posture slightly and Ravi lets his hand fall from Shaffiq's shoulder.

"Come on, tell me. You don't look very fine right now," Ravi insists.

"It's just that, well, I don't think Salma is happy here." Shaffiq gets up and paces back and forth in front of Ravi. "She is having trouble feeling settled, you know. And suddenly she is changing. Developing a new interest in religion. Spending time at the *masjid*. That's not normal for her."

"It takes a while to feel at home here. I, myself, was homesick, very badly homesick for three, even four years. And what's the problem with her going to the *masjid*? That's good for women, no?"

"It doesn't feel like my Salma." Shaffiq stops his pacing. "Something is bothering her and she is turning to religion instead of talking to me about it."

"Give it time, Shaffiq. Things have a way of working out in time. Maybe for me too."

Shaffiq sits down, suddenly feeling tired. "*Inshallah*, Ravi. Listen, I've been meaning to invite you over for dinner sometime. Salma is eager to meet the man who eats her *samosas* and compliments her on her cooking. Maybe you and your Angie could come over sometime soon? Maybe next week Sunday or the week after?"

"That's very nice, Shaffiq. I was wondering when I was going to meet your family. And now you can meet Angie. I'll ask her," he answers, obviously pleased by the invitation.

"Good. Salma will like meeting some new friends. It'll do her some good. These days she only meets the old biddies at the mosque."

Chapter 12

"NASREEN, IT'S YOUR FATHER. Call me back." Nasreen pushes the delete button on the answering machine and goes to the kitchen to make a cup of tea. She fills the kettle, opens the cupboard door and scans the selection of teas lined up in their colourful boxes. She considers Raspberry Fields, Chamomile Dreams, Licorice Lullaby. She reaches for a big tin of mint and then hesitates. This was Connie's favourite, the tea that accompanied them during evenings together on the couch, watching movies, or after dinner talks. Of course that was before, while they were still good together, before the relationship went bad. Did we pass our expiration date? Nasreen wonders. She chooses a mug that flirts with her in small, insincerely shy letters, "dip me in honey and feed me to the lesbians" and drops in a bag of decaf orange pekoe. She scans the cupboard for something sweet and hastily eats three chocolate chip cookies. She starts on a fourth when the phone rings. She munches down the cookie, wipes her mouth and then answers the phone.

"Nasreen, it's me, your father."

"Hi Dad."

"I called earlier, did you get my message?"

"I haven't had a chance yet, I just got in a few minutes ago." She pours the hot water into the mug, watches it slowly turn from amber to brown.

"I just called because I wanted to know if your work has travel insurance in the health plan. I bought insurance for me and thought you should get some too."

"I don't think I have that in my plan. What were you thinking? Health insurance?"

"I bought everything: health, cancellation, lost baggage, the works."

"We need all that?"

"Yes, just in case. You never know what will happen. We forfeit the free trip if we have to cancel at the last minute, but there's no loss if we have the insurance. Given everything is free so far, I thought we might as well buy the expensive insurance. I'll call the travel agent and get it for you then."

"Why would we need to cancel at the last minute?" Her father rarely does anything at the last minute.

"Well, you know, it doesn't hurt to plan for the unexpected. I'm getting older, and well, who knows what can happen," Bashir says, hurriedly.

"What, Dad? What are you worried about? Is something wrong?"

"*Arré*, I'm not saying that. There is nothing to worry about. We all get house insurance in case we get burgled, or there is a fire, or something like that, but we don't know if or when it might happen. Cancellation insurance is like that. It is simply a precaution. Nothing to worry about. Speaking of that, have you made an appointment to get your shots? You should do that soon."

"Right, I've been meaning to do that." After a few minutes of small talk Nasreen hangs up. She absent-mindedly leaves her tea in the kitchen and goes to bed. She is grateful when Id joins her there.

Later in the week, Shaffiq checks his watch and calculates the time left in his shift. Just two hours and ten minutes to go. He deserts his cart and takes the elevator up to the fourth floor to share his break and snack with Ravi. He doesn't feel like keeping his own company tonight.

He surveys the east wing and then the west but doesn't find his fellow janitor, who must have moved on to another floor by now. Disappointed, Shaffiq eases himself in a metal waiting room chair and unwraps the aluminum foil from around the *pakoras* Salma fried yesterday. He happily bites through the spiced *gram* flour coating to a slippery onion. Salma cooks better than his own mother, a compliment Shaffiq has learned does not impress Salma much. Early in their marriage Salma impatiently rolled her almond eyes at him and said, "Yeah, thanks a lot. Really, Shaffiq, as though I aspire to perfect every one of your mother's recipes," and returned to marking some grammar assignments. Shaffiq knows what does matter to his wife and pays her compliments accordingly: her teaching, her quick wit, and her mothering, in that order.

He uncaps his thermos and pours himself a cup of tea. Not hot anymore, but still warm. He wonders if his daughters will care about Indian cookery, if they will want to learn this craft from Salma, or if they will be more interested in hamburgers or pizza. For Salma, there was no question that she would learn to cook even if she was a teacher. But for his young daughters, he is not even sure what the choices are, what the options will be for them once they become more Canadian than Indian. In just two years, they are beginning to seem different. Will they turn out to be like that Nasreen with her polished boots and Canadian accent, familiar yet so foreign to him? Does Nasreen even know how to fry a *pakora*?

Leaving behind his thermos and snacks, Shaffiq meanders down the hallway and stops at her doorway. What impulse takes him there? Why this strange curiosity in a woman he has met briefly, exchanged pleasantries with, who is really not so interesting? Come on, he chides himself, it must be simple attraction, right? She has long hair and a curvaceous young body and he is a man. Isn't that how it goes? He sighs. It's not as simple as that. Something about her bothers him, even repulses him slightly. She is too western for him, too un-Indian. And yet at the same time he wants to draw nearer, to understand this strangeness. His mind lingers on these thoughts only for a moment before he reaches for his master key. He inserts it with his right hand and turns the doorknob with his left, taking care to avoid touching the door with his greasy fingers. He has a moment of hesitation in which he imagines the protagonist of a crime show hunting him down, his oily fingerprints the telltale clues left behind. He pushes the door open, switches on the desk lamp, and shuts the door gently behind himself. He takes a moment to quickly wipe his hands with his handkerchief.

In the dim light of Nasreen's office, Shaffiq spies the gold box resting at the back corner of her desk. Sitting down in her ergonomic chair, he reaches for it gingerly, lifts the lid and looks inside. He sifts through the box, scanning the photos within, seeing nothing very interesting. There is a photo of her with some friends at what looks like a party in someone's home. He wonders if that is where Nasreen lives. Then there is a glossy of a big brown cat, looking menacingly into the camera, a snap of some flowers, a postcard from someone writing with a messy hand from Vancouver. He flips through them all a second time, coming back to the party shot. It's missing. Where is Nasreen with the blond girl? He replaces the box to its original place and disappointed, he gets up to leave. He pushes the chair back in and knocks over the garbage can under the desk. As he rights it, he sees that it has already been emptied.

When Shaffiq returns to the waiting room, he finds Ravi looking keenly at the aluminum foil package that holds Salma's *pakoras*.

"Ah, there you are. I was just walking the floor to see if I could find you. Have you had your break yet?"

"No, I wanted to finish upstairs first," Ravi says, gesturing to his cleaning cart heavy with two large garbage bags. "I see you brought some goodies?"

"Yes, go ahead, finish them off. I should get back to work in a minute or two. My break is over. Why don't I take those bags for you on my way back down?" Shaffiq says, trying to affect a casual manner.

Ravi pops a large *pakora* between his teeth. His mouth full, he holds his hands up in a show of resistance. "*Arré*, no need to do that, Shaffiq. I'll do it later."

"Absolutely no problem, my friend." Shaffiq hoists the bags and waves at Ravi as he hurries to the elevators.

"Alright then, thanks. And tell Salma that she makes truly great *pakoras*! Oh by the way, dinner next Sunday works for Angie. Is that day still available for you and Salma?"

"Sunday? Oh yes, perfect. See you then." Shaffiq smiles as he enters the elevators and presses the 'B' button. He is away before Ravi can call out to him about his forgotten thermos.

Shaffiq leans over the large stinky bins, letting the contents of Ravi's fourth floor bags drift slowly to the sticky plastic bottom. With his right, rubber-gloved hand, he sifts through it, searching. After the first bag is emptied, he opens the second, hoping to find treasure amidst filth. Halfway through, he discovers it. Nasreen's face is smeared with something sticky, which he wipes clean with his glove. The other girl's face is scratched up with the deliberate marks of a pen, as though someone has tried to scribble out her image. He drops the photo into his pocket and throws the rest of Ravi's second bag to the bottom of the bin. He doesn't stop to consider what a middle-aged Indian man digging in the garbage must look like to anyone who might be watching him.

Chapter 13

MIRANDA ARRIVES FOR HER third session dressed in a tight black lycra top with dark blue pants. Shiny silver and black mandalas circle the thin cuffs at her ankles. Nasreen recognizes the designs from her last trip to the mall. Recently the fashion industry has exploded with India chic, splashing Sanskrit, Hindu icons and sub-continental designs over belts, t-shirts, dresses, and now, the cuffs of pants. She nearly bought the same pair herself last week, but Mona dissuaded her from the purchase, complaining about neocolonialist forces appropriating and profiting from their cultures and religions. She added that the designer in question also had poor labour policies and sweat shops in Guatemala. Nasreen put the pants back on the rack and bought a pair of Levis instead.

Chunky silver bangles matching the mandalas on her cuffs circle Miranda's wrists, clanking against each other with each movement, creating an effect that strikes Nasreen as deliberate chaos. At the same time, Miranda's wrists and ankles somehow balance each other with a measured symmetry. Nasreen wonders if she wore this outfit on purpose, for her benefit.

Miranda takes off her coat, snaps open her Palm Pilot and then sits down. "I thought we could schedule the next few sessions ahead of time. My schedule is really quite tight in the next couple of months, so I need to have these sessions locked in well in advance." Nasreen rises to get her black, vinyl covered agenda book. Is this a sign of commitment, Nasreen asks herself.

"That's fine with me." The two women negotiate times for the next few sessions. This takes close to five minutes, with Miranda juggling her schedule out loud. "No, not the twelfth. I have a big deadline then. How about the thirteenth after three p.m.? No, the thirteenth won't work either. I'm planning a surprise wedding shower for my friend … OK, then the fourteenth at ten a.m.? Perfect." When they finish, Nasreen puts her book down and waits for Miranda to put away her electronic agenda. She doesn't. Instead, she clutches it tightly in her lap.

"Some people consider me kind of anal. Type A, you know. My life is scheduled so far in advance, it doesn't leave much room for spontaneity. You must think I'm obsessive."

"Well, I don't know you very well yet, but I would say that there is nothing pathological about wanting to schedule our sessions in advance. Do you view yourself the way yours friends would? Or differently?" Nasreen deftly skirts the question. This is not about what I think, she reminds herself.

"I suppose I do sometimes. I trust my friends mostly. I take lots of jokes for being the one who they need to book three weeks ahead. Or when I start yawning at nine o'clock. I start my day at four-thirty a.m. I need to go to bed by ten." Nasreen calculates the number of hours Miranda sleeps. Why would anyone get up at four-thirty, she wonders. Without at least seven hours, she can't manage to get through the day without looking like a zombie. The last time she got up at four-thirty was probably to catch at flight to India. Her mind wanders to the details of her upcoming trip: will the departure be at some god-awful time? Will she have to stay over in Mississauga the night before? She brings her focus back to Miranda, who has just said something she missed. She guesses, or rather hopes, from Miranda's bland expression, that the comment wasn't very significant.

"Last time you were here we started talking about your mother and the impact that she's had on you. Shall we continue with that this week?" Nasreen knows she may be rushing Miranda to get to the important issues, but she is impatient. She wants this therapy experience to be better than Miranda's last. Actually, Nasreen has been considering Miranda all week, her mother's suicide, and what she imagines to be its impact. She even brought Miranda's case to her peer supervision session this week.

"Yeah, OK. I spent some time thinking about that this week, as you suggested. I made some notes in my organizer but I forgot to make a copy for you." Miranda holds up her Palm Pilot but doesn't open it.

"That's all right." Nasreen says, leaning forward slightly. "Why don't you just tell me what you came up with."

"Well, I know I drink to keep those feelings away, but I think I also try to control everything as a way to cope," Miranda says, almost cavalierly, "But that would have started when I was much younger. My mother's depression may have contributed to that. You know, when I was younger I used to label all my bookshelves and sort my books by genre," she adds looking over at the bookshelves above Nasreen's desk, which are orderly, but definitely not in alphabetical order.

"What in your current life is like that?" Nasreen asks, following Miranda's eyes roving from the bookshelves, to Nasreen's messy desk, and back up toward the bookshelves.

"Well, my schedule is one of the things I order, as you can see," she says, making eye contact again with Nasreen, "and my drinking is pretty orderly too. I keep it fairly secret, I even measure my drinks, I buy only the best wines, which I research and keep track of in my Palm." She holds up her electronic organizer. "This thing holds everything together. I am probably the most controlled drinker you'll meet. Except that I can't seem to control my drinking." She smiles at Nasreen, who is pleased with the direction of their conversation.

"Kind of a paradox, isn't it?" Miranda nods and then gazes at the wall behind Nasreen. "Miranda, I think that it is important that we keep on the topic of your mother and her death. It may be difficult to talk about and very tempting to avoid the topic, but I recommend that you try to stay with it." Nasreen feels compelled to push. "What feelings came up this week about her?"

"Well, I thought a lot about what she might have been like the few hours before she killed herself," Miranda says quietly. She pauses, looking past Nasreen, and then continues, her eyes glassy and unfocused. "I wondered what she was thinking and feeling and why she did it, especially since she seemed so much better, you know, more alive than she'd ever been. I wondered if she liked being depressed more than, well, normal," she says without emotion. She sniffs, then coughs.

"What's your feeling about that?"

"Well, I think so. I think she did like being depressed," she says, her voice growing stronger, more angry, "It was what she knew how to do. And she knew what to expect from it. She was good at it."

"So, depressed was more familiar and easier for her," Nasreen nods, not wanting to interrupt Miranda's thoughts.

"Yeah, and maybe she didn't want to stop being depressed. It was me and my father and all the doctors who wanted to change her. I suppose we never stopped to find out what she wanted," Miranda says, blinking hard, as though realizing something for the first time. Nasreen feels a swell of excitement building within herself, and she presses on.

"How would you have felt if that were true?" Nasreen holds her breath.

"Then it means that we all drove her to her death," Miranda says, dropping the Palm Pilot in her lap, her hands traveling up to her face.

"By wanting her to get well?"

"By wanting her to be so-called normal. Maybe depression was her normal. Maybe being neurotic and alcoholic is my normal," she exhales, her hands covering over her eyes, "I never asked her what she wanted. I kept on hoping that she would transform into the mother I wanted and needed." Miranda rubs her dry eyes, which have started to feel itchy.

"That seems like a reasonable thing to want," Nasreen asserts. She looks away from her client, glimpsing a tree branch, almost barren now, most of its leaves already fallen, knock up again the office window.

"Yeah, I needed a mother. I still do. But now I know I won't ever get that. At least she did me a favour by not letting me continue with a futile hope," Nasreen looks back at Miranda, watching her hands grip her electronic organizer, noticing that her face has returned to its previous expressionless state. "Hoping that things would be different was exhausting."

After Miranda leaves, Nasreen sits at her desk, staring at the wall for a few moments. The intensity of the session tired her, but it is a good kind of tired, like the fatigue after thirty minutes on an elliptical machine. For the first time in a long time, Nasreen feels like a good therapist instead of a distracted, burn-out case. What she doesn't know now, what she is yet to sense, is the workout's hangover. It's the residue that is about to come, the pain-after-the-gain, the emotional onslaught that arrives a day or so after the endorphin rush.

She flips open her agenda, scanning the empty pages of her future, wondering when she should see her own therapist again. They didn't schedule a follow-up appointment after the last session because Nasreen had left her agenda at work. She was supposed to call right after the session to rebook. That was a week ago. She makes the call and leaves a message on Therapist's voice mail, requesting an appointment.

Salma stands back from the couch, scrutinizing the painting she has just hung, a little crookedly, on the wall. She studies the *raani's* serene face, and notices for the first time that the servant's gaze is not really averted away from her queen, but directed out at the viewer, at Salma. That's strange, Salma thinks, why hadn't I noticed that before? She matches the servant's stare, appraising her as she feels she is being appraised. Salma imagines the servant standing slightly taller, steadying her posture, her brown nipples pushing against the thin fabric of her blouse. Salma views herself in the painting's glass reflection, wondering what the servant might see in her. Salma too stands more erect, and brushes her hair back with her fingers. Then she shifts her gaze from her reflection back to the painting beneath and it seems to her that now the *raani*, too, is glancing her way. The weight of both stares makes Salma inexplicably self-conscious and so she backs away, averting her gaze. She checks to see if the painting is hung level, and out of the corner of her eye thinks that she sees the *raani* turn and wink at her. She follows the movement with her eyes but once again the *raani* and her servant have returned to their original positions.

She hears movement in the next room, the predictable outcome of her recent hammering; her husband is awake. Shaffiq shuffles out, his pajama pants slightly askew, hanging just a little to the left like the painting.

"Salma, what have you been doing? So much noise –" She knows from his surprised eyes that he has just answered his own question.

"Well, you know, the wall has been bare for a while, and we kept talking about getting something to put there –"

"Where did you get this? It's nice. Reminds me of some of the paintings I used to see back home." He draws closer to have a better look at it.

"Yes, I like it. Asima Aunty gave it to me. She and Quaid Uncle bought it last year in India, but had no room for it."

"Yes, of course, they bought one too many, as usual?"

"That's right," she says with a laugh, "But let's not complain, Shaffiq, this apartment is filled with their 'one too many' purchases."

"That's true," he says, moving even closer to the painting, his eyes squinting, "*Arré*, Salma, this painting is a little naughty, no? Look, when you look at it closely, this woman is half-naked!" Shaffiq, says, pointing and laughing. "Are you sure Asima bought this? It's almost pornographic! No, it must have been Quaid who picked this up, the old dog!"

"Pornographic? No, it's not, Shaffiq! It's art. And you can hardly see anything, just a little hint of her breast," Salma says, crossing her arms over her own chest.

"OK, OK. Don't get upset. I'm just kidding around. I'm glad we have some Indian art. The wall needed it. Hey, wait a minute is she …" He draws nearer to the painting again, "Just look at the way the *raani* is looking at her. Salma, she's looking straight at her nipples!"

"Maybe it is not the painting, but your own mind that is so dirty."

"*Arré*, it's so obvious! Just look here, at the line between her eyes and her chest." He says, pointing, drawing an imaginary line between the *raani's* gaze and the servant's nipples. "Come on, you can't tell me it's not obvious!"

"OK. That's enough, Shaffiq," she says, straightening the painting. "I like my *raani* and her half-naked servant."

"I didn't say I didn't like it," he counters, laughing.

Chapter 14

THAT NIGHT, WHILE SALMA snores, Shaffiq roots around in the kitchen for somewhere to hide his most recent treasure. Instinctively, he knows that he will not show this new photo to Salma. It's not like that other picture he picked out of the wastebasket in the vice-president's office; that nameless woman had nothing at all to do with Shaffiq's life. Her photo was only a novelty item, a simple anonymous curiosity. This photo of Nasreen's is a different matter altogether, something he stalked, hunted, and found in the institute's garbage bins.

He hears a noise and looks out into the living room to check if anyone is awake; he thought he heard whispering. He tiptoes to the girls' room and pauses to watch them sleep. They look so peaceful, he thinks. For a moment, a feeling of calm brushes through him. *They will be OK.*

He sneaks back to the kitchen, traversing the dark living room and the agitation returns, and soon his is sweaty from his own nervousness. He looks up at the painting on the wall, notices the *raani* illuminated by a shaft of moonlight coming in through the drapes. Her image distracts him for a moment, but he knows he must not dally. He has already taken unnecessary risks; he should have hidden the photo last night after his shift, but Salma seemed to be sleeping lightly when he came home. Tonight, she seems dead-asleep. But still, he will have to be quiet.

He looks through cutlery drawers and underneath piles of coupons and decides that the kitchen is Salma's domain and probably not a good hiding spot. In fact there is no place in the cramped apartment that is not Salma's, nor is there any place that is solely his. Even the top drawer of his bureau is shared with her jewellery. He returns to the living room and scans its clutter for a nook or cranny to hold his photo. He examines a small bookshelf that once held encyclopedias in Asima's home. He touches the Indian knickknacks, running his index finger over a small mirrored elephant that has lost a few of its shiny tiles during the journey to Canada. His mother gave him the little elephant on his sixth birthday – Shireen's age. Funny how his children have not attempted to play with his treasured elephant.

On the shelf above, the gold cover of Salma's Koran beckons to him. He picks it up and holds it, feeling its weight in his hands, dusting off its jacket. He considers hiding the photo within it but changes his mind. He would not want to defile the book with his weird fascination with Nasreen Bastawala.

Shaffiq is not a very religious man, but he is not a non-believer either. He doesn't like the structure of it all, the heavy rule-making, the way that some people use religion for their own gain or to pass judgement on others. But he does like the Koran. He admires how some of the passages read like poetry and agrees with the fair-mindedness in most of the prescriptions for daily living.

He lets the Koran's binding fall open and it lands in two equal piles at page 246. He scans the page, his eyes slowing to read a passage about adultery. He ponders the words for a moment, then re-reads the passage. *Am I a kind of adulterer?* He turns the question over in his mind. He has certainly never cheated on Salma, never touched another woman since he married her. And God knows that he barely touched a woman before her, unless you count the smooch from that girl in college and the one adolescent kissing session with his cousin-sister. So it is clear to him that he has never physically cheated on Salma. But why has he been so focused on Nasreen? Why has he been gathering things that belong to her, things that should be of no concern to him at all? He considers his collections: the itinerary, the earring, which he has lost anyway, and now the photo. The first two items landed in his path and it was just his curious nature to pick them up, he rationalizes. Fate brought those things to him. But the photo is different. The photo he procured through more illicit means, behaving like a shameful garbage picker. And for what? So that he could possess this damaged photo? Is this a type of cheating, perhaps an emotional adultery? He doesn't want Nasreen for romance or sex. That's not it. He doesn't see her in that sort of way. It's something else entirely. It maddens him that he doesn't know what.

He turns to look at the *raani*. "Where shall I put this, what do you think?" Shaffiq examines the painting, gazing at the queen, and in the early morning light, he thinks that he sees her eyebrows rise at him. When he looks over at the servant, he detects her smiling. He shakes his head. Ah, what rubbish. I must be dead tired. But he feels compelled to turn back to the canvas until his eyes begin to ache from the inside out. Finally, the painting releases his eyes and he moves decisively to the kitchen. He slides a top drawer open and feels for the plastic tape dispenser lying sideways behind the knives and spatulas. Back in the living room, he takes the painting down from the wall and turns it over on the couch. In the bottom left hand corner he tapes the photo face down on the cardboard backing. Satisfied that it is secured, he backs away from it and surveys his work. A glint of something shiny catches his eye and he sees what he had not noticed before, a piece of clear plastic attached to the bottom right hand corner of the frame. He hovers above it for a moment, and then tugs at the plastic until it slips out of the frame. Holding his breath, he grasps the delicate package close to his eyes. He unwraps it carefully, knowing that he has just found something that he was not meant to find, aware that he is intruding upon someone else's secret. Now unwrapped, he sees that between the layers of plastic lies a small silver teardrop. It is his silver earring, the one he found outside Nasreen's office. The one he lost. Well, really the one that Nasreen lost. His exhausted mind scrutinizes the meaning of this little piece of jewellery hidden behind the painting. His heart pounding, he removes the photo from the frame's backing, hastily replaces the earring back within its plastic wrap and shoves it into the frame's edge. He puts the painting back onto the wall and stashes the photo between the pages of a rarely looked-at book about the *Life and Times of Mahatma Gandhi*. He rushes to bed, falling sideways into a deep sleep, a slumber that grabs him and drags him under before he has a chance to pull the covers around him.

"Miranda, why don't you share with me what you wrote this week?"

Nasreen's client looks down tentatively at her cream-coloured stationary, and then shuffles the pages, reordering them. She pauses, studies her red canvas shoes and Nasreen notices for the first time today that her usually well-coordinated client looks different. Inside the red shoes are black sport socks, which are topped by a pair of faded blue jeans resting below a crumpled grey silk shirt. Nasreen looks for the usual one-of-a-kind jewellery and tastefully applied make-up and sees none.

"Sorry, I forgot to make a copy for you again. I've been forgetting to do a lot of things this week, actually."

"Has something been preoccupying you this week, Miranda?"

"Well, it's going to sound really simple, but it has actually been really disturbing …"

"Yes, go ahead, Miranda," Nasreen readies herself for Miranda's words, taking a deep breath, as though preparing herself for a blow. An emotional body-check.

"Well, I just realized, I mean really realized, that I have no mother and I won't have one again."

"That is a big realization. What's it feel like?" Nasreen's insides begin to twist, and at first she wonders if she'd hungry. No, she thinks, I had a big lunch just a couple of hours ago.

"It feels like I am … empty. Or sort of hollow … right here," she says, rubbing her flat stomach.

"Like something is missing?" Nareen says, bringing her own hand to her stomach, empathetically miming Miranda. And that's when a force within her abdomen brushes up against her fingers, making itself known. A wave of nausea follows and Nasreen, a little alarmed, checks her watch. Reflexively, Miranda checks her own.

"Listen, can we end early today? I'm not feeling so well. I think I might be coming down with the flu or something," Miranda says, not hiding her need to bolt the room.

"OK, Miranda," Nasreen nods, knowing she is ending the session too easily, but she is relieved. "I'll see you next week."

The next morning, Nasreen takes her journal from her bookshelf and blows a fine coating of dust off its cover. She has not yet done her therapy homework and her appointment with her therapist is tomorrow. She can recognize resistance in her clients and she certainly sees it in herself now. What was the question she was supposed to write about? Patterns. Patterns in relationships. Nasreen's mind feels as blank as the page in front of her. And something about the session with Miranda is bothering her too, something she is not ready to name. She gets up, puts the kettle to boil and returns to her bed with a cup of orange pekoe.

The phone rings. Nasreen stares at it a moment and then picks it up on the third ring.

"Hello?"

"Nasreen, it's me, your father. I just thought I'd call you today."

"Hi Dad. What's up?"

"Well, you know what today is, don't you?" Nasreen hates these types of questions. She gets them from her clients and sometimes her father drops them on her too. They are like not-yet-exploded emotional bombs that she is supposed to detonate. She thinks hard, knowing she has forgotten something.

"Today? Uh, well, I just got up, I haven't really looked at the calendar –" Then it comes to her.

"Nasreen, it is your mother's birthday today. Didn't you remember?" She hadn't. Until just now. Nasreen hears the hurt in her father's voice.

"Oh, I guess I wasn't thinking about it really. And I just woke up. It probably would have come to mind sometime today." Or this week, or sometime, Nasreen hopes.

"Well, yes, maybe that is the better way of coping with things. But I can't help it. I started thinking about her birthday last week, the way I would have when she was alive. You know, I actually had a moment of panic yesterday when I realized I hadn't bought her a gift yet. And then I remembered that I didn't have to." Bashir's voice is soft, almost a coarse whisper, "I bought her perfume last year and the year before that too, you know, her favourite kind. It was strange, but I had to buy her gifts even when she was gone. I resolved to not do it this year." He pauses, and Nasreen is quiet, unsure what she should say, or even if she should interrupt him. He continues, "The bottles are still here in her drawer. Sometimes, I take them out and spray a little of her perfume in the house, just to … just to be able to have something of her here with me." Nasreen thinks she hears him holding back tears, or maybe they're the leftovers from tears already cried. She understands now why the smell of her mother still lingers in the house, two years after her death.

"Geez, Dad, why didn't you tell me?"

"I don't know. Because it made me feel silly, I suppose. And I didn't want you to feel bad too."

"I think it's normal to remember, Dad. It's only been a couple of years, right? That's not a long time when you consider that you lived with her every day for over thirty years." Nasreen feels her therapist voice emerge and she is suddenly more confident, "You know there have been studies about how bereaved people unconsciously remember significant dates and anniversaries related to the person who died. It's called the Anniversary Effect." She wonders why the anniversary effect passed her over this year. But then she remembers the strange feeling in her stomach yesterday during Miranda's session. Maybe I wasn't just empathizing.

"Really? I thought maybe I was just not getting over her death," Bashir answers, his voice heavy.

"I don't think we ever will get over her, Dad. But maybe the pain gets less bad over time." Or maybe it will be worse before it gets better.

"Well, it's good to have a psychologist in the family. Look at me, I just got a free session, or are you going to charge me for it?" Bashir laughs softly.

"It's on the house, Dad." But she doesn't feel like laughing, or counselling him anymore.

"No, at least let me take you out for lunch. I don't wish to abuse your services. I'll come in to Toronto and see you. We could go to Gerrard Street. What you think?"

"OK, what time? I have a few things I need to get done today –" Nasreen thinks fast to try to head off this unexpected request.

"How about one o'clock. I'll come pick you up. Don't worry, I won't take too much of your time. I want to go to the *masjid* a little later today anyway."

"I'll see you at one then," Nasreen says, sighing. As they say their good-byes, Nasreen ponders her father's plans to go to the mosque. She thought that he had stopped going a long time ago. Suddenly fatigued, she abandons her journal and flops back into bed.

Across the Don Valley, under the fluorescent bulbs at Moti Mahal, Nasreen and her father sip *lassis* while they wait for their orders to be ready. Bashir likes a salted *lassi* while Nasreen prefers a sweet one. Nasreen's mother, their absent lunch partner, usually drank orange soda with her *thali*.

And because memory is strong and habits difficult to break, Bashir sometimes reflexively orders a Fanta for his deceased wife, only catching himself after the impatient counter staff has already rung up the order. For the past two years, a bright orange soda can has sat unopened and conspicuous between Bashir and Nasreen during their many father-daughter Little India lunches. Both parties usually avoid acknowledging the mistake, the Fanta, a simulated orange-flavoured elephant on the plastic laminate table. At the end of their meals, Nasreen has observed her father deftly slip the can into his deep coat pockets, sneaking away with his embarrassed grief.

Once, when visiting him at the house, Nasreen caught a glimpse of an orange soda at the back of his fridge. She had an urge to do something with it, perhaps to toss it into the garbage, pour it down the sink, or just steal it away. But to take such action would mean trespassing the corridors of her father's sorrow, a territory she is reticent to enter. In the end she left the Fanta there, standing beside the ketchup and Shanti's mango pickle.

To Nasreen's relief, today of all days, her mother's birthday, Bashir somehow manages to remember not to order a drink for his deceased wife.

"So Dad, you're going to the mosque again? Is that something new?" Nasreen asks, sucking the thick *lassi* through a not quite wide enough straw.

"Yes, well, your mother and I stopped going when she got sick, and then I didn't feel like going back after that. But then recently I just wanted to go again."

"Number Four, Number Four," the server at the counter yells into the microphone.

"They got a sound system since we were last here." Nasreen observes.

"Oh, that's us." Bashir says, checking the number on his receipt. He hurries to the counter to retrieve their *thalis*. He returns to the table and the two metal platters land on their table with a light thunk.

"These are both vegetarian, Dad. You didn't order a meat *thali* this time?"

"Well, it's supposed to be better for the cholesterol," he says, with a slight grimace.

"I don't think any of this food could be good for anybody's cholesterol levels." Nasreen scoops up some *matter paneer* with her *chapati*, taking care to avoid the oil pooling around the edge of the dish. "You're turning vegetarian and going to the mosque. That's a real change, Dad."

"I wouldn't say I am 'turning vegetarian'. That's going too far. I'm just having less meat these days. And, as for religion, you know, it can be comforting. At least for me. I often feel more at ease after I leave the *masjid*." He scoops some rice into his mouth. "Maybe it would be good for you too."

"I don't think so, Dad. You know how I feel about organized religion. I don't like the *ridah* and the fact that the women are segregated from the men. It feels so archaic to me." Nasreen takes in a mouthful of *aloo gobi*.

"I suppose all religions are old-fashioned. It's how they are. They have old origins. Well, it's your choice. I think it's a good thing. Maybe you'll feel differently when you are older." Nasreen rolls her eyes. "No really, things are different now at the mosque. So many new faces. I only recognized a few people in the crowd. But then my crowd tends to go on the special days only."

"Do you see your friends much these days?" Nasreen attempts a casual tone. So many of his friends seemed to desert him after her mother died.

"Well, a little bit. Last week the Shahs, you remember Fatima Aunty and Asif Uncle? They invited me for dinner. They asked about you, wanted to know how you were. Rahim and his wife just had their first baby. A boy." Nasreen remembers hearing that their son had married a couple of years ago. Their families used to be so close.

"The Shahs? You haven't seen them for ages."

"Yes, it was nice that they called. You remember we tried matchmaking you and Rahim when you were teenagers," Bashir smiles at the memory while Nasreen winces on cue. It was the predictable, awkward joke that came up each time the families visited one another.

"Yup, I remember. That was lots of fun," she says sarcastically. For her part, Nasreen had always been more interested in Rahim's older sister, Rehana, on whom she'd had a crush for years. "What's Rehana doing these days?"

"She's married too. To a doctor. Gastroenterologist, I think. But no kids. Fatima and Asif are disappointed, naturally." Nasreen pushes away her empty *thali* knowing that she shouldn't have asked the question. She doesn't enjoy these discussions, the chronicles of upwardly mobile South Asian kids she knew as a child.

"Yes, well, I always thought she was a lesbian." Nasreen knows she is saying this for shock value, but she can't seem to stop herself. "Maybe that's why there aren't any children. She and her husband probably don't sleep together." Both she and her father squirm involuntarily at this mention of Rehana's sex life.

"Well, I don't know about that. She's always seemed normal, I mean, she is just like anyone else," Bashir feels his face flush. How to say the right words after saying the wrong ones? He tries again. "Not that you aren't normal, that's not what I meant to say. I just wouldn't suspect Rehana of being ... gay."

"Well, none of your friends 'suspected' that of me either. Neither did you for that matter," Nasreen says sharply, a slow heat rising in her chest. She looks at her watch. Bashir sees the obvious gesture and reaches into his pocket for his handkerchief.

"Are you ready to go? Had enough to eat?" He so badly wants to avoid an argument with his daughter, especially today.

"Yeah, I have to go." She is a little ashamed for being mean, knowing what this day means to her father, but not ashamed enough to stop herself.

"How about some tea and a *dil bahar*? You want some sweets to take home?"

"No, I really have to go. You get some if you want, I'll go wait by the car," she says, pulling on her coat, turning away from him.

"No, no sweets for me today. I have to watch my cholesterol," he says, trailing behind her out of the restaurant.

Chapter 15

AT SEVEN P.M. ON Sunday night, the buzzer rings, signaling Ravi's arrival. Shaffiq pushes the intercom to open the lobby door, five floors below.

"I hope he's brought Angie. I want to see what this girl is like. He's head over heels about her," he says to Salma, who peeks out at him from the kitchen. "Everything ready?"

"Everything ready and warming. Saleema, Shireen, come out of your room. Ravi Uncle is here." Shireen emerges first, excited by the arrival of guests. Saleema joins them in the living room a few moments later, carrying *The Lion, the Witch and the Wardrobe*. "Saleema, leave your book for just a little while. It is not polite to read while guests are here. You can read again after dinner." Saleema crosses her arms over her chest, holding the book against her body like a shield.

There is a knock at the door and Shaffiq opens the door to Ravi and a small woman with shoulder length brown hair. Shaffiq looks into her blue eyes and smiles while she hands him her coat. She's short, just like an Indian, he thinks. After a round of introductions, the four adults and two children sit in the living room, smiling at one another through an awkward silence.

"So finally I get to meet all of you! Shaffiq is always mentioning your names and now I get to find out that he has actually not been lying all this time about having a beautiful wife and children." Ravi breaks the ice, his face opening up into an infectious grin.

"We're so glad you could come," Salma replies warmly, "Shaffiq talks about you all the time too."

"And such a nice apartment, huh Angie? Maybe we'll have a place like this in not too long."

"Yeah," says Angie, her eyes scanning the drab living room. She searches for something nice to say. "This painting here is really nice," she says brightly.

"Thanks. It is quite a classical piece, very common in India," Shaffiq says, rising from the sofa. "What can I get you to drink? Angie, we have juice, soft drinks, beer. Ravi, you'll have a beer, no?"

"Actually, Angie, I just put that up recently. A relative of mine brought it back from India last year," Salma adds, pleased that her guest noticed her new painting.

"Daddy laughs at it. He makes faces when he looks over there," Shireen stage whispers to Angie.

"Yeah, he says it's too revealing," Saleema joins in, "Because you can see through that girl's top." Ravi and Angie follow Saleema's finger to the offending blouse.

"Children, don't say that! It's not true! It's fine art. Artists for centuries have admired and painted the human form," Salma admonishes. She turns back to her guests, "So, how long have you two known each other?"

"We've been dating each for just over six months," Angie says, "Ravi rents from us, you know, and so we actually met before that. But we didn't start going together 'til later." Salma watches the couple smile at one another, sees the look in their eye that tells her that maybe they'd rather be alone tonight.

"As soon as I met her, I knew she was the one for me. I fell in love straight away," says Ravi, puffing up proudly. "Of course, she didn't know that, I was just the renter until we officially met and started talking. Yes, very convenient, our living arrangements. We get to see each other all the time! No travelling time is a bonus," Ravi gushes. He reaches over and takes Angie's hand in his, rubbing her fingers with his palm, as though the apartment is too cold for them. She leans over and gives him a quick kiss on his lips.

"And just a little risky too, right? You have to watch out for the parents, no?" Shaffiq teases, handing beers to Angie and Ravi and a soft drink to Salma. He wonders if his daughters should be watching the display of affection. He notices that Saleema has long abandoned her paperback to the coffee table. Shireen, for her part, sits beside Angie, looking up at her in awe. Angie reminds Shireen of Miss Lewis, her first grade teacher at St. Clair Public who she thinks is one of the prettiest ladies she's ever met.

"Yes, Shaffiq mentioned that your parents are not aware," Salma says to Angie.

"Yeah, but it will be fine, they're not so bad. We'll tell them eventually, and they won't really be able to stop us. I mean, they'd prefer I was with someone Italian, but they'll have to deal with it when the time comes." Angie smiles at Ravi. She kisses him again. Salma notices that Ravi makes slight smacking noises when he kisses Angie back. She wonders if he is a sloppy kisser, the way Shaffiq used to be before she taught him how not to give such wet kisses.

"Girls, come, you want some pop? Come let's go to the kitchen and get some." Shaffiq corrals the girls out of the living room. Doesn't Ravi realize how inappropriate it is to carry on this way? And in front of the children!

"Yes, you're right. If it is what you want, then that is the most important thing. No one can really control you unless you let them. My parents were trying to get me married off for years before I was ready and I resisted them until it was the right time. And when we met." Salma looks toward Shaffiq, who is frowning from the kitchen door. "Our parents were so glad that we were finally making the match. They'd given up on us. Of course, Shaffiq and I didn't have cultural differences for them to protest."

"That's true. You two are from the same community. But we're not really so worried about Angie's folks. It is my mother who is expecting me to return to India one day to find a bride. Sometimes we Indians can be so old-fashioned. Although she is so far away, it is she who is weighing heavily on my mind. I don't wish to hurt her, but I'm afraid there is no choice. I just hope she will do all right with it."

"Come on Ravi," Angie says, "let's not talk about this depressing stuff. We're here to have a good time," she says, nuzzling into his shoulder. He grins at her and takes a gulp of his beer.

"Well," Salma says, feeling like she is intruding upon the pair, "I'm going to make the final preparations so that we can sit down and eat. I'll just be a few minutes."

"OK," trills Angie, not looking away from Ravi, "Let me know if there is anything I can do to help."

"That's fine," says Salma, "You two just sit. I won't be but a minute." Just try to remain vertical, Salma thinks.

Therapist looks at Nasreen intently, waiting for a response to her challenge. Her age-spot speckled hands are folded in her lap and her foot taps the floor lightly, making the only noise in the office. Nasreen studies Therapist's face, notes that her lipstick has almost worn off, leaving a still intact and clownish-looking lip-liner ring.

"I guess the answer to my question is a difficult one for you Nas. So, have you been thinking about your mother lately?"

"Yeah, a little. It was her birthday this past week." Nasreen questions Therapist's motives. *Why take me down this road? What a waste of money this is. And now I'm feeling nauseated.* Nasreen knows these thoughts are a little off, and that her feelings are likely misdirected. She ventures out loud, "your question pissed me off. I feel pissed off with you, with me, with her. The question is difficult because it is difficult to think about her. I feel guilty about that."

"What do you feel guilty about?"

"I intentionally try to not think about her sometimes. Delete her from the files, my father would say. And he's another story. He called me yesterday and you know what? I forgot that it was her birthday. I felt embarrassed and resentful that he would call me. What does he want from me? I mean, what am I supposed to do for him?" Nasreen takes a breath, "so I talked to him, and reassured him and told him that he's normal, as though I have any clue what that is. Talked about the Anniversary Effect and blah, blah, blah. You know he started going to the mosque, I guess he's turning to God now to cope with his loneliness." She laughs miserably, "at least now I'm not the only one he turns to. Let God take on some of that work. I don't want it." Nasreen takes another deep breath, sees that Therapist has an encouraging expression on her face. Nasreen looks down at her hands again. She doesn't feel like making eye contact today.

"Let's try to separate out your father for just for a second. How about focusing on your own feelings regarding your mother. What do you think makes you want to not think about her?"

"Well, I suppose I must be wanting to avoid the sadness."

"What do you feel when you say that?" Therapist leans forward in her chair.

"Like I want to give you the right answer," Nasreen says, smiling self-consciously.

"And that's the right answer? What else would there be if you weren't concerned with that?"

Nasreen looks at her fingernails and notices that they have begun to grow longish. They look almost like straight-girl nails. A sign that she hasn't had sex for awhile. She curls her fingers in and the points jab into the flesh of her palm.

"I dunno. I'm drawing a blank." Therapist waits and watches Nasreen for twenty seconds. Nasreen counts them out silently.

"Are you aware that your fists are clenched? What feeling goes with that?"

Nasreen imagines her fingernails digging deep into her palms, cutting through the fine layers of skin and fleshy tissue, reaching hard bone beneath. And then what she sees next are no longer her hands, but her mother's, not as they were before the cancer, when she was still healthy, but after, with IV tubes poking through green veins, translucent skin sagging away from stainless steel. She remembers that the nurse hurt her mother when she inserted the needle and her mother gasped, flinching slightly. Then the nurse covered over her hand with a new piece of white adhesive tape, the bandage like a denial of the pain just inflicted.

"I remember that I always felt like yelling when she was in the hospital. She hated it there. I hated it there." Nasreen feels her breath grow ragged. She inhales deeply but can't seem to get enough air. "The staff was always in a rush and I wanted to scream at them to stop and take better care of her. I wanted them to keep her alive a little longer. I wanted to yell at her so that she would try harder to stay alive just a little while longer. I wanted to smack my father so that he would stop crying all the time." She forces herself to breathe, and finally, cool air reaches her lungs, and she continues, "I wanted to get home each night and have Connie hold me. And when she couldn't be there I wanted to yell at her. But there was nobody to yell at and so I didn't yell at anyone, not at all and now that yelling is still there. And it gets too loud for me." Nasreen's lungs heave, and she notices that her stomach no longer hurts.

"So maybe it's time to yell a little."

Nasreen looks up at Therapist, feels the edges of her eyes moisten, then fill, and before she can think to find a way to stop it, they overflow.

"That was entertaining," Salma says, just after Ravi and Angie said their goodbyes, "You can tell that they are new together."

"*Arré*, they couldn't stop mooning and kissing, even when we sat down to eat dinner! And then she started to spoon-feed him! If I had known that they would behave like this, I would not have invited them! I bet they were even playing footsies under the table!"

"Yes, they were, actually. I noticed when I got up to clear the dishes. But don't be so angry, Shaffiq. They are just young. I thought it was a little funny." Salma sits on the couch, and pats the spot beside her.

"I'm not angry. It was just so uncomfortable. And with the children watching." He sits on the opposite end of couch as though being chaperoned by a prim Aunty.

"Yes, I saw. You kept dragging them to the kitchen for more soda. It's a wonder they got to bed with all that sugar."

"Hah! It was the only safe place!"

"You know," Salma says, smiling at him, "We used to be affectionate, too, once upon a time."

"What do you mean once upon a time?" Shaffiq says, turning towards her, "We are still affectionate, but just not in public! It's a question of the correct time and place," he says, jabbing the couch with his index finger to emphasize his words. "Time and place, time and place."

"I'm just saying that things are not the same for us. Not like they used to be," Salma sighs.

"What, are you keeping count or something? Yes, we're not newlyweds, but we are not –"

"When's the last time you kissed me like they kissed each other, you know, with passion, or held my hand while we sat together on the couch?"

"You know, I've tried a couple of times, if you recall. And you are the one doing the resisting. But that was in private. You want me to be like them, looking like fools in front of other people? I can do that, if you want!"

"Of course not, Shaffiq. I'm not saying that anyone should do that while at a dinner party. I agree with you on that point. But, it just made me think that we could be a little more … you know … romantic, just sometimes," she says, biting her bottom lip and looking at him shyly. Shaffiq shifts closer to her on the couch. He plants a warm kiss on her mouth.

"How is that? Is that good?"

"Yes, like that," she says, moving closer to him. She holds his face and kisses him longer, soaking in the warmth of his lips. She closes her eyes, and in the dark behind her eyelids, an image of Nasreen pops up, first small and unobtrusive, and then in full screen view. Salma opens her eyes in alarm and pulls away from Shaffiq.

"What? What's wrong?"

"Nothing, nothing." She moves her hands down his neck to his chest and hurriedly unbuttons his shirt. She rubs her hands against his hairless chest and takes care to keep her eyes open. He kisses her again, on her face and neck and then, eyelids fluttering shut, she lets herself relax a little.

"The kids are asleep, right? Even with all the sugar?"

"Yes," she murmurs, now kissing her way down his chest to his soft belly. This time, her own private cinema shows her another image she hasn't seen in a very long time: two young women in Jogger's Park in a suburb of Bombay, embracing on a park bench. She opens her eyes to see Shaffiq looking dreamily at her. Once again, she pushes away the obtrusive image and with an almost single-minded determination, fixates on undoing Shaffiq's belt buckle.

Shaffiq is over the moon with passion for his wife. He marvels at how excited and full of vigour she seems to be. It was a good idea to invite over Ravi and Angie after all! *We must socialize more often!* Out of the corner of his eye, he glimpses the *raani* staring down at them intently. He pulls Salma up.

"Come, let's go to the bedroom. Let's get off this couch."

"No Shaffiq, let's stay here. Let's be a little crazy." She is worried that if she stops now, it will interrupt her focus, permitting other distracting thoughts to enter her mind again. She falls onto her back and pulls him down on top of her. She wriggles out of her pants, kicking them off and onto the parquet floor. She grabs at his trousers while he shifts and squirms to help her pull them off.

"I just hope the children don't wake up."

"They won't." She grabs his shoulders and pulls him to her, kissing him again. She feels his resistance withering and his excitement mounting. Soon, he is panting over her, moaning her name. She clasps his buttocks and looks up at the *raani* and her servant. She feels Shaffiq's sweat on her skin, feels his frantic movements inside her and observes the *raani's* strange expression, a slow smug smile moving across her painted face. Her eyes travel to the servant's, whose lips are pursed in school-marmish disappointment. Shaffiq collapses onto her, a few minutes too soon for her. She holds him maternally, protectively, the way she thinks a good wife should.

Chapter 16

SALMA AND SHAFFIQ SLEEP fitfully after their lovemaking. The next morning they awake to their younger daughter tugging at the sheets and threatening to get into bed with them. Still naked from the night before, Salma's modesty overpowers her honesty. She manages to trick Shireen into leaving the room with a "go find your surprise in the kitchen" while she pulls on a dressing gown. She passes Shaffiq his pajama pants and he takes them groggily, struggling with them under the covers.

"Where, where is my surprise, Mummy?" Shireen yells as she re-enters her parents' bedroom.

"Oh, that's right! I haven't made it yet! I must have dreamt that I made the *thuli* in my sleep. I'd better put in on the stove now." Salma prepares the wheat dish very irregularly, and somehow it has become her younger daughter's favourite breakfast.

"Quick thinking," Shaffiq whispers to his wife.

"*Thuli! Thuli!* I'll tell Saleema!"

"Yes, go wake up Saleema," Shaffiq says, getting out of bed.

"I'm awake already. And I heard. Who wouldn't have, with you yelling like a maniac all the time," Saleema says menacingly to her younger sister.

"Saleema, Mummy is making *thuli* for us! Aren't you happy?"

"I don't want any. *Thuli* sucks," she says, testing out the new word she has heard recently, in fact, just this past Thursday, in the playground.

"What did you say?"

"She said *Thuli* sucks," Shireen reports obediently.

"That is not a nice word, Saleema. Don't ever say that word again!"

Salma responds predictably to Saleema's provocation.

"It's not a bad word. Everyone says it." Saleema sniffs defensively, while her eyes well at the possibility that her mother might be angry with her.

"Shaffiq, where are these children learning such things! What are they exposed to at school? You know the education system here is very different, so substandard compared to Bombay." Then turning to Saleema, "In my family, we did not talk back to our parents and we did not use bad language!" She faces Shaffiq again, "the children are so different here!"

"I just meant that I don't like *thuli* anymore," Saleema whines, a few tears escaping.

"Why do you say that Saleema? You always liked *thuli*. Why use this language?" asks Shaffiq. He puts his arm around her and rubs her small, stiff back.

"I don't know. Can't we get any Fruity Flakes or Frosted O's or something like that? No one in my school eats *thuli*."

"I like Frosted O's too," Shireen says, her tone conciliatory.

"I'm making *thuli*. If you want something else, then you will have to make your own breakfast. And why are you so concerned about what everyone else is eating, anyway? Those kids are different from you. Their families are different. It makes sense that they eat different foods," says Salma, now in the kitchen, noisily opening and closing cupboard doors.

"Saleema, I'm sure there are other children in your class from India. I saw them when we came to your music night. There were plenty of kids like you."

"Yeah, and they're the geeks, at least the ones that just came from India. They bring chutney sandwiches or *pav bhaji* in their lunch boxes and the rest of the kids make fun of them."

"Have they been making fun of you?" Salma asks, her worried face poking around the kitchen door. "You see Shaffiq, this is how people are here."

"No, they don't make fun of me," Saleema says, "But that's because I take cheese sandwiches."

"Sounds like lunch-box tyranny to me. Well, let's strike a compromise, OK? You can eat *thuli* at home. No one will see you eating it here. We'll keep it a secret amongst ourselves. Then you can have cheese sandwiches for lunch at school. None of the kids in your class shall ever know the truth about breakfast in this home," Shaffiq says, his arm around his daughter, trying to cheer her up. A small smile emerges from Saleema's pouting expression.

"Yes, *thuli, thuli!*" Shireen says, sensing the tension dissipating.

"Shut up, Shireen. Stop screaming all the time!" Saleema says, stamping to the kitchen.

Nasreen awakes early Monday morning with the weight of memory still in the air. She lifts her head an inch from the pillow and sees the red light of the clock telling her that it is still too early to get up. She closes her eyes, and then the dream comes back to her again. She rarely dreams of her mother and wants to hold on to this one a little longer.

Nasreen's mother talks to her over some kind of video-conference phone, her image projected on a white screen high upon the wall of the bedroom. Nasreen notices a small dimple in the centre of the screen causing her mother's nose to look slightly crooked and she forces herself not to be annoyed by this defect. Her mother speaks softly, almost inaudibly and Nasreen strains to hear. Zainab says, "It's so good to finally get through, to make a connection. You know the lines in Bombay are not so reliable. The wiring is still so ancient that phoning is really very difficult. I have been trying for years now to make the call, but I never could get through." Nasreen thinks she hears a note of regret in her mother's voice. Her mother continues, "But I've been OK, you know, surviving, earning money from some odd jobs, living with relatives. Don't worry Nasreen, don't worry about me. I am fine and I will see you again one day. I hope you will visit me when you come to India."

Nasreen is speechless as she stares at her mother's projection on the bedroom wall in disbelief, trying to find the right words. Then, before she knows it, her mother's image begins to shrink until there is only a white dot left on the blank wall, like the receding image on an old black and white TV switching off. Nasreen begins to panic and fumbles with the dials and buttons on the video-conferencing equipment, but nothing brings her mother back to the screen.

Nasreen wakes with a start and with Id sitting on her chest, gazing intently at her. "Can you believe it, Id, my mom's been alive all this time! We've just been separated due to the crumbling state of the telecommunications industry in India," she says, sleepily.

Cheated, the dream leaves her feeling cheated.

It's still dark out but she pushes back the covers, upsetting Id from his rest, and stomps to the kitchen where she opens a can of wet cat food. Id forgets his rough and tumble start to the day and circles Nasreen's feet flirtatiously. Then, ravenous herself, she makes a pot of macaroni and cheese, simultaneously feeling delight and disgust while mixing the artificial cheese powder into the butter, milk, and pasta. When it is ready, she eats it from the pot in front of the TV, digging furiously into the orange macaroni with a fork, her eyes glued to a four a.m. infomercial about an exercise machine that can give her better abs in just one amazing use.

Later that day Nasreen sits in her office, listening to Miranda. Surprisingly, Miranda has quit drinking and is on her fifth sober day.

"Actually, it has been five days, fifteen hours and twenty minutes. I've rearranged all of my books. The books used to be alphabetical by author, but you know, I really only ever remember the titles, so now they are alphabetical by title. I am thinking about creating subsections to separate them by genre like I did when I was a kid. I can do that now because I sorted them and gave away about one-eighth to the Sally Ann. So there's more space."

"Uh huh," Nasreen says, absentmindedly. She feels guilty for being distracted today, but she can't help herself. She has been emotionally checked out since noon due to her lack of sleep, managing to go through all the various head-nodding, empathy-conveying, interest-showing motions of therapy. Miranda, on edge herself, doesn't seem to notice Nasreen's lack of focus.

"On day one I put away all my summer clothes and ironed all my shirts. Tomorrow I'm going to organize my CDs."

Nasreen's mind travels to her grocery list. Juice, bagels, eggs.

"You know, my mother gave me lots of my CDs. She liked to buy them when she wasn't so depressed. I think that's why I left them for last. I don't know if I can go through them. Some of those CDs will make me think about her, when she bought them, what the occasion was, you know? But I guess I should get to them." Nasreen makes her head bob up and down. Her left hand rises to meet her left earlobe, feeling for the gift from her mother that is no longer there.

"You know, I often wish she were alive, but not the way she was in real life, I mean, I sometimes think of her, fantasize a different kind of mother altogether. You know, one that wasn't so sad all the time." Nasreen bobble-heads again, looking past Miranda and to her computer screen. A fragment of last night's dream, the receding image of her mother on the television, flashes to her mind.

Nasreen directs her attention back to Miranda, who has started to cry softly. She reaches for the tissue box and offers it to Miranda, who takes one and blurts out, "When am I ever going to get over this?" Nasreen waits for Miranda's breathing to regulate and then asks one or two appropriate questions. After that, she checks her watch, which signals to Miranda that she should wipe her face and her nose. She leaves the office with a incongruously cheery, "Well thanks, I'll see you again next week. Have a good weekend."

Nasreen waves and smiles blandly and then moves to her desk to write a session note. She observes that Miranda is opening up and managing to do so well, ironically on a day when she feels so shut down herself. And she hadn't expected sobriety so soon from Miranda. She writes in blue ink, "Client states that she has not drank for five days. She is actively grieving her mother's death." Grapefruit, cereal, apples. She shuts the file and puts it into her filing cabinet.

At eight p.m., Nasreen walks north to the Imperial grocery store on Bloor. It takes her a moment to adjust to the florescent glare of the overhead lights after being outside in the autumn night. She picks up a plastic basket near the door, then, changing her mind, inserts a quarter into the cart dispenser and pulls out a large shopping cart with stiff wheels. In the fruit section, she chooses two grapefruit, four apples and two bananas. She pushes her cart past the junk food aisle, telling herself she can go back there later if she needs. She hovers in the dairy section for some time, trying to find low fat gouda. She settles for low fat havarti. Next, she maneuvers past a young man moving slowly amongst the jams and jellies and then stops in front of the tall displays of cereal boxes. She scans the endless variety of products, and then reaches for the house brand of granola, eighty cents cheaper than the prettier box beside it. You must comparison shop, save your money, a quiet voice in her mind tells her. Nasreen wonders if that is her mother embedded in her mind, or her own sensible voice. She pushes the cart down the aisle and another voice chides, that one doesn't taste good, why do you have to be so cheap all the time? This one is louder and sounds like Connie's frustrated complaints. She's not sure how Connie's voice seeped in and took root in her brain. Perhaps it's just a matter of time. If you spend enough time with someone, does their voice begin to infiltrate your own? And how long does it take for it to leave? Nasreen stands there, in aisle three, her hand in midair between brightly packaged boxes, suspended in indecision. *Come on*, she tells herself, *I can't be doing this over boxes of granola*. In the end, she takes down both boxes and tosses them into the cart. She thinks this will appease both voices, and it does. She circles back to the junk food aisle, the stiff wheels of the shopping cart whining noisily in reply.

The subway is uncharacteristically deserted for a weekday evening. Nasreen looks down the long platform and studies two young men standing at the far end. They talk animatedly with one another, the arching movement of their muscular arms telling their stories for them. She picks up a few of the louder words about boxing or wrestling, but she is not sure which of the two sports their swinging and punching arms mime. The platform across the tracks is similarly empty except for a South Asian woman and her small daughter sitting on a bench. Their train approaches first and the woman carries the child on while an opposing warm wind throws Nasreen's hair up and then back down over her eyes, unsteadying her for just a moment. As the east-bound train leaves, Nasreen watches the woman and the child slide into a seat by the window, the little girl staring out from behind the glass.

An instant later, the westbound train rumbles from around the corner, its headlight preceding it, filling the long tunnel with bright light. Nasreen glances down at the waste-strewn tracks and feels a force drawing her to them. I am just so tired. She steps across the yellow safety line. She thinks: this is the moment. This is the moment that could change everything and nothing at all. This would be the end and a beginning. Closure. She clutches her grocery bags, eager to hold onto something tangible, the plastic handles slippery in hands. Her eyes rooted to the metal tracks below, she envisions herself being pulled down by gravity, her body landing heavily onto the rails, steel growing warmer by the train's approach. She feels herself being pressed forward and down at the same time; what direction is that? A body no longer feeling, a body joining with the heat and metal around her.

A man approaches from behind, hesitates a moment, and then reaches for her. He tugs her backpack, pulling her back from the yellow line.

"Careful, there, the wind from these trains could knock over a young lady like you." She turns to see a middle-aged man, his pale face made ruddy by a recent blush. The doors of the train chime open and the man says, "after you, miss." She walks past him and looks for a seat at the back of the car. She wants to be far away from him and his good Samaritan's concern for her. The doors chime closed and the train readies itself to leave again.

Chapter 17

IT IS ANOTHER MONDAY evening and Nasreen rushes to finish her case notes before Asha comes to pick her up. She feels guilty that it's been at least a couple of weeks since their last class. Both she and Asha have been busy, Asha with her papers and she with work and therapy, and they've had to cancel on Salma. Nasreen hopes she will have some time to review her Gujarati notebook on the way over in the car. She glances at her watch, shuts down her computer and turns off her desk lamp. The phone rings, and guessing that it is Asha calling from her cell outside the front doors of the building, Nasreen picks up.

"Psychotherapy program, Nasreen Bastawala speaking," she says automatically.

"Hi," the quiet voice makes Nasreen pay attention. "It's me, Connie." Nasreen stays silent a moment, a haze of emotion stopping her from responding. Anger and relief form a fog so thick she can't see through it to speak. She turns the desk lamp on again but it doesn't help.

"I'm sorry to call you at work, but I've tried you at home a few times and haven't been able to reach you. I needed to ask you about something," Connie speaks quickly, as though she is afraid that Nasreen will hang up. Her tempo signals to Nasreen that this is a possibility. *I could just hang up*, she thinks. The haze in her head clears.

"Yes?" She hopes her voice sounds cold to Connie.

"I think I left my passport back at the apartment." Nasreen makes the correction in her mind – *my apartment*. "Can you check for me? I'm going to New York next week. I started looking for my passport and I couldn't find it anywhere, so I figured I must have left it behind."

"OK, I'll check for you. Where do you think it is?" But Nasreen already knows the answer. She saw the passport in a desk drawer a few weeks ago. She fingered its pages and read its contents like a prime time TV detective hoping to discover some clue to the mystery of their break-up. She'd planned to hold onto this piece of Connie unless she asked after it. A petty act of vengeance. *It's my apartment.*

"Check the desk." My desk. "I think it's in the middle drawer. By the way, if there is anything else there that's mine, could you give me that too? I can come pick up everything later this week, if that's alright with you."

"This week? Um, what day?" The fog rolls back in.

"Well, how's Thursday night, maybe around eight?"

"Thursday? Um ... I think that's fine."

"Thanks Nasreen. So," she says awkwardly, "How are things? You OK?"

"Yeah, just fine. I have to go. Asha's picking me up."

Nasreen steps out of the building just as Asha's car pulls up.

"Hey, you don't look so good. Did something bad happen at work?"

"Yeah, I'm fine. I haven't been sleeping well lately. Lots of stuff has been going on lately." Nasreen tells her about the phone call from Connie.

"She's coming to your house? You're going to let her in?" Asha asks, a tone of disapproval in her voice.

"Yeah, I guess so. I mean ... it will just be a short visit. She just wants to get a few things. Her passport and some other papers. She said she's going to New York." Nasreen says matter-of-factly, trying to convince herself that Connie's brief visit won't be a big deal.

"Why now? I mean, doesn't she still have a key? She could have done this weeks ago." When Connie moved out, Nasreen had not thought to take the key back and Connie did not offer it up.

"I don't know. I guess she realized she was missing the passport when she starting planning her trip. I suppose I'll have to get the key back when she comes." Nasreen never imagined Connie coming back to the apartment, at least not in this way. Not just to pick up a passport.

"Is that going to be OK? Maybe you should have someone with you. What time is she going to be over?"

"Eight."

"I've got a class until nine. Maybe you should ask someone to be there, though. You could ask Mona," Asha suggests, knowing that Nasreen isn't likely to ask anyone for help.

"Yeah, maybe. I hope she doesn't show up with anyone. Would she do that? Bring the new girlfriend? I bet she's going to New York with her."

"Who knows. That would be just the kind of thing the big jerk would do. Like I said, you should have someone there with you," she says firmly, hoping her friend will listen to her advice for once.

"Yeah, someone to pose as my new girlfriend," Nasreen sighs, "Or maybe not just pose. Maybe one will magically appear by Thursday." Asha rolls her eyes.

"Speaking of new girlfriends. Let's go see our Mrs. Paperwala, oh, I mean, your Salma," she quips sarcastically.

"Hah, hah, very funny.... But hey, let's do some vocabulary practice before we get there. I don't remember much from two weeks ago," Nasreen says, attempting to change the subject. She flips through her notebook.

"Fine," Asha says, giving in, "*Gujarati waat karwanoo.*"

A few minutes later, Asha pulls into the parking lot at Salma's building and fits her hatchback into a guest parking spot. They quiz one another on the previous class's material as they walk into the building and ride the elevator up to the fifth floor.

Later, in the Paperwala apartment, Nasreen and Asha pour over Gujarati-English flash cards, Salma cajoling her students through the vocabulary game. So far, Asha is winning by a small margin.

"Nas, concentrate. How do you say this one, 'Take care of your health'?"

"Umm, OK, I remember this one. *Tabiyat jalavjo.*"

"Great!" Salma squeezes her arm and Nasreen feels it grow warm under Salma's slim fingers. She looks away from Salma and catches Asha's mischievous smirk.

"Now just watch your pronunciation." Salma mouths the words slowly and her students repeat them. "OK, since you two are now even in score, let's go for one last question, a tiebreaker." She flips through her homemade cards. "Ah here's one. 'Are you married'?"

Nasreen and Asha look at one another, both knowing this question by heart. They respond simultaneously, competitively, "*Tu paranelo cho?*" The two students erupt into laughter.

"So you know the question well. Now we need another tiebreaker.

How about you both try to answer in Gujarati?" says Salma, laughing with them.

"Finding the right answer to that would be worth a lot. It's guaranteed that the question is going to be asked by one nosy Aunty or another," Asha giggles.

"I agree. An answer that would stop the questioning forever would be priceless," Nasreen turns to Salma, "Maybe you can help us find the words for this one."

"Yes," Asha continues, "Something along the lines of will you stop asking me that bloody question, or –"

"It's none of your goddamn business!" Nasreen exclaims. Unsure whether she understands the joke, Salma watches the interchange with an uncomfortable smile.

"Or, even if it is legal for me to marry my partner, I still don't want to get married because it's a patriarchal institution!" Asha announces triumphantly, "actually, I want to say that I am in a common-law relationship with my female lover. Yes, I want to know how to say that!"

Nasreen looks over at Salma, and sees that she is no longer participating in the joke. Salma gazes at something in her lap.

"Well, you could say something like, '*Na hajo to vichaar nuthi,*'" Salma says, her eyes still averted, "which means that you aren't thinking about marriage right now. That would be one way to answer the question."

"But not really the point, is it?" Asha counters.

"So you'd want to say that you are living with a woman?"

"Well, yes, and that we are in a relationship."

"Or that I'd like to be but I haven't had any good offers lately," adds Nasreen, laughing, trying to ease the new tension in the Paperwala kitchen.

"I don't know how to say that. And I don't think you really should anyway. At least not to your grandmothers," says Salma, gathering up the cue cards and pulling an elastic band around them. "OK, good work. I declare this game a tie."

But the conversation didn't end there, at least not for Salma, who stands in her living room, looking at the *raani* and her servant at four a.m. She has been up for hours, transfixed by her own memories, and voices from within the painting. *Could it be possible that the painting has been talking with me for the past few hours?* Except for brief interruptions in which Salma stopped herself, scolding herself for acting like someone insane, the dialogue between her, the *raani* and the servant, has been continuous, unbroken. Sometimes, they've spoken in English, and at other times have broken into a Gujarati-Marathi blend she has to strain to comprehend.

What has she been discussing with them through the night hours? Her scandalous disclosures began with a story from long ago. She's crossed the ocean and many years with her confessions, dredging up history she has not considered for over a decade. When she is finished with her tale, she takes in a hungry breath, inhaling deeply, as though she has been starved for air all night. She decides that she has said enough for now, and feels a little lighter and more innocent. She unhooks the painting from the wall, sets it down on the couch and kisses the *raani* on her painted cheek in thanks for her listening ear, leaving a small greasy smudge on the glass. This gush of gratitude leaves her feeling a little silly and she hastily wipes the glass clean with the edge of her sleeve.

She is about to return the painting to the wall again, but hesitates. She scrutinizes the servant's eyes, blinks and then turns the painting face side down on the couch. She looks at the back of the canvas, searching for the treasure she hid there weeks earlier. In the dim light she spies the shine of plastic and metal and carefully removes the earring from inside its wrapping. She takes the silver teardrop into her palm, rubs her index finger over the smooth metal, the earring a kind of talisman to another place, another world, a reality different to her own. After a few moments of this devotion, she replaces the package from where she found it, turns the frame over again and returns it to the wall.

She inspects the painting to ensure that she has hung it plumb and notices from the servant's strange expression that something is amiss. Yes, it seems her face has changed. Her eyebrows have arched, her eyes have widened and her red lips have pursed as though she is trying to tell her something. But what? What could be bothering her? She studies the servant's odd countenance. Although it is still not morning and the living room is dark, Salma thinks she is able to lip-read the servant mouthing the words, "It's been moved."

"What?" Salma gasps, peering more closely at the painting, but the servant's lips are still, the warning unrepeated. Hurriedly, she takes the painting down from the wall and turns it face side down once again. She calculates the position of the plastic bag with its hidden treasure and sees it. Yes, that's what's different. The earring is in the wrong place, relocated to the opposite corner from where she had placed it days before.

She knows, is in fact positive of this fact, because she had put it in the right hand corner of the photo, where she surmised her Highness's heart would be. She had not placed it under her feet, where it lies hidden now. Was this her mistake, made just a moment ago? She tries to remember. No, she is sure this is where she found it when she first searched for it tonight. She turns the painting over again and examines the women's visages for anything that will give meaning to this relocation, this trick being played on her. The *raani* tells her nothing and neither does the servant. She anxiously turns the painting over again and snatches the plastic package out from the frame's edge, sure that her hiding spot has been violated. Shaffiq. Her heart pounds so fast now, she is forced to sit down on the couch beside the *raani* and the servant.

Trying to find a place of calm within herself, she fingers the smooth silver earring and considers the soft ear to which it once belonged. She rubs the teardrop slowly against her cheek, feeling a warm flush spread across her face. She furtively guides its stem through the tiny hidden hole in her earlobe, feeling the metal sliding through, penetrating it. The heat from her cheek prickles her ears and rushes down her neck, across her chest before heading down through her stomach and between her thighs. She closes her eyes, exhales languidly. She runs her fingers through her hair, thinking about Nas's tresses, so lustrous, long, and shiny and then the hair in her imagination starts to change form, becoming short. It morphs in thickness, develops waves and takes on a hint of sandalwood. Raj.

She opens her eyes, interrupting the reverie and pulls the earring from her ear. She replaces the plastic wrap and her body slowly begins to cool itself. She tells herself that she should be reasonable. She is not that kind of woman, not like her two students.

And this is really the heart of the matter, the spark that ignited her insomniac night with the *raani* and the servant. Salma is truly caught off guard by her students' recent disclosures. She never thought that Asha and Nas were that way. Lesbians. Well, maybe Asha, but not Nas, certainly. Not that she is an expert about women with queer ways; she had only known a couple like that in India.

Now that she knows about her students, does it change anything for her? Maybe. Before she puts the *raani* and the servant back on their perch, she takes some tape from the kitchen, and repositions the plastic pouch. She fastens it to the centre of the backing, making a kind of bull's eye. Yes, that's how it changes things for her. Her students' desires make her own longing, the longing she has been feeling all her life and now so recently with Nas, all the more visible. It gives it a name.

Salma told the *raani* and her servant something that no one else knows:

Salma and her closest friend, Ritu, used to meet after work at a little Bandra café. Not only was Ritu her oldest friend, but she was a neighbour, an old schoolmate and now a fellow teacher. Just as they had walked to school together when they were young, the two women continued on a similar path as young adults, both going to teacher's college and becoming primary school teachers at local schools. Baldev's was a convenient place to meet one another at the end of the teaching day.

Despite their similarities, the two friends had developed vastly different opinions on many of life's questions. Perhaps it was their fondness for one another that allowed them the comfort of expressing their opposing views with such vehemence.

That day, they found themselves arguing about the topic of marriage: Ritu's upcoming wedding and Salma's determination to never wed. The argument was becoming quite heated.

"You are only marrying Madhu, who you know is so incompatible with you, so that you won't end up an old maid. You're bowing to your parents' pressure," Salma scolded her friend.

"Well maybe my parents do know what's right for me. After all don't they seem happily married? And look at us! We're already twenty-four. We need to settle down soon before we get too old. You'd better start taking this seriously yourself."

Back then, Salma and Ritu were firmly wedged in an age group where all their contemporaries were either already married, or were about to be wed. So, just a few months earlier, Ritu had celebrated her engagement to a young engineer from their neighbourhood. Salma found Madhu to be somewhat square, the opposite of fashionable Ritu who loved to go out to watch all the new films, listen to the latest music coming from Britain, and challenge her parents' rules. But somehow Ritu had acquiesced to her parents' conservative choice and was even showing a measure of excitement about her upcoming betrothal. In fact, all she talked about those days was Madhu this, Madhu that. She could spend entire afternoons talking non-stop about how pretty her sari would look and how much delicious food had been ordered for the celebrations. Salma yawned through these discussions and wondered what her friend could possibly find interesting about Madhu or the elaborate wedding arrangements.

Each year since completing her A-levels, Salma had become more vocal about her anti-marriage sentiments and she loved having this familiar argument with Ritu. It made her feel sure about herself, articulate, progressive. In truth, Ritu was an easier target for her diatribes than her own nagging parents. With them, she was more passive. She went along with their plans to meet this cousin's cousin or that uncle's friend's son. She got dressed up in her best clothes, made small talk and then one by one rejected each suitor. This strategy, although admittedly labour intensive, was easier than being honest with her parents. They would never understand her views. Rather than trying to convince them, she hoped to tire them out until they finally gave up on her.

Salma and Ritu did not only have arguments. They sometimes talked about the children they taught, a mutually pleasurable topic of discussion. They also liked to watch the stylish crowd that packed Baldev's after work. While they sat eating *mango kulfi*, Ritu and Salma eyed the smart-looking couples and handsome men drinking coffee. The two entertained one another with their appraisals of the customers around them.

One day Ritu pointed out a woman sitting in the corner of the café. She had short hair, cut in a style that was mannish, and she wore loose jeans and a plain *kurta*. Ritu whispered her assessment to Salma, "Oh, see her, over there, she wants to be a man. She was in my maths class years ago. I think she dropped out of college. I heard that she had a girlfriend in Pune who left her for another girl and then she became so upset and that's when her studies suffered. Can you imagine that, Salma? That one for sure will never find a husband."

"Good for her!" Salma snorted, warming up to return to their previous argument, "Maybe she doesn't want to find a husband. And how do you know so much about her anyway?" Ritu sighed in exasperation and turned her attention to a tall man who had just entered Baldev's. Salma did not doubt Ritu's information. She always seemed to know so much about other people's private business. She was her best source of gossip.

While Ritu whispered about the other patrons at Baldev's, Salma surreptitiously watched the mannish woman drinking her *chai* in the corner. She studied her hairstyle and the way she sat, one leg crossed over the other knee like a man would. Her clothing was also different from Salma's own feminine *salwaar*. Why would she dress that way? Did she really want to be a man? Had she really been with a woman? And what type of woman? Were they intimate? The questions circled Salma's mind a few times, distracting her until Ritu's voice finally brought her back. She joined her friend in watching a foreign couple standing at the counter, so tall and pale, conspicuously towering over everyone else. When Salma looked back toward the corner, the woman had left, her seat empty.

Later the same evening, while Salma sat marking her fifth standard students' compositions, she found her mind drifting back to the woman in the café. What made a girl turn that way? Salma could understand having crushes on girls – hadn't she experienced that from time to time? She especially admired some of her teachers in school. There was Miss Shah and Mrs. Ghandi. They were both pretty, young women who seemed so modern and smart to her. She would volunteer to help them after school so that she could spend more time with them. But these attractions were nothing like Ritu's gossip about that woman in the café.

A week later, Salma arrived at Baldev's and searched the busy café for a table, weaving through the narrow space between the crowded tables, looking for an empty place. A voice called out to her from behind, "I'm just about to go, you want this table?" She turned gratefully toward the helpful voice and found herself looking at the woman who had piqued her curiosity the week before.

"Yes, thanks. You sure you're ready to go?" Salma looked down at the woman's half-filled teacup. "Finish your tea. I'm still waiting for my friend to arrive. I can wait."

"OK, then sit down and wait here. Join me for a minute before your friend arrives." She extended a hand toward Salma, "I'm Raj Patel. I've seen you before."

"Salma Pittawalla. Yes, I noticed you last week." She felt herself warm under the cotton armpits of her blouse.

"Quite a melee here, no? Just two years ago this place was a good place to come to study, it was so quiet then."

"Yes it was less fashionable back then. Don't tell me you still try to study in this chaos?"

"No, I'm not in school," she looked up at Salma self-consciously. "I was taking journalism at Xavier, but I still have anotheryear to complete. Maybe I'll go back. Right now I don't have much use for what I learned working in my father's shop."

"Which shop is that?" Salma found herself wanting to gather as much as she could about this woman before Ritu arrived. For once she could impress her friend with some bit of gossip. "Is it near here?"

"Yes, we own a computer supplies shop – Patel's Computers, just down the road."

"Oh yes, I know it. I don't think I've ever been in, though. I don't even know how to use a computer. I suppose I should learn, it's supposed to be India's future, they say."

"Well, for the sake of the business, I hope so. Do you work?" Salma nodded. "What type of work are you in?" she asked, her eyes curious, and friendly.

"I teach Standard Five. English mostly, but –" Salma looked up to see Ritu pushing her way though the café. "Oh, there's my friend now." Raj gathered her things and stood up. "Wait, why don't you stay? I'm sure we can find an extra chair," Salma said, craning her neck to look for what had turned into a precious commodity. "Ritu, this is Raj. She was just sharing her table with me. Can you see any more chairs to pull up?"

"No, no, I've got to get back to the shop anyway. Ritu, I think we've met before. Did you go to Xavier?"

"Yes, I think you're correct," Ritu said stiffly.

"Well, nice chatting, Salma. Maybe we'll run into each other again."

"Yes, I'm sure. See you. And thanks for the table."

As Salma watched Raj leave the café, Ritu whispered, "What were you thinking?"

"What do you mean?"

"You'd better be careful. Sitting with her, you never know what people will think. Do you want people to say you are her newest girlfriend?"

"Don't be silly. We were just talking. She offered a seat to me. Look around. You can't find a free table anywhere. She was being nice."

"Still, people will talk. It's alright when you are younger, but not now. I know you don't care about marriage options, but you might one day. You need to be careful."

"You sound like my mother. I don't care what people talk about. And, you're quite correct, I don't much care about getting married either."

"Well, that's your business. But you should make sure your options remain open." Ritu signaled for the waiter and ordered a *kulfi*, then changing her mind, she ordered tea and said, "I don't want to be too fat in my wedding photos. Did I tell you that we managed to get one of the best photographers in this city?" Salma nodded, pretending to listen, her eyes following Raj move down the sidewalk, disappearing into the crowd.

Now, over a decade later, Salma is married, a mother, and barely a teacher. She watches the sky brighten slightly from her place on the couch. A twinge of guilt creeps through her and she allows herself to wonder where Raj might be now. She uncurls her legs from under her and stands up on the couch, facing the *raani*.

A few minutes later, Shaffiq comes home and finds his wife in this strange position, her face so close to the painting that she is fogging up the glass with her breath. He shakes his head. What is she doing? She looks like a crazed apostle listening for advice. What has come over his Salma? Eventually, she turns to him, her eyes glassy and tired.

"Salma, why are you up? What's happening?"

"I just woke up a little while ago," she says placidly, "I was just admiring our painting in the morning light. It's nice, no?" She doesn't care that she looks crazy. She feels tired but unburdened, as though she has been in the company of good girlfriends. Better than she's felt for some time.

She asks him to join her for a cup of tea. Together they sit down at the kitchen table for a few minutes. He tells her about his shift, she talks about what the children did the night before. They share their plans for the day. Shaffiq stands and stretches and tells Salma that he is heading to bed. "You know, I had my Gujarati students again last night."

Shaffiq sees averted eyes, a look of shyness uncharacteristic for Salma.

"Oh, yes. How was that? Are they progressing?" Shaffiq sits down again.

"Yes, more or less. It's better now that I decided to send Shireen and Saleema next door to play. I can concentrate much better."

"It's a pity that they are not interested in learning."

"They're too young to pay attention. They just seem to want to stand around and gawk at Asha and Nas. I guess they must seem a little glamorous."

"Tell me about them. What are your students like? Are they glamorous?"

"Well, I don't know," she pauses, "Maybe a little. They are both very modern types, you know, trendy. Asha, the student who came first, is kind of mischievous. A Master's student in Political Science, I think. And Nas –" Salma pauses a moment, looking up to into space. Shaffiq follows her wandering eyes to a place on the kitchen wall, trying to discern what she is looking at.

"Nas is a psychologist. She's planning a trip to India with her father soon, so she wants to learn Gujarati. And she is from our community too, which is a big coincidence."

"That is a coincidence," Shaffiq says, his blood rushing to his head, a flurry of questions at his lips. "Are you sure? Where does she work?" He is almost afraid to ask.

"I don't know. I think she said some type of hospital. Why do you ask?"

"Oh, just curious. It's nothing really. I should get some sleep. Are you coming back to bed?" he asks, rising and placing his teacup in the sink.

"No, I'm up now. Sleep well."

Salma sits alone at the kitchen table and in the half-light of morning the memories come unbidden.

Salma needed to see Raj again, she just had to. The next time she was to meet Ritu at the café, she purposely arrived early so that she might run into Raj, who must have had a similar idea. By their third "chance" meeting at Baldev's, Raj suggested that they meet at Jogger's Park, a local seaside oasis in the middle of Bandra where the trees and garden provide privacy to lovers. Salma understood that the invitation to meet at a more intimate venue would herald a shift in their casual relationship, and although she was nervous, she readily agreed. She'd been asked out on dates before, but she'd never wanted to go and so never had been on one. She knew, felt, that Raj's invitation was, unmistakably, a date.

As they walked the pebbly paths together for the first time, they pointed out pretty plants and manicured shrubs to one another, revealing to one another their favourites. She remembers that she and Raj stood on a low arching bridge that crossed a small pond and looked up at a Gulmohar tree. Raj described to Salma how she would look forward to May, when the tree would bloom into red flowers. She called it the "flamboyant tree," one that wasn't afraid to show its full colours for all to see. As for Salma, her favourite thing about the park was how it managed to keep the clawing city at bay, the trees, joggers and lawns providing a quiet haven to be alone with Raj.

Soon, they were seeing one another nearly every day and when they could not arrange to meet, they spoke on the phone. They took chances and like teenagers too involved in their own heady feelings, often forgot to be discreet. In their haste to be close to one another, they sometimes chose a not very secluded bench in Jogger's Park. Often, they were surprised by someone jogging or strolling leisurely around a corner, and they had to move apart quickly, releasing one another's hands, putting some distance between their warm bodies. When Salma thinks back, she remembers how innocent, yet thrilling it felt at the time. They would hold hands and talk about their families, their jobs, their hopes. Raj said that she wanted to open her own shop, or take over her father's one day. Salma shared her dream of one day being the principal of a school. Both talked about being pressured to marry and how they had managed so far to resist their families' pressures. At the time she thought, so this is what courting feels like. This is what it is like to desire someone.

The sound of the bathroom door opening and a bedroom door closing, the noises of Shaffiq getting ready for bed, rudely returns Salma to her family's Toronto kitchen. She gulps back the rest of her tea, and then stares into the bottom of her teacup looking for patterns in the dregs left behind.

All is quiet in the Paperwala apartment while Salma and Shaffiq sit awake, thinking about all the clues that tell them they need to mind their marriage.

Chapter 18

A FEW DAYS LATER, Nasreen is checking her messages. The automated voice tells her that there are nine messages. She patiently listens to the first eight, noting them, deleting them. None are important. The ninth is a message from Miranda, who explains in monotone that she no longer wants to return to therapy, is doing very well now, and thinks the sessions have been a success. She doesn't want Nasreen to call back and she plans to make a large donation to the Institute in appreciation for all her help. Nasreen replays the message twice, makes a note about the phone call, and saves the message.

Nasreen then distractedly reviews a case file of a client booked for the next day. She is irritated by Miranda's message and quells the urge to call and encourage her back into therapy. In the end, she decides to take a few days to consider what her professional response ought to be. Perhaps she will take it to her peer supervision group this week. She digs through her purse and finds a jumbo box of chocolate covered peanuts she bought the previous night, only half-finished.

She checks her watch and sees that it is already five p.m. Connie will be at her place in three hours. She finishes up, tucks her work into her desk and looks out the window, observing that the evening sky is already darkening, the effect of the season changing and the days shortening.

She exits out the back doors of the Institute and onto College Street, which is already crowded with other nine-to-fivers on their way home. She hurries toward the streetcar, which is overflowing with passengers. A few people, pressed against the doors, struggle for better footing. She thinks she will walk one stop, and then the next one, until she decides to power-walk all the way home, hoping that the exercise will burn up some of the restlessness coursing through her. Her mind races with what she will say to Connie and what to tell her supervision group about Miranda. Intermittently, she finds herself counting to forty in Gujarati, part of her homework practice for this week.

Quickening her pace, her eyes dart at the store windows she passes: computer equipment at discount prices, greasy diners, a health food store. She strides by a sex shop, does a double take, startled to see a scantily dressed woman waving to her. The woman is window-dressing, a live mannequin wearing a red French maid's outfit. Two prepubescent boys walk by, giggling and nudging one another with skinny elbows. Nasreen waves back at the woman who smiles and pouts out her lips at her, and the gesture leaves Nasreen unexpectedly flushed. She continues her brisk pace but glances over her shoulder again to catch another eyeful of cleavage and bare inner thigh.

She's home by six o'clock, relieved that it is still early enough to prepare herself for Connie's arrival. Although she agreed on principle with Asha's recommendation to ask a friend over during Connie's visit, she has chosen, more or less, to ignore the advice. Nasreen does not want an audience for whatever could happen between her and Connie, nor does she feel that she needs a witness. Not that she has anything specific planned. She's been too confused to organize a plan of action in advance; instead, she is hoping for the best. She is aware that this is not the best of strategies, and that perhaps she should have called Mona and made sure she wasn't alone with her ex-girlfriend.

First, Nasreen tidies up the living room. She unwedges the TV remote from between the couch cushions and places it on top of the television. She wants to erase any evidence of the nightly sitcoms, game shows, and talk TV programs that have been keeping her company since Connie left. Then, she opens her desk drawer and finds the passport. There is also a university transcript, old bank statements, and an envelope from a credit card company that arrived three weeks earlier. She puts all the papers, except for the transcript, into a large envelope. She wants something of Connie's to keep, something that may require a future visit. Who knows, she thinks smugly, maybe Connie will want to do a Master's degree someday. She places the neatly folded transcript back into the desk drawer, beneath some other papers, and sets the envelope on the coffee table.

She notices a thin layer of dust coating the wooden surface and gets a rag from the kitchen to wipe if off. She hates dusting. That was Connie's job when she lived here and Nasreen can't remember the last time she dusted, or polished, or shined anything. She finds a second cloth and some furniture polish and gets to work dusting every surface in the living room: the bookcases, television stand, end tables, stereo, and even the picture frames on the wall. Id watches Nasreen intently for a few moments and then saunters away, no longer interested. When she is finished, Nasreen opens the window wide to clear the air so that Connie won't detect the fresh furniture polish fumes. There should be no evidence of the visit's preparation; Nasreen wants to appear as informal and unstirred about Connie's arrival as she imagines Connie to be. Will my performance be at all convincing, she wonders. And then, how pathetic am I?

Next, Nasreen goes to the bedroom and switches on the light. She looks at the messy, unmade bed and the mound of clothes strewn all over it. There is a pile of clean, unfolded laundry in a chair and an unsteady stack of books beside the bed. Nasreen sorts the clothes, hanging the clean ones in the closet, filling her hamper with dirty laundry. She piles the books on the white IKEA bookshelf beside the window. She surveys the bed and tries to calculate how long ago she last changed the sheets. Two weeks? Three? She tears the sheets off and then makes the bed with a set of her favourite red percale. Finally, she moves the blue dolphin vibrator, left sitting on the side table from its last use a few days ago, back into the bedside table's top drawer.

She empties the garbage in the bathroom, gives the vanity a quick swipe and puts out fresh towels. Nasreen looks at her watch. Seven-ten. She pulls the vinyl shower curtain across the tub to hide its brown ring of grime; there's no time to clean up. She washes her face and brushes her hair, then reapplies her lipstick. She looks into the bathroom mirror, checking herself, looking for anything on her face that would reveal her emotional state. She surveys the small pimple just beginning to surface on her chin, the shadows under her eyes, the one or two grey hairs that have sprung up near her temples. Mona pointed them out the week before, telling Nasreen that they contrasted nicely against her black hair. Nasreen wonders if she should pull them out. In the end, she decides against it. Perhaps it is good that she has matured a little since the break-up, she thinks.

She backs up from the mirror and scans her body. She feels fat today. She pinches the loose flesh on her arms and around her waist. She wonders if she has gained weight since she last saw Connie. She changes into a loose fitting green blouse that holds up her heavy breasts well. Then she squirts some perfume into her cleavage. She takes one last look at herself and recites the positive self-talk she has trained herself to say each day, the one gem of good advice she picked up from her first therapist years ago, "Yes, you are a beautiful woman." Today, she's not quite sure if she believes the affirmation, but she knows it is worth saying regardless. *Maybe one day I will believe this self-inflicted brainwashing. Whatever.* She turns off the bathroom light and sees Id watching her in the hallway. He mews loudly at her. Nasreen picks up the overweight cat and cuddles him, happy for his attention and diversion.

"Is that a meow of love, or are you just hungry again?"

At five minutes to eight, there is a knock at the door. Nasreen opens it and there Connie stands, holding a small plant in her hands. A peace offering.

"Hi Nasreen. Here, this is for you. It's a Christmas cactus. It's easy to look after. And it should flower soon." Nasreen takes the plant, looks at the small, tight red buds and then steps back.

"Come in."

Connie does, and Nasreen closes the door behind her. She sets the plant down on the coffee table. "Thanks. It's nice," she says blandly, unsure if bland is what she wants to sound like.

"It's almost impossible to kill. Just water it a couple of times a month and it should be OK." Connie stands awkwardly, shifting her weight from one foot to the other. "Everything kind of looks the same."

"Yeah, it is," Nasreen says woodenly. How is it that this woman who was once her lover is now like an alien to her? "I guess it must be weird being back here."

"A little. Oh, there's Id." Connie sits down on the couch, puts out her hand to the cat, coaxing him closer. Id circles Connie's ankles seductively and Connie strokes his back. Nasreen watches their easy familiarity with a lump in her throat, and sits down on the couch too.

"Do you want some tea? Do you want to stay a little while, or you in a hurry?" Nasreen wants to offer Connie an exit strategy, or perhaps a way out for herself. Door Number One, she leaves with her envelope and the world returns to normal again. Door Number Two, she stays, and we talk. About what?

"Sure, if that's all right with you. I can stay a little while. I mean, I wasn't sure if you would be open to that after the last time we saw each other." Connie looks uneasily at Nasreen. "You know, at Tango's."

"Yeah, well, I'm not sure what I'm open to, but a pot of tea would be OK." She says, bristling for what feels like no good reason. She walks away to the kitchen and puts the kettle on. Id remains in the living room with Connie, basking treacherously in her attentions. Nasreen takes down a small blue teapot from the cupboard and puts in two bags of peppermint, the way she has done many times before. She doesn't have to ask Connie what kind of tea she wants. Nasreen stands at the counter, closes her eyes a moment, pressing her eyelids together. Numb. No, sad. It feels sad and strange. I should be angry, she tells herself. She reviews her mental inventory of things she hates about Connie, the injuries she will never forgive, the wounds inflicted that she doesn't know how to heal. She remembers the quiet nights when Connie came home late, too late, the many little lies that made a fiction out of their relationship. The kettle whistles at full blast and Nasreen opens her eyes again.

"Do you need any help in there?"

"No, the tea's ready. Just a sec." Unnerved, she pours the boiling water into the teapot and carries the mugs and pot to the living room on a small wooden tray. Id lounges in Connie's lap. Nasreen sits down beside them, a couple of feet away. "It will take a minute to steep."

"Id seems the same as usual. And you're looking well, too."

"Thanks, you too." And Nasreen means it. She looks shyly at Connie's muscular arms, bulging slightly out of a tight navy blue t-shirt. She registers her flat stomach, her short, spiky blond hair, her languid amber eyes ringed with dark brown lashes. Nasreen can easily imagine her naked, her small breasts, the angles in her collarbone, ribs, hips. Their sex life had been the easy part of their relationship, even close to the end. Lesbian Bed Death did not even come close to looming over them as it had with other couples Nasreen knew. She and Connie folded easily into each other and even the stress of work, or her mother's death did not interfere with their lovemaking. Nasreen wonders if Connie is the same with other women, or if it had been something special between the two of them.

"So, you're going to New York?"

"Yeah, it's a short trip. I start a new job in two weeks, so I wanted to go somewhere before I have to build up vacation time again."

"A new job? Really? You're not at Starbucks anymore?"

"I'm still there for another few days. I got a better paying job with Coffee Love. I will be doing more or less the same kind of work for them, you know, PR, some advertising."

"Coffee Love? Connie, there are huge boycotts against them." Wait until Mona hears about this, Nasreen thinks.

"They're not as bad as other companies. I did some research." Connie reaches for the pot and pours them each a cup. Id jumps to the floor.

"I don't know about that." While they were a couple, they had often disagreed about politics. They had also learned how to avoid arguing about politics. "Well, I hope it works out for you there."

Connie follows Nasreen's lead out of the contentious subject to other topics: Nasreen's job; gossip about some of their friends in common and Nasreen's plans to go to India with her father.

"I'm glad to hear that you are taking a vacation this year too. How long has it been since you went anywhere?"

"Probably not since we went to New York."

"That was a couple of years ago. I liked that trip. Do you remember that neat restaurant we went to, in Soho? They had amazing mussels."

"And grilled shrimp. I do remember. We sat on the patio for hours." Nasreen allows herself to enjoy the moment. Since the break-up, she hasn't given herself permission to tread into the fleeting warmth of Good Connie Memories.

Nasreen observes Connie reaching for her hand, senses Connie's warm fingers intertwining with her own, feels Connie's thumb pressing lightly into her wrist.

"I'm really sorry for the way things turned out. If I could go back and do things differently, I would. I didn't mean to hurt you, Nas. I mean it, I'm sorry. I hope you'll be able to forgive me some day." Nasreen looks into the dark irises of Connie's eyes and sees in there a well of hope. She means it. Her own dark eyes become wet.

Connie takes the mug from Nasreen's hand. Her vision blurred by tears, Nasreen doesn't see what comes next. She feels strong arms pulling her, hot breath on her neck and then soft lips on her cheek, forehead, and mouth. Nasreen becomes uprooted, Connie the gale force wind snatching her up. Caught in this tornado, there is only motion now, the force of legs and arms, the crush of eager lips and hungry mouths, the whoosh of clothing being unzipped, unbuttoned and discarded. Nasreen struggles to hold on. By the time she opens her eyes again, Connie is kissing her from somewhere above, and Nasreen is flat on her back, her hands gripping Connie's hips tightly. Her brain registers that things are too far gone for her to bother stopping now, so she runs her greedy hands over Connie's back and pulls her weight down onto her, whispering teasing, bawdy words into Connie's receptive ear. Id watches them from the pile of still-warm clothes on the living room floor.

"You what?" Asha exclaims, her mouth full of penne. A 501 Queen streetcar rattles by their window table and Nasreen wonders if Asha hasn't heard her. Then, assessing Asha's expression, she guesses otherwise.

"OK, I admit it. It was poor judgement. I know that. I just don't know what came over me. It happened really fast."

"I can't believe you'd sleep with her after everything she's done to you!"

"I know, I know. It was stupid. It was weird. One moment I was feeling all cool and confident about her and then next, I was melting. It was because," Nasreen looks up at her friend's frown, and then back down at the cooling *pad thai* in her plate, "she said that she was sorry."

"Just sorry? That's what it took? That's what got you into bed with her? Oh, Nas…" Asha shakes her head disapprovingly.

"Hey, you don't know what's it like with her and me. When she started to talk, and seemed so sincere, well, that's what got me. I guess I needed to hear her apology."

"But do you think she was really sincere?" Asha's tone softens for a moment and then hardens again, "Come on Nas, it can't be that easy. 'Hey, I slept with my best friend, I betrayed you and now I'm sorry, so let's fuck?'" Nasreen looks around to see if anyone else has noticed the increasing volume in her friend's voice.

"I know it's not that simple. Something about her apologizing made me weak or something," Nasreen says quietly. "There were two things that were really good between us. Sex and … well, her taking care of me … being nice to me. And that combo was there again on Thursday night." Nasreen doesn't look up, but hears Asha sigh heavily.

"That girl is a snake and she just bit you. There's something about her that makes you way too vulnerable. I'm not sure you should be spending time with her." Nasreen stares out the window at the busy sidewalk, avoiding her friend's probing eyes. "Are you going to see her again?"

"No, I guess not. You're right. I just don't hold my own when I'm with her. She just … I don't know what it is about her. And anyway, she's going away for a couple of weeks. That should be enough time for me to suffer through the withdrawal. Again. When she's back I'll be strong again."

"Nasreen, should I remind you that two months have passed between the break-up and your passionate evening with her this week? I think you need a longer Connie Moratorium to get yourself rational again.

Her venom stays in your blood a long time." Asha spears a sausage and pops it into her mouth.

"Geez, what's with all the serpent metaphors?" Nasreen jokes. "OK, OK. Yeah, I know you're right. The next time she asks to see me, will you remind me that I can't?"

"Yeah, as if you'd listen to me." Asha says, her mouth full of sausage.

"Try harder to convince me next time. I can't go through another evening like that again. It feels like the way it did when she first left me."

"You mean when you kicked her out after being a two-timing slime-bucket." Asha looks at Nasreen. Nasreen is silent and stares sullenly into her noodles. "What? What's wrong? What'd I say?"

"It's not what you said. It's what I haven't said. The truth is that I didn't kick her out. I don't know why I said that to everyone. Maybe that's the version of things I would have preferred. I wish it had happened that way."

"So what happened then?"

"She cheated. That part is true. And then I pleaded with her to stay. I begged like a desperate person. I told her that we'd work it out. And then she left. I was pathetic, a mess."

"Oh wow, Nasreen."

"I couldn't tell anyone that I'd been left. I couldn't believe it myself. I didn't want to believe it. So I started telling the story in a way that sounded better to me. I almost started believing it. Wow, am I delusional, or what?"

"Maybe a bit of a revisionist, but not delusional. Don't be so hard on yourself. I mean, it's not so long since you lost your mother, why would you want you lose Connie too?" Asha tries to be soothing, but her tone only sounds condescending to Nasreen.

"It didn't have anything to do with my mother," Nasreen says defensively, "I wanted her to stay because I loved her."

"OK, well … you know there was no shame in asking her to stay and work it out," Asha says, trying to placate her friend.

"Yeah, I suppose so," Nasreen says, her voice softening.

"I bet there are plenty of couples who work things out after a bout of infidelity. I would have been lucky if one or two of my exes would have been open to that possibility."

"Yeah, that's true, you big philanderer," Nasreen says, at last a glint of mischief in her eyes.

"Hey girl, I am no philanderer. The proper term is polyamory queen, thank you very much," Asha grins.

"I should remind you that it is only polyamory when there is agreement between, I mean, among the partners involved. Otherwise, it is cheating. What would your girlfriend say about that?" Nasreen asks, eyebrows raised.

"I know, I know. I am a reformed woman these days. But how did this become about me? We were talking about you and your good-for-nothing cheating ex-girlfriend, weren't we?"

"Yes, we were. That good-for-nothing cheating snake of an ex-girlfriend" she says, laughing, "OK, I declare a Connie Moratorium starting today and going forever. I mean not forever. Well, for a long time. A really long time."

"Uh huh. OK, if you say so", says Asha, raising her glass and eyebrows in a toast to Nasreen.

The next morning Nasreen awakes from a dream so vivid, its clarity endures through the beeping of the clock-radio alarm. She closes her eyes, expecting to be pulled under by the thick dark night of it, but it has moved on, has already released to the day. She reaches for the pad of paper beside her bed and writes it down.

She was trailing Connie happily through their neighbourhood, following a few steps behind her. Only she wasn't herself in the dream, she was smaller, like a puppy. Her nose was wet, and close to the ground. The smell of warm asphalt and garbage filled her nostrils. Her palms scratched up against the rough pavement and her knees were stained and raw, unprepared for such mistreatment. Despite the discomfort, she felt happy to be with Connie.

During the walk, she began to find money all over the street in front of her. She wanted to jump up and down with excitement, but couldn't manage it from her all-fours position on the ground. The money was in large denominations, crisp red fifty-dollar bills and brown one-hundreds. The money was so pretty, reminding her of autumn leaves. She scampered toward the money and gathered up the notes in her right hand. This caused her to fall once or twice, until she figured out how to balance on one hand and two knees. She yelled out excitedly to Connie about her discovery, urging her too to look for the treasure. Connie bent down and tried to grab the money too, but just as she reached for it, the paper dissolved into the asphalt, disappearing as though it hadn't been there in the first place. Nasreen watched helplessly as Connie tried again and again to gather the vanishing money. Connie grimaced and looked at Nasreen angrily, as though it was somehow Nasreen's fault. Then, she bent down and grabbed the bills from Nasreen's hand. This unbalanced Nasreen and she crashed down to the ground, skinning her cheek. Connie marched away from her, leaving her alone on the pavement.

Nasreen puts down her pen and rubs her cheek, feeling wounded, but finding no injury there. Leaning over to her left, she pulls open the drawer of her bedside table, feeling for a thick bundle of notes and cards held together by an aging rubber band. She started this collection when Connie sent flowers and a note after their first date. No one had ever sent her flowers before. The pile of love notes continued to grow over their years together. She pulls aside the rubber band, and it ungracefully snaps open and springs across the room. Id races to capture the runaway elastic, and snarls with it.

"Stop that, Id! You can't eat that!" The cat stops chewing the elastic to study her dully. He jumps onto the bed and sidles up against Nasreen, the elastic still between his teeth.

Nasreen turns to the bundle of cards that she has read and reread, an archive of her life with Connie. At the top of the pile is the small florist's card that says, "Thanks for the lovely evening. I'd love to get to know you better." There is a Valentine's card full of sexy sentiment, a birthday promise of everlasting love, and an anniversary letter that once spellbound her with its romantic prose.

She gathers the pile together, and with a deep inhalation, she begins to tear each card and love note, one by one, until there is a small pile of little paper scraps in front of her on the bed. She scoops up the shredded paper in her pajama top and carries it carefully to the bathroom and then dumps them on the cotton bath mat. She drops a handful into the toilet, watching as the paper soaks up the light blue water, becoming saturated, heavy, unreadable. She flushes. She repeats this again and again until all the paper scraps have disappeared. Then, she rests a moment on the side of the bathtub and stares vacantly into the blue water of the toilet. To her surprise and relief, something about this has worked, has helped. She feels as though she has lost five pounds. She has cleared away something, created a little bit of space in her bedside table drawer. And within herself.

Chapter 19

SALMA UNDOES THE METAL latch of her old, metal trunk and breathes in its slightly musty, closed-up smell. It was shipped from Bombay along with a few boxes they could not carry with them on the plane, and its delayed arrival in Canada carried with it heavy expectation. Now, loaded up with bits and pieces that have no other place in the small apartment, it sits at the foot of Salma and Shaffiq's bed, mostly ignored. It is the one piece of furniture in the Paperwala home that is from India.

Upon landing in Canada, the Paperwalas experienced the immigrant's optimism, the heady, hopeful feeling that everything can be better in this new place. For most this sentiment lasts perhaps half a year and then the excitement, this faith in the new country, begins to dissipate when dreams become sidelined by the wearying challenges of looking for a home, finding a job, and searching for belonging. It's as though the new country can only participate in the charade for so long, and eventually tires from the heavy expectation placed upon it.

For Salma, her Canadian honeymoon barely lasted three weeks and she remembers it like a summer vacation. She felt like a tourist in Toronto, carrying an open map wherever she went, marveling at the new things that delighted her: the huge selection of shampoos in the Shoppers' Drug Mart, the rows and rows of books in the quiet of the Lillian H. Smith Library, the Music Gardens by the lake. Then, homesickness descended upon her slowly, manifesting in ways she didn't understand. At first, she found herself growing irritated by silly things, like the cost of a ten-pound sack of Basmati rice or the unfamiliar quiet outside her window at night. Later, she found herself criticizing nearly everything that was different from home: the smells of Toronto pavement after a rain, the slow pace of the downtown pedestrians, the way she had to repeat her name three times before the Canadians seemed to be able to hear it.

She tried to hide her feelings from Shaffiq, who reveled in the newness, the freshness, the adventure of being out of India.

"Look Salma, see how clean everything is here! Not a speck of dirt on these sidewalks." This was a month after they had arrived in Canada and the family was out for a walk through Yorkville, touring the city on a sunny Saturday. Shaffiq had wanted to check out a variety of Toronto neighbourhoods and so Asima had given them a TTC map and told them to get off at Bay Station. "Everthing is so clean and white here."

"I remember, before Asima's family came here, people used to say that the sidewalks in North America were lined with gold," Salma scoffed.

"Yes, now we are more realistic, no? We just want clean. And we have that much. Bombay could never be like this."

"Mummy, is that a beggar?" Saleema asked, as they passed a panhandler sitting in front of a fancy dress shop.

"Yes, I think so. Children, don't stare like that. I suppose there are poor people here too," Salma whispered.

"Yes, but not like in India. Here the beggars collect money from the government and then ask for money on the street. Remember what Quaid told us?" But Salma wasn't so sure it was true. The man on the sidewalk didn't look so different from Bombay beggars. "And anyway," Shaffiq continued, "There are so few of them here. In Bombay you can't walk one meter before hearing *"paisa, paisa, paisa."* Look, an ice cream shop. Children, shall we have some ice-creams?"

Although she tried, Salma could not share Shaffiq's optimism. While he looked back with disdain at India and forward in anticipation to their lives in Canada, she could not stop thinking about what she was missing back home. How were her students doing? Was the new teacher treating them well? Had her friend Ritu had the baby yet?

During her second month in Toronto, as she willed herself to push aside her homesickness and focus on settling in Canada, her nostalgia for home morphed into an obsession with her delayed trunk. She began to fixate on its arrival and felt that perhaps she would begin to feel better, more like a happy immigrant, if she could only have this last piece of luggage with her. She would do mental inventories of the items inside, trying to remember all of her belongings yet to come. At night, she dreamed about its contents: her old college books, an ancient shawl given to her by her *nani*, her wedding sari. Sometimes the dreams transformed into nightmares of her prized keepsakes being lost forever: a plane crash where her trunk sinks to the bottom of the sea; a corrupt agent stealing it away and handing out her possessions to his family; a mistake in the address label that sends it forever to the opposite side of the globe.

On nights when she awoke in the dark, these bad dreams fresh in her mind, her chest and neck wet with perspiration, she told herself, it's coming, it will all be here soon. The rest of our things will come and then we can finally settle down.

When they got the call that their shipment had arrived, Salma was elated. She watched as Shaffiq and the Pakistani driver loaded the trunk and some boxes into a cab at the airport. For a moment she wondered if they had picked up the right trunk because it seemed smaller and shabbier than the one she had remembered. But of course it was hers; it had her name on it and it had been her imagination that made the trunk larger than life. And what was inside it anyway? She scolded herself for placing so much emphasis on this trunk full of useless keepsakes. Her eyes filled with tears and Shaffiq held her hand on the way home, confused at his wife's distress.

She unpacked the boxes first, emptying their contents into closets and drawers. After a few days, she opened the trunk and decided to leave it in the bedroom as a storage box. She didn't need any of the superfluous things in there anyway.

Today, she digs through the trunk knowing that it holds something of value. She takes out her old teaching textbooks. She flips through them, remembering her college days. She unfolds her *nani*'s shawl, holding it to her nose for the smell of India beneath the mustiness. Then, she finds what she has been looking for under her marriage sari. She pulls out an old photo album, its binding weak and its cover peeling, and flips through the plastic-covered pages.

She is not entirely sure why she packed this particular photo album at the bottom of her trunk, instead of with the others that came with them on the journey. Perhaps it was because this album is filled with memories of her life before she met Shaffiq, before the children came, before she really grew up. When people get married, their belongings stop being his or hers, mine and yours. They become ours. This album is about a life before this one, a lifetime ago. It is *hers*.

Inside, she looks at a photo of herself as an infant. In black and white, she sees how similar she looked to Saleema at the same age. She smiles at the possibility that her eldest daughter will grow up to look very much like her. She knows that Shireen will resemble her father more, as she already does.

There are photos of herself and her older brother, Rahim, at Chowpatty beach, drinking Thum's Up and smiling into the camera. She looks to be five or six, while he is almost a man, tall, lanky, and clumsy in his body. A few pages later there is a graduation photo of her and beside it, one of herself and Ritu standing proudly together on their final day of classes.

She continues to turn the pages and holds her breath. And there it is. A photo of Raj, herself, and two of Raj's friends in Lonavala, during a weekend trip they took together. They stand together like pals, each woman slinging an arm around the other, looking happy. She never showed that photo to her family.

Over a year later, when she packed up her belongings to be shifted to Shaffiq's flat after their marriage, she found the photo and slid it into her photo album. She wanted to file the memory of Raj away in this book, put the photo in its place, so to speak. Later, when she unpacked her boxes in Shaffiq's room, she showed him the album and explained that the photo was of a group of friends she hadn't seen in many years. He looked closely at the photo, inquiring about her friends and why they lost touch. He commented that they all seemed close at one time.

Now, she pulls the photo from its sticky plastic sheath and holds it up to the light. There she stands beside Raj, her arm around her and holding her waist, while Raj's left hand grazes her shoulder. She can't see her own left arm, but it looks like it is behind Maya's back. And beside Maya is Anjali, who is pulled in close to Maya. The four women pose good-naturedly for the camera, but there is a measure of tense caution in their stances. Everyone shines white teeth smiles at the photographer, except for Raj. Her round, young face tilts toward Salma at an angle that obscures her expression.

Chapter 20

SHAFFIQ IS DREAMING. He is wet all over, sweating through his cotton pajamas. Still asleep, he throws off the covers to cool his warm body. He wonders why Nasreen's office is so bloody hot. He sits down on a red upholstered chair, resting in her muggy office. Drops of sweat roll down from his forehead into his thick eyebrows. He reaches for his handkerchief and finds his pant pockets empty. Nasreen sits opposite him in her ergonomic chair, looking placid and cool, a yellow steno notepad ready in her lap. He is aware that she is waiting for him to speak and so, finally, he begins to talk.

At first he is unsure what to say, after all, he has never been to see a therapist before. He explains why he brought his family to Canada. He tells Nasreen that even though Salma had not wanted to come, it was the best thing to do. Nasreen doesn't look up at him, continues to write on her notepad. He glances over and sees that she is writing in Gujarati, a language he can speak, but is unable to read well. She has not once made eye contact, has not shown any sympathy whatsoever for him. In fact, she appears to be bored. Then, it occurs to him that perhaps she doesn't believe him, so then he starts to yell, his dream logic telling him this is the best way to have her take him seriously. In his loudest voice, he insists that coming to Canada was the best thing to do. He gives her all the good reasons for leaving India, the same arguments he gave Salma and his friends, trying to convince Nasreen, make her see his point of view.

She stares back at him vacantly, disinterested. She looks at her watch. This inane gesture makes him furious and he yells even louder, standing over her, waving his fist at her, demanding that she listen to him.

Eventually, she turns away from him and faces her computer and types something. He shouts, "But this is my home now." Still she does not respond, so he grabs her shoulders and shakes her roughly, and her head wobbles back and forth on her neck, like a newborn's. She points to the computer screen, directing him to read what she has typed. He does so, but he cannot understand the writing. It looks like gibberish to him. He tries to remember his elementary school lessons, to sound out the Gujarati script, the way he instructs Shireen to do with difficult words in her school reader. But still, Nasreen's writing is incomprehensible to him. Then he watches as Nasreen presses Control-Alt-Delete and the screen goes empty. Then she picks up her phone and dials Shaffiq's home phone number.

Salma picks up the phone after the first ring and soon he is awake. Shaffiq turns over in the bed and pulls the blankets up to his chin; his drying sweat has chilled his body. The heavy curtains are drawn shut, but he can just make out a sliver of sunshine invading the dark. He hears Salma's voice talking to someone on the telephone while the television murmurs quietly from the living room. He goes to the bathroom, empties his full bladder, flushes and then follows Salma's voice to the living room. She glances up and after a few moments, hangs up the phone tiredly.

"You're up early."

"Yes, I woke up and couldn't get back to sleep."

"Oh, was it the phone that woke you up? I tried to get it fast so it wouldn't ring too long."

"Must have been. It's OK, I was having a bad dream. Who called?"

"It was Asima. She wanted to know if I am going to join her this week. Shaffiq, maybe you should come along. It is soon going to be Ramadan."

"I don't know, Salma. You know I don't get much out of going to mosque." Shaffiq feels himself growing irritable. He studies her face and wonders if this will turn into an argument.

"Well, I think I'll start taking the girls. Just on the important days for now, and then if they are interested I'll take them more often."

"Were you interested in going to mosque at their age? I can't think of anything more boring for a child. But take them if you want." He says tiredly, wanting to return to his bed, "Let them decide."

"You will come with us at least one time, won't you? At least do that."

"Yes, alright, if I am not working. You know in this country they don't give us a holiday to go to the mosque."

"They didn't in India either. Or don't you remember?" She watches Shaffiq retreat into the hallway, and then she says to his back, "I think I'll do the *rosas* this year."

"Fasting? Really Salma, this is such a change I'm seeing in you! When have you ever fasted?" Shaffiq feels himself waking up, alarmed at his wife's changes, and warming to the idea of a big argument with her.

"When I was younger, before we met, I fasted a few times. Not the whole month, but part of it anyway. You know even though we weren't so devout, my family did observe some of our traditions."

"OK, whatever suits you Salma. But the children will not fast. They are too young for that. I don't understand this change in you. Aren't we supposed to be moving forward in Canada? Instead you are turning back, acting like an old woman, behaving like they did in our parents' generation. What for?"

"I am just going to the mosque, Shaffiq. How is that going backwards? And what do you mean about moving forward? How have we gone forward in this country? You clean toilets for a living in the middle of the night. I work in a dry cleaners. Moving forward? If I want to fast or go to the mosque, can you blame me?"

Shaffiq stares at his wife's reddening face. His own fury and fear blocks his words and so he stares silently at her angry, strange expression. Has she looked at him this way before? Has he ever provoked such ire? A new, unfamiliar feeling grips him as she turns away from him. He is about to respond, to fight back, or maybe to try to appease her but then, just as he opens his mouth, the lock turns, signaling the return of Shireen and Saleema, back from school. He stomps off to the bedroom.

Salma attempts to swallow her anger and greets the girls as they enter the apartment. As she walks past the painting of the *raani*, she feels the servant's eyes following her. She takes a long look at the painting, sighing, interpreting the servant's and the *raani's* expressions to be sympathetic toward her.

Nasreen sits in a circle among her peers, explaining her confusion about Miranda's phone message.

"So I guess my question is, should I call her back and try to engage in a dialogue about her decision to terminate therapy?"

"My instinct would be to respect her wishes at face value. Let her call you again when she wants to resume contact. Allow her the control," says Michael, Nasreen's next-door office neighbour.

"I think it might depend on what kind of rapport you have with her," suggests Joan, the most senior therapist on their team. "I would only challenge her decision – which, by the way, I agree with your analysis that she is terminating early because she is afraid of her own grief – if you have a strong rapport with her. Otherwise she will not be able to hear your point of view."

"Well, I've only seen her a few times. I don't think we have a strong rapport. But would it do her any harm for me to challenge her decision? I mean, she clearly cannot see that she is once again repeating a pattern of dumping therapy just when she is getting somewhere. Isn't it my job to point that out?"

"Nasreen, what I'm hearing is that you feel very strongly about this client, perhaps more than you normally would. Is there any counter-transference going on here?" Noseywendy says this with the pleasant-looking smile she uses when wanting to avoid seeming critical.

"Um, I don't think so. I just think that she is going to go round and round until she shifts her pattern. Her problems clearly stem from her unresolved mother-grief issues. I'd like to help her understand that," says Nasreen defensively.

"And that's what bothers you?" asks Noseywendy. "Her grief issues?"

"Bingo," says Michael.

"Bingo? What does that mean?"

"Sorry Nasreen, but I have to agree with Wendy. What do you and Miranda have in common?"

"Oh, right. I guess I'll have to think about that," says Nasreen quietly. The three other psychologists study their shoes until Wendy suggests they move onto another case.

On the next Monday, Nasreen arrives at her Gujarati teacher's apartment a little late, very wet, and out of breath. Saleema appears at the door and opens it wide for her, averting her gaze in a flush of nine-year-old shyness. The girl says a muffled hello and then disappears to the far corner of the room. Shireen skips forward, takes her place and asks, *"Khem, cho! Khem cho!* How are you! How are you! See I know Gujarati too!" The words fly out enthusiastically, along with a spray of spittle through the gap between her front teeth.

"Uh huh, *majama chun*. And I see the tooth fairy has come to visit you," Nasreen says, wiping her face and smiling at the girl.

"Yes, I only got a quarter. My friend Melanie got a toonie."

"Next time, if you keep being so greedy, you will only get a penny," says Salma, standing with her arms folded across her chest. Shireen pouts theatrically, and Salma sends her to play in her room. She takes Nasreen's soaking wet coat and hangs it in the hall closet and then steers her into the kitchen.

"As you can see, the children are home tonight. Their playmates down the hall are out, but I've told them to leave us alone."

"Oh, I don't mind. They're very sweet."

"Sometimes a little sour too. But where is Asha? She didn't come?"

"No, she's not feeling well. She's got that bad cold that's going around."

"Too bad. Well, you'll get my undivided attention tonight." As though uttering an unexpected faux pas, Salma looks away uncomfortably, "I mean, we could focus on the vocabulary you'd like, if you want."

"Great," says Nasreen, now also feeling awkward. She hasn't given Asha's comments about Salma's crush much thought, but suddenly, without Asha in the room, the notion that Salma could be attracted to her seems to take up all the space in the apartment.

"But look at you, you are drenched. I will find you a towel."

"With the rain, I thought I'd be really late. The TTC took forever."

"Well, at least it is rush hour. Lots of buses. My husband comes home from his job each day around five a.m., and if he misses his bus, he has to wait a long time." She hands Nasreen a red and white flowered towel.

"Thanks. Wow, five a.m.? What's he do?" says Nasreen, searching to make conversation and relieved to be discussing Salma's husband.

"He used to be an accountant in Bombay, but in Toronto he is a janitor, at a hospital downtown," Salma says, scrutinizing Nasreen's face. It reveals nothing. "'No Canadian experience', they tell him when he applies. You know he has looked for a more suitable job for two years, since we first arrived."

"That's awful, Salma. And you were a teacher in India, right?" Salma nods. "Our system needs to change. You know, every other cab driver in Toronto is like, a doctor or engineer," Nasreen adds sympathetically.

"Well at least the hospital pays over minimum wage, and has some benefits."

"Oh yeah? Which one's he at?"

"The Institute of Mental Health."

"Hey, that's where I work! You mean on College Street?"

"The same." Salma arranges some Gujarati flash cards on the kitchen table, busying herself. "I wonder if you have met him. Though you work such different jobs, maybe you would not have crossed paths." She looks directly into Nasreen's eyes.

"What's his name? I've seen a couple of Indian janitors there. There's one guy who's very friendly ... I can't remember his name," Nasreen's face scrunches up in concentration.

"Shaffiq," says Salma.

"Shaffiq," says Nasreen, a quarter second later. "Wow, that's amazing. I wonder if he's the same one? I probably talk to him once a week. What a coincidence if his wife's my Gujarati teacher!"

"Yes," says Salma, her back to Nasreen. "That would be quite a coincidence. Here, let me help you." She takes the towel from Nasreen and rubs her wet hair with it. Salma is a bright woman. The synapses in her brain flash double-quick, linking Shaffiq with Nas through the crumpled itinerary and the teardrop earring.

"Oh, that's OK, I'll do it." Nasreen reaches up for the towel but Salma steps aside, moving behind her and out of reach.

"Look, the water soaked right through your coat and blouse." She slips the towel down the back of Nasreen's green blouse and wipes her wet skin. "This won't do. You'll get sick." Nasreen's back warms under Salma's towel strokes. "Come, let me give you something to change into."

"Really, I'm fine, I'm just a bit damp."

"No, no. Follow me, I will find something for you to put on."

Nasreen obediently follows Salma down the hall. They pass the kids' room, the sound of girlish arguing leaking from beneath the door. They enter the master bedroom, really just a room large enough for a double bed, a chunky dresser, a trunk and an ironing board. Salma pulls open the closet door and roots around, looking for something while Nasreen scans some framed family photos on the dresser. There is a small bottle of Fleur de Jardin, her mother's favourite perfume sitting amongst a circle of moisturizers and lipsticks. The sight of the perfume makes her catch her breath for a moment and her mind troubles over why she hadn't identified Salma's familiar fragrance before. She rubs her forefinger over the smooth glass of the bottle. A garden path opens up in her mind and her mother walks through it, arranging her sari as she readies herself to go out to a party. She uncaps the Fleur de Jardin, and holding the bottle out a foot from her arm, spritzes her left wrist. She offers her wrist for Nasreen to sniff, and smiles while pink azaleas and white roses bloom in Nasreen's nostrils.

"I'm sure there is one back here. Just a minute, Nas." Nasreen exits her mother's garden and returns to Salma's bedroom. She averts her gaze from the perfume bottle and tries to steady her mind by looking at a black and white photograph of stern looking elders. Then, there is a photo of Salma, standing formally beside a man, their serious expressions incongruous with the white garlands hanging garishly around their necks.

"Oh hey! That's Shaffiq."

"So you do recognize him. I guess he is your janitor."

"Weird. We'll have to tell him about this! Is that your wedding picture?" Salma's brain registers the guiltlessness of Nas's enthusiasm. So whatever Shaffiq's interest in her, it is not shared by Nas.

"Yes. We both look younger, no? I was twenty-six. Shaffiq was already thirty-two. Your age, yes?" Nasreen nods. "Marriage ages you. Oh, here is something." She hands Nasreen a sweater. "Having kids ages you."

"I dunno. You don't look so different from this photo. And that wasn't so long ago, was it?"

"It was … eleven years ago, no twelve. We waited three years before having Saleema and she is nine now –"

"So you're what, thirty-eight now? You're not that much older than me. You look great."

"You are trying to flatter me. Go on, try this on, I think it will fit. It is from my younger, thinner days." Nasreen hesitates a moment.

"Try it on. If it does not fit, I will look for another." Salma considers turning her back, allowing Nasreen a moment of modesty but doesn't manage to move in time.

Nasreen turns, peels off her damp blouse and pulls on the sweater. Salma watches as Nasreen's head disappears through the neck hole, averting her gaze only when the knitted fabric comes down over her belly. She commits to memory a small dimple just below Nasreen's breast bone, a mole just to the left of her navel.

"Looks like it fits you." Salma says, her voice cracking with nervousness, "Why don't you keep it? It is too small for me."

"Oh, I can't take it from you. Maybe it will fit Saleema in a couple of years."

"No, no. Please take it. The styles will have changed. They have already. Teenagers wear everything short and tight. They barely like to cover anything up over here." Salma laughs, but isn't sure if what she's said is funny.

"Are you sure?" Nasreen asks. Salma nods. "Thanks. I'm warmer already."

"Good, so let's start the class. *Chalo.*"

Bashir sits on a prayer mat in his living room, facing the blank scree n of the television, which stands in his direct path to Mecca. He distractedly contemplates moving around the furniture, mentally rearranging chairs, sidetables, and electronic equipment. He worries that the involvement of the idiot box may ruin or nullify his prayers somehow.

He has somehow lost track of his prayers, something interrupting his flow, side-tracking him from his faith. It just isn't working for him today. Maybe it is just old age, he thinks, the mind wandering.

Prayerless, he looks at his reflection in the TV screen. He sees an old man, his hairline receding, most of the black hair turning to grey. He breathes in and out, in and out, considering his lungs and heart, envisioning them working hard in his sixty-one year old body, trying to push around air and blood, each year this endeavour becoming slightly more laborious. He imagines his arteries, not pink and rubbery like the diagram in his doctor's office, but as he feels to be realistic: slowly becoming encrusted with yellowish plaque. That's the word his doctor used and Bashir recalls wondering if the blockage in his arteries is the same stuff that dulls his teeth. He'll have to ask his cardiologist this question when he goes for his follow-up appointment next month. Or maybe he will ask his dentist when he has his six-month check-up.

His mind circles back to the television screen and its effect on his prayers. It's hopeless. He'll have to ask Nasreen to help him move the chesterfield, and television next time she is here. He abandons his prayer mat and stands facing the window. It is still raining outside. A bolt of lightning illuminates the sky and his suburban neighbourhood. He scripts a more direct line of conversation with his God and reasons that perhaps a personal entreaty will work better than the ritualized, common ones He hears from the mouths of the masses. Yes, a private prayer might just work. He clears his throat and says aloud, "Dear God, I want to ask You," he pauses then, feeling self-conscious. How silly I must seem. He tries again, "Dear God, please just grant me this one thing – " he hesitates again, looks around at the familiar room, at the drapes and furniture and trinkets, the result of years of decorating by his now deceased wife.

He becomes aware that he has occupied this house for over twenty-five years, that it was the first and last house he bought with his Zainab, and is the place where his daughter grew to be a woman. A place that was a home while Zainab was alive and that is nothing more than a house now. He wonders if she listens in on his thoughts and prayers from time to time. *Are you there Zainab? Can you hear me?*

He shakes his head, feeling even more foolish. I am just a man, like any other man and I am afraid to get old. I am scared to get sick and to die. "Please, God, help my Nasreen to be happy. Don't condemn her for her choices. Let my dear Zainab's soul rest peacefully. Help me to stay well and to live a long time still. I don't want to leave my Nasreen alone. Don't let the plaque in my arteries get too thick. Thank you for listening, God."

He bends to sit down again on his prayer mat, his knees noisily protesting this sudden movement. Changing his mind, he takes a seat at his computer. Within moments he is logged on to his favourite "free stuff" site, the magic of the Internet freeing him from his failing body and providing him a limited measure of peace.

An hour later, Nasreen stares blankly at the vocabulary sheet Salma has placed before her. Her fingers drum against the metal kitchen table while she strains to remember the words she learned last week.

"You didn't study this week?"

"Well, I did, but I'm drawing a blank for some reason."

"Try again. Come on now, how do you say 'I would like to have lunch'?" Nasreen stumbles through some phrases in her mind, wishing that Asha were here to deflect some of Salma's intense energy away from her.

"I'm not sure what's wrong with me today. I just can't seem to remember much."

"Let's take a break then. You want some *chai?*"

"Yeah, that would be good. Maybe the caffeine will wake me up."

Salma turns away from Nasreen and fills the kettle, welcoming the distraction. For the last hour, she has avoided Nasreen's eyes. She has tried not to focus on the butterfly feeling in her stomach, or Nasreen's lips, or her bare neck, or the wisps of hair drying in tight coils around her soft ears. *Is this what Shaffiq sees too?*

Nasreen, too, takes a moment to settle herself. Something has been different today and a part of her brain has been busy, working hard to interpret the vibes coming from Salma. What would Asha say? Is she really right about the crush? No, it can't be true, Nasreen thinks. *What would a nice, married woman like Salma want with me?*

"Nas, I've been curious about something," Salma turns around and leans against the counter. She crosses her arms in front of her chest. "Maybe it is none of my business. If I am being too nosey, just say." Nasreen leans back in her chair and nods to Salma, giving her permission to continue. Here it comes, she thinks.

"Mummy, Saleema is being mean to me!"

"No I'm not! She should just leave me alone. I'm trying to read and she's bugging me!" Both children burst into the room.

"Both of you out of here! Shireen, you go play in the bedroom and Saleema, you read in the living room. I don't want any more interruptions. Go!" The girls listen to the seriousness of her tone and follow her pointed finger out of the kitchen. Salma continues to chide them in Gujarati and then closes the kitchen door firmly behind them. "Sorry about that. They are always fighting with each other, always at each other's throats."

"That's OK. They seem like pretty normal kids to me. What were you going to ask me?"

"Well, last time you and Asha were here, you talked about being attracted to women.... Are you both, well ... gays?" She says the last word quietly, as though it requires a delicate touch.

"Yes, well, actually we call ourselves lesbian or queer. What would you like to know? You know it is alright to ask questions about this. Most people are a bit curious." Nasreen is back on solid ground. *This is why Salma has been so strange with me. Of course she would have questions after the way we carried on last time.*

"Well, I am curious. I'm not sure about what exactly. It just got me thinking you know, about attractions to women. Remembering. You know, I am married and I am very happy with my husband, but there was a time when ..." she says very quietly, "well, I had a relationship with a woman. It was long ago, in India."

"Really?" Nasreen is the one who is curious now.

"It's silly, I don't know why I'm thinking about it now. I shouldn't be telling you this."

"Have you told anyone?" Nasreen asks, understanding that Salma has revealed a big secret.

"Well ... no. We had to keep things hush-hush. No one knew. But it was just a short affair," Salma says, her voice hesitant. She hears the gurgling of boiling water and she turns to remove the kettle from the stove before it whistles. She is relieved to be able to turn away from Nasreen's gaze. She transfers hot water from kettle to tea pot, placing it on the table between them.

"Tell me about it anyway. I bet lots of married women have experimented with women at some point in their lives." Nasreen tries to sound reassuring.

"Shhh! Please speak softly. My nine-year-old out there likes to listen in on everything. It was only for a few months, when I just starting teaching. It was a kind of a phase, you know, a curiosity, I think. I broke it off when she started to get too serious. And then there was quite a lot of pressure to settle down and get married. I was already turning twenty-five by then."

"It must have been hard to keep it a secret, you know, to sneak around?" Nasreen says in a stage-whisper.

"Well, I don't know how hard it was to keep it secret. We just knew we had to. I didn't even tell my best friend, Ritu. Although she may have suspected something. She disliked Raj because Raj was sort of known to be that way. She was sort of mannish … and people spread rumours – you know how people can be about things like that."

"Sounds like Raj was butch. People always give the gender-nonconforming queers the hardest time. It's so stupid."

"I don't really know about all that. But, well, she did stand out. She was obvious … not like how you are." Salma pours tea into two ceramic cups. "I can't believe I'm telling you this. It was a long time ago. We were young, and she was more serious than I."

"It sounds like it was a big deal. How do you know it was just a phase? That's what my parents said when I first started dating women. This phase has lasted a long time."

"Well, we did care about each other, but we both knew that it was only temporary, that it wouldn't last long, or couldn't last very long. But still, she was very hurt when I broke it off." Salma sits down at the table and passes Nasreen a cup. "I felt bad about that. Maybe it wasn't a phase for her. She was more that way than me. More, you know, lesbian," she says tentatively, as though testing out the new word, "more lesbian than me. If I am really at all that way myself." Salma shrugs, uncertain what she is driving at, why she is making this confession.

"What does that mean, Salma? Let me ask you this," Nasreen says, leaning in a little closer. "If there had not been a need to keep it a secret, and if you hadn't been expected to get married, would you have broken it off? Did you like being in a relationship with her?" Nasreen watches as Salma wrinkles her forehead and takes a sip of her tea.

"I don't know. That is how the world is. I made the decision to put a stop to it based on what the reality was then," she says, trying to sound sure of herself. *But is this true? Was it just my own fears?*

"But if it hadn't been the reality? If things had been different?" Nasreen presses her.

"But things weren't different. Don't you see? It was India almost fifteen years ago, not Canada today," Salma replies, realizing that Nasreen cannot possibly comprehend. She grew up here.

"But I've heard that there are plenty of out lesbians in India. One of my friends was there for a while and made contact with all these lesbian and gay groups in Delhi and Bombay. And in Calcutta."

"I don't know. I don't think those things existed back then. Or at least I didn't know about them. If things had been different maybe Raj and I would have stayed together. I can't say. I did care about her." She looks up at Nasreen, her eyes watering. "I did care about her. If it were Canada today, I might have made some different choices." Nasreen reaches out for Salma's hand.

"But Salma, it is Canada today." Salma feels the warmth of Nasreen's hand on hers and heeds the electricity that prickles across the expanse of skin between her wrist and shoulder. The sensation continues all the way to her groin, and ends up somewhere in her stomach. She reaches out to touch Nasreen's cheek and without thinking, without looking for Nasreen's startled reaction, presses her mouth against soft lips. They yield to her and pure sunshine radiates over Salma when she feels Nas drawing closer. The bright light thaws something frozen within her, and she feels her insides turn to liquid. And then, as suddenly as it appeared, the sunlight is gone, refracted by the dark pupils of Nas's eyes and the force of her fingertips, gently pushing her away.

Chapter 21

NASREEN RIDES THE OSSINGTON streetcar home, her lips still tingling from Salma's kiss. She closes her eyes, tries to replay the incident in slow motion. Did she do something to encourage Salma? Did she flirt a little, play into the crush, maybe? *I suppose the possibility of a crush was kind of flattering ... God, I'm ridiculous!* Salma's lips felt warm and demanding and Nasreen kissed her back, wanting to receive and meet the pressure and heat of Salma's mouth. She liked it. Then Nasreen remembered where she was and with whom and pulled away. She left soon after that, feeling uncomfortable and vaguely guilty. She looks down at the sweater Salma lent her. *Damn, why'd I leave my favourite blouse behind?*

At home now, she calls Asha. It rings twice and then her friend picks up, her voice thick with a cold.

"Hi Ash, how are you feeling?"

"A little better. But I am so bored. Do you know that *Days of Our 'Restless' Lives* is still on the air? I've been watching it the last few days and some of the same characters are still there from when I was a teenager. And there are still no lesbians or people of colour. Some things never change."

"Sounds like you are almost back to your old self, except that you're deconstructing the soaps instead of your course texts," Nasreen scoffs.

"They are of similar quality, I think. How was class tonight? Did I miss much?"

"I'd say so. That's why I'm calling. Something weird happened tonight."

"Weird?"

"Yeah, you were right about Salma having a crush on me."

"Really? No way! What happened?" Asha asks, excitedly.

"Well, she started asking me about being a lesbian and then told me that she had had a relationship with a woman over twelve years ago –"

"Wow! I did miss a lot!"

"That's not all. Then, when she got a bit teary about ending that relationship, I touched her hand, you know, to offer some sympathy and then she started kissing me."

"What? Hold up. She kissed you? How did that happen?" Asha asks, gasping into the receiver.

"I don't know. It happened really fast. She reached over and started kissing me. And then I left."

"Wow, you sure are getting a lot of action lately. Did you like it? Where were the kids?"

"They were there in the apartment, but not in the kitchen with us. I think I did. I mean … it's nice to be kissed. Maybe I liked the attention. But … but, she's a married woman, our Gujarati teacher, for God's sake! And she isn't really my type."

"I guess so, she is like the polar opposite of Connie, isn't she? Although, I hate to mention it …"

"What?"

"In terms of being confused, sending mixed messages, being inappropriate, that's Connie all over again."

"Well I am sure about not being attracted to Salma. Really sure. I didn't come on to her, remember? She was the one who kissed me," Nasreen says defensively.

"Hmm. So what next? Did you talk about it after? Are you going back?"

"No, we didn't talk about it. She apologized as I was leaving. I don't know if I should go back. I have to think about that." Nasreen ponders the potential awkwardness of going back to Salma's apartment.

"Didn't I tell you she was hot for you? Wow, but this is bad. Who're we going to get to teach us Gujarati now?" Asha asks, laughing.

Salma listens for the children in the other room. There is the sound of a flushing toilet and a child padding her way to bed. Instinctively, she waits until there is silence again before returning to the *Ladies World* resting in her lap. The magazine, which Asima passed on to her, is chock-full of petty Bollywood news and advice for women, and is strangely calming after the humiliating day she has just had. She reads through Ms. Madhuri's column, scanning the counsel given to women who cannot get along with their in-laws, or who suspect that their husbands are cheating. *At least I don't have those problems,* she thinks.

She peers at the well-thumbed matrimonials page, likely poured over by someone already. *Perhaps Asima has been busy seeking a match for one of her cousin-sisters or another self-chosen cause in her family,* Salma thinks. Her attention is caught by a large, bold ad in the men seeking women category.

Bangalore issueless Muslim divorcee. Looking for a decent post-grad/professional/teacher/doctor match. Slim, fair girl preferred. Dowry no bar.

Salma smirks at this ad. *How many rupees per word did he pay to find just the right kind of match to satisfy himself and his family? And did the ad work for him? Did he find love?*

She closes her eyes, leans back and wonders what Shaffiq would say if he knew that she kissed Nas tonight. *Would he be scandalized? Jealous? And if so, would he be more jealous of her or Nas?*

She will never tell him about the kiss, that much she knows for sure. It would raise too many insecurities and perhaps also open up doors to questions she would prefer to remain shut and locked. He might ask her to stop teaching, or at least stop teaching Nas. She doesn't want that. After all, it is the only activity that provides her with some intellectual stimulation.

But why did she have to kiss Nasreen? Chances are that Nas will never come back, and maybe Asha too. Salma pulls her knees to her chest and lets a few tears escape. She despairs for her ridiculous desires, for the likely loss of her students. *How could she jeopardize her teaching like that?*

Salma looks down at the magazine in her hands, imagining what Shaffiq would ask for in a matrimonial:

Muslim man, previous accountant, and now a janitor, seeking smart, slightly plump woman who will fry tasty pakoras while gracefully bearing his children.

She puts the magazine down. *Perhaps his needs are simpler than her more complicated desires. But maybe he is more complicated than she* knows. What is his interest in Nas, anyway? She holds her head in her hands, considering the bizarre reality that both she and her husband might have an unreciprocated crush on the same woman.

Nasreen's questions echo in the small bedroom: what if things had been different? What if she had never married, but could have stayed with Raj?

What if she had not become a mother? What if she were still teaching, rather that working in the Blue Dove dry cleaners, sorting through the dirty clothes of the upper middle class? What if things had been different and she did not have to keep things secret with Raj?

Salma sighs heavily, tired from too many impossible questions. She pulls the covers up over her chest. Why think about what did not happen in her life? Her life is what it is. She should be more positive, like how Shaffiq is. Her negativity must be hard on him. She resolves to stop thinking about Raj.

But despite her efforts, Salma cannot shove aside her memories, for memory has a presence of its own, perhaps even a mind of its own. She has tried to compartmentalize the parts of her past that are difficult to accommodate, imagining them like cards to be filed away into a dusty wooden library drawer, a kind of card catalogue of her existence. But the drawer that is her time with Raj, and the cards that hold the most potent of her memories, never sat well and still don't. They have a way of resisting being filed in any kind of orderly way, and now, more than ever, are jamming the drawer, making it impossible to shut.

She stumbles from her bed to the dark living room and searches the *raani's* face. Salma notices that the queen's mouth is turned up slightly as though she is enjoying a joke at her expense. Salma curses the *raani* and her smirk. *Guuderhoo!* Donkey! She pulls her down and rests the bottom edge of her frame against the couch cushions. I should put you back in the closet, she thinks. Flipping her over, she studies the packet containing Nasreen's earring, sees it twinkling in the half-light of the living room.

She composes the only matrimonial that makes sense to her:

Muslim woman, 38, with issues and husband, current dry cleaner and past teacher, seeks love match in all the wrong places.

Chapter 22

SHAFFIQ IS EXHAUSTED. He has been waking up in the quiet apartment, reaching for Salma and feeling panicked when she is not there sleeping beside him. Once fully awake, he soon realizes the reality of his life, knows that it is daytime, that he is sleeping while his wife is at Blue Dove Dry Cleaners, and that his children are still at school. He is the one missing in action, not his wife or children. After these mid-day awakenings, he finds it difficult to fall back asleep, the uneasiness still with him in his bed.

At work a few hours later, Shaffiq looks at his watch and groans inwardly at the hours ahead. How do people survive such boring, menial labour, he wonders. *How will I survive it*? He thinks that talking to Ravi might help, could take his mind off Salma and perhaps there is an entertaining update about his situation. Is he still dating the landlord's daughter? Has he told his mother yet? Has Angie's father found out? Shaffiq finds himself smiling and marveling at his friend's romantic antics.

He takes his lunch bag to the fourth floor and roams the silent wing. It looks to Shaffiq that Ravi hasn't started cleaning there because the garbage cans have not yet been emptied. He decides to check for his friend on the fourth floor and walks toward the elevator, passing Nasreen's office on the way. With the door slightly ajar, he can hear her talking to someone. He listens to her Canadian accent, the way her voice sounds so solid and confident.

"What time would be good for you?" she asks someone on the telephone. And Shaffiq repeats the sentence silently, endeavouring to erase his Bombayite lilt from the sentence. *Whaat tyime wood bee good for you?*

He hears her say good-bye and hang up the phone. *Ol rright then, tek cere. See you Wed-nes-de, Walerie*, he mimics silently. He hears Nasreen pick up the phone again and dial another number. Shaffiq glances around furtively to make sure no one is around in the empty hallway, and not really knowing why, he lingers a moment longer. He listens.

The phone rings twice and Salma picks it up while steadying a load of laundry on her hip. A pair of white boxers threatens to escape from the unbalanced basket.

"Hullo?"

"Hi Salma. It's Nasreen." *Hi Sulma, it's Nusrin.* Shaffiq stops mouthing the words.

Salma puts the laundry basket on the couch and sits down heavily. She deftly grabs hold of the boxers and settles them back with the other clothes.

"Oh Nas, how are you? I wasn't sure if I'd hear from you again. I feel bad about what happened last time you were here."

"Yeah ... that's what I'm calling about. I thought we'd better talk about it. Can we meet sometime?"

"Of course. Again, I'm sorry. I don't know what happened. You must be angry with me."

"Not really. I was just surprised, I guess.... Are you free tonight? Uh, will your husband and the kids be home?"

"No, Shaffiq has a shift tonight. He is probably there by now. And I can ask the neighbours to watch the kids, but it will have to be fairly soon so I can get the kids to bed early enough. Maybe we could meet out for coffee instead of here? There is a nice coffee shop a block from Ossington subway. It's called Coffee Love. Can we meet there at seven-thirty?"

"OK, I'll see you later, Salma. Oh, and could you bring me the blouse I left behind? You remember the green one I was wearing that night?"

"Of course. I washed it today. I'll bring it for you."

"Thanks, Salma. Alright, see you at Coffee Love at seven-thirty then."

Nasreen replaces the receiver in its cradle and checks her watch. Already almost seven p.m., she puts off finishing her report-writing and shuts down her computer.

Shaffiq skulks away from the office. Salma had not mentioned that she was teaching tonight, Shaffiq recalls. And what could be so urgent that her student would want to meet her tonight? What do they need to talk about? Shaffiq turns these questions over in his mind, wondering what kind of mystery this is, and what the clues could possibly mean. Suddenly, he doesn't want to look for Ravi anymore.

Twenty minutes later, Nasreen walks up the filthy steps of the Ossington subway station. Toronto's subways aren't what they used to be; litter everywhere and the escalators perpetually out of service. Nasreen regards a poster informing customers that the cost of a token is going up. At a minimart at the top of the stairs, she buys a package of mints and pops one in her mouth.

She walks north two blocks to the coffee shop. It's windy and Nasreen buttons up her coat and pulls her scarf snugly around her neck. Candy-bar wrappers and discarded sections of newspaper swirl across the sidewalk, threatening to tangle at her feet. Most of the stores' lights are turned off already at this hour, but the neon orange Coffee Love sign casts a sunny glow on the dark sidewalk ahead. Nasreen wishes she had suggested a different coffee shop to Salma, one that is neither being boycotted nor the current employer of her ex-girlfriend, but she was too nervous during the phone call to raise the political or moral implications of the meeting place. For a moment she wonders if she'll run into Connie at Coffee Love: *What if PR people visit their franchisees? That's possible, isn't it? What should I say to her if I see her there?* She speculates on the question with some alarm, but when she reaches the coffee shop door, she inhales deeply and manages to brush the irrational thought aside. She checks her watch and sees that is is seven twenty-two. That's just like her isn't it? Always showing up for nerve-wracking situations early enough to further raise her anxiety levels. But when she walks in and looks around to find a quiet corner, she sees Salma already there, waiting, looking up at her with expectant eyes.

"Nas, hello. You want a coffee or something?" Salma holds a white ceramic cup between her hands.

"Yes, I'll get one." She turns away from Salma's strained, smiling face and is glad for the moment away. Nasreen is more nervous than she thought. She breathes, orders a cup of decaf, and then sits down across from Salma.

There are a few minutes of small talk: about the cooling weather, how neither woman likes the cold and will never get used to it no matter how many years they live in Canada.

Salma takes a deep breath, decides to say the words she has been rehearsing for days now, and looks directly at Nasreen, "Nas, look. I want to say I am very sorry about what happened. I must have made you feel very uncomfortable. I don't know what happened to me to make me act that way. I feel embarrassed about it all."

"I'm not really looking for an apology. You didn't do anything that bad. You kissed me. It was just a kiss. I guess I just wanted to talk to you about it. And well, to find out how do you feel about me, Salma? I mean, was it just a spontaneous thing, or have you been feeling something for me?" Nasreen fixes her eyes on Salma's, searching for what they might reveal.

"I don't know, Nas." Salma looks down and Nasreen thinks she sees Salma's eyes begin to fill with tears. Nasreen has an urge to comfort Salma, to touch her arm or rub her shoulder, but she holds back. "I'm not sure how I feel. I haven't stopped to think about my feelings for some time," Salma replies softly. "You know, I never even stopped to think that I should be thinking about this! Am I making any sense?" Nasreen doesn't think so, but nods encouragingly so that Salma will continue.

"My life hasn't allowed much time to feel since we came here. Until recently, I only had time to see myself as Shaffiq's wife, the girls' mother. That's it. Until I met you and Asha, I had almost given up on myself being a teacher, even. Since leaving India, there has not been any time to really feel what I want, who I am ... do you know what I am saying?"

"I think so," Nasreen nods. "Things must have been so different for you in India. And even before you got married. I mean, you had a female lover! What was her name? Raj?"

"I was single, with only a few responsibilities. I was experimenting with life. I saw her as a very dear friend. She was very special to me. But there was no future in what we had together. I knew that at some point we would have to stop being together. While we were together I was just trying to enjoy it as long as I could."

"I find that sad. Did you ever wish you could have stayed together?"

"Sometimes, I don't know. Nas, I am a very practical person at heart. Wishing for things doesn't do much good if it can't happen."

"This might be personal, but have you been attracted to other women since Raj?" Nasreen asks.

"Maybe. I don't know. If I did I never let myself go anywhere with those feelings."

"Until last week, with me. When you kissed me," Nasreen says, smiling.

"Yes. Until with you. But you have to know I didn't plan it like that. I guess I have been a little attracted to you since I first met you. And then when you and Asha talked about being that way I started to think about Raj and somehow all the feelings came up for me. But I never meant to kiss you that day. You have to believe me." Salma looks pleadingly at Nasreen with wet eyes.

"Relax Salma. I believe you. And I don't think you did anything wrong. You didn't commit a capital crime or anything."

"Yes, but I do feel guilty, and a little silly. Yes, I find you attractive, but like I said, I am a practical person. There is no practicality in being attracted to you. Besides me being married and having children, I don't even know if you feel that way for me," Salma looks pointedly at Nasreen, holding her breath. *There, I've said it. I have to ask it, to know.*

"I'm a practical person, too, Salma," Nasreen says gently, sensing the vulnerability in Salma's question. She thinks about how she is about to tell the first of many lies, knowing that lies help to smooth out feelings and friendships and that she wants to be kind to Salma. "Salma, I think you are attractive too. I really like you. I don't think that I ever allowed myself to go beyond that because you are married. It's kind of my policy to not pursue women who aren't available. If you were single too, then maybe that would be a different story."

"That would be a different story. Maybe you are more practical than me. That's a good thing, Nas." She smiles weakly at Nasreen, who smiles back.

"I still need to learn Gujarati. And you are still a great teacher. Part of why I wanted to talk to you about all this is to find out if we can put it behind us, or if it would be too awkward. Do you think we could continue to meet? There are just a few weeks until I leave for India. Or would that be too weird?"

"No. Yes. I mean I would love to continue teaching you. And you know what? I forgot to pack up your green blouse to bring it to you tonight. I even washed it for you, but forgot to bring it. I think I was too nervous about coming to meet you. If you come back for classes then you can pick it up next time, can't you?"

"Yeah, sure. There's no big rush to get the blouse."

"So, then, we will go on as normal."

"I can if you can."

"Yes, of course I can." Salma hopes that she is telling the truth.

That night, Salma awakens to the sound of a toilet flushing. Must be

Saleema. She drank too much juice before going to bed. At least it is not like a few years ago when she would wet the bed and then Salma would be up, changing sheets, bathing her child in the middle of the night. Salma turns over, curls into a fetal position and pulls the blanket to her chin. Her mind takes her back to the dream she was having before her sleep was disturbed.

She is walking hand-in-hand with Raj through Jogger's Park in Bandra. Inside the park, there is a welcome reprieve from the noise and anxious movements of the city surrounding it. The lush trees and grass cool her skin and the air smells sweeter than normal as though the Bombay smog respects the hedge borders of the park and stays out.

Raj's face looks somewhat more angular and masculine than in real life, so the other walkers and joggers assume that Raj is a man out walking with his girlfriend. The pair pass two middle-aged, plump women in saris who look at them disapprovingly, but their censure is not about them being women, but about their public show of affection. It doesn't look proper. Raj notices the matrons' glance and guides Salma toward a more isolated area of the park where they find a granite bench on which to rest. Raj turns toward Salma and tells her earnestly,

"We must find a way to be together. We are in love, aren't we?" Salma looks into Raj's round, brown eyes and smiles at the simplicity of the statement, of the joy she sees in Raj's face. It magically and instantaneously changes back to its more feminine form. Salma kisses Raj on her cheek.

"Yes," she says, "I suppose I agree now. I couldn't back then. I wish I had been able to." Salma wants to say more, to explain about the past, but Raj puts a finger to Salma's lips and smiles at her forgivingly. Raj then pulls out a notebook and tells Salma that she will write down a secret plan in which they will elope in one month's time. Salma strains to see what Raj is writing, but Raj teases her by pulling herself and the notebook away each time Salma leans close. She tells Salma to wait. It feels like forever, but Salma waits patiently while Raj writes, her brow furrowed, her body tense. Salma looks around at the pink flowers to her right and continues to wait for her love to finish writing out the plan.

Salma sleeps peacefully. Her face is that of a woman who is calm, contented, in no hurry to change anything. All is still in the Paperwala home. The living room has been left clean and orderly. The only thing that might seem out of place to an outside observer of the Paperwalas' lives – if such a witness were to exist – would be a bright green blouse sitting on the edge of a laundry basket.

At two a.m. Shaffiq has finished all his floors ahead of schedule. He knows that his mind is not on the cleaning, and very likely, he has not done a tip-top job at the Institute tonight, but he doesn't care. He has been preoccupied with two particular questions. The first is derived from his painstaking dissection of the one-way conversation he overheard between Nasreen and his wife. At least he assumes it was with his wife. What did the conversation mean? Why would Nasreen ask Salma for a blouse she left behind?

The second question is how he will find the answer for the first question once he gets home. What clues should he be looking for? Should he ask his wife outright whether and with whom she has been out tonight? Should he ask the children what they know? Might they be witnesses to whatever is going on? His mind is muddled. He can't imagine that Salma would lie to him about anything.

If Nasreen had been arranging to meet Salma, it was very likely something innocent, Shaffiq reassures himself. Perhaps Nasreen needed some extra tutoring? No, that can't be it. The tone in her voice was all wrong for that. Perhaps she and Salma have become friendly and Nasreen had something she wanted to discuss with an older woman? Salma has not mentioned that she was becoming friendly with one of her students. She would have mentioned this, wouldn't she?

If their meeting was not so innocent, then what could be happening? Shaffiq thinks hard about Salma's ability to do something illicit with Nasreen. After all, Nasreen is the kind of woman who likes other women. Could it be that she has taken an interest in Salma? Developed a crush on her teacher? Surely that is not impossible. This kind of thing must happen all the time with women like Nasreen. Salma is a good-looking woman, after all, and a teacher. Shaffiq smiles to himself. He believes he has cracked the phone call's code, sorted out the only plausible possibility. Yes, Nasreen has a schoolgirl's crush on his beautiful wife! Salma would be gracious about such a thing, Shaffiq thinks. She would try to avoid hurting Nasreen's feelings but make it clear that she is not interested. Very likely, when Shaffiq gets home, Salma will tell him the story and they will laugh about Salma's ability to attract a young woman. They are liberal, open-minded people, after all.

A couple of hours later, when Shaffiq comes home, he checks in on

Salma and the girls. They all sleep soundlessly and he is reminded of how wonderfully peaceful his life can be. He feels silly for all his anxieties and mental sleuthing. There is nothing to worry about. He changes into his pajamas and makes a cup of tea, decides to stay up to watch the sunrise. With his tea propped on his knee, he rests his head back against the couch, and turns to look up at the *raani*, admiring her handsome, placid face. Her smile seems accepting, loving to him in the early morning light. He thinks that he really does like looking at the painting and that he must remember to tell Salma this. Perhaps it will be a small goodwill gesture that she will appreciate, a movement toward closing the distance between them. He doesn't want to argue with her so much. He must learn to be more understanding of her situation. She has had a tough time here too. With this resolution of matrimonial peacemaking, he leans his head back against the couch and after a few minutes, dozes off.

When he wakes, Salma is across the living room, bending over the laundry basket. In her hand is a bright green blouse. He blinks twice, clearing the sleep from his eyes and says, "Is that a new blouse? I haven't seen that before."

"No, it's not new. Shaffiq, what are you doing sleeping out here? It's bad for your back." She puts the blouse back into the basket, helps him to his feet and leads him into the bedroom. She tucks him into bed maternally, the way she does for Saleema and Shireen, and Shaffiq smiles with contentment. As she leans forward to kiss his cheek, he grabs her tightly and pulls her down into the bed. He climbs on top of her and kisses her in the way he imagines the heroes in Bollywood films would. In this moment he is Amitabh Bachchan and she is Zeenat Aman in *Don*.

Except that she doesn't kiss him back like Zeenat Aman. Rather, she lies still, unresponsive in his arms. He pulls away from her and she gets up out of bed.

"What's wrong?"

"Nothing's wrong. I'm just not in the mood right now. I have to get the girls up and ready for school."

"Sorry, no problem," he says, disappointed. "I suppose we are on opposite schedules, aren't we?"

"Yes," she says, straightening her nightdress, "quite opposite."

"So whose blouse was that?" His worry returns.

"Which blouse?"

"That one in the laundry basket. The green one. You said it wasn't new." In the pause that follows, Shaffiq wonders if his wife has ever lied to him before.

"It's Nas's. You know my student? It was raining the last time we met and she was wet, so she took it off and I gave her a sweater of mine. She left it behind. I guess she forgot it." Salma looks up at her husband and then down at her nails. "Not the sweater, the blouse, I mean. She wore the sweater home. I gave it to her to keep. It doesn't fit me anymore." She laughs, nervously. He decides to ask one more question.

"It was raining the last time you saw her?" He remembers the bus ride to work last night and doesn't recall any rain.

"Yes, last week. You remember the big storm we had? She got drenched that day." Salma walks out of the bedroom, leaving Shaffiq to his questions. She picks up the green blouse and puts it on a metal hanger in the hall closet.

Salma can't wait to get out of the apartment and to work. Normally she would not relish the thought of going to Blue Dove dry cleaners, where she mechanically goes through her day, mindlessly sorting jackets and shirts, making change and manufacturing smiles for her customers. But today she needs time alone, time to think, to contemplate her feelings, the green blouse, Shaffiq, and Nas. She also needs to get away from Shaffiq, who, although asleep, threatens to wake at any moment and ask her more questions. His queries from this morning muddled her enough.

She cannot stomach the thought of lying to him. But did she lie? Maybe through omission? She tiptoes into the bedroom and gathers her work clothes. Shaffiq lies still on the bed, his head resting on his elbow. It's a naturally uncomfortable position and so she knows that he is only pretending to be asleep. She thinks she hears him sigh while she chooses her clothing from the closet. She leaves the bedroom silently and dresses in the girls' room. As she pulls on the reinforced-toe panty hose she likes to wear on cool days, she spies Shireen's doll, Memsahib, gazing at her from the lower bunk. What does Shaffiq know? What could he suspect? What will she tell him? She tugs the nylons up over her hips and stomach and wonders if her last two weeks of dieting have paid off. Perhaps she's lost a pound or two because they don't feel as tight today. She pushes her head through the neck of a navy blue cotton *salwaar kameez* she has selected. Over this, she wears a white cardigan. She inspects herself in her daughters' dresser mirror and feels old, matronly, in this outfit. Cardigans just don't go with *salwaars*, she thinks. In Bombay, she rarely wore sweaters, but here in Canada she almost always feels cold. She has seen Nas wear long cardigans that hang to her calves. Those must be in style, Salma thinks. She will have to buy one.

Nas. Salma's face flushes hot with the embarrassment she felt at the coffee shop. Nas asked her so many questions for which she was not prepared and she felt so confused, so silly and she doesn't want to ever feel that way again. She resolves to ensure that all will return to normal. She won't say anything more to Shaffiq. After all, she is Salma, his wife, the girls' mother. She is not a crazy woman who has crushes on other women. She is not in love with Nas. She is just Salma, who works at Blue Dove Cleaners and she must go now so that she will not be late.

There have been few lies between Salma and Shaffiq, mostly tiny falsehoods and inconsequential fabrications that have helped to mend the small frays arising from time to time in their marriage. These tiny ruptures, and the white lies that patch them, exist in all relationships. The Paperwala marriage is not so different from others. Their fibs have never been meant to create distance or cause distrust or make either out to be a fool.

But these new lies that have cropped up in their marriage feel more dangerous to Shaffiq, as though they might be tearing away at his previously intact home. Shaffiq wonders if he is responsible for the damage or if it is Salma who is to blame. Perhaps neither is at fault. Perhaps it is just their chance encounter with Nasreen that has put them both off balance, causing them to be wary of telling the truth. Maybe, just maybe, he thinks, it is Nasreen who is ripping at the fabric of their relationship.

Chapter 23

SALMA GETS THROUGH THE day at Blue Dove and then the evening with the children without focusing on her worries. But in the silence that night-time brings, she is alone again with her thoughts. There is no girlfriend close by, no family except for Asima Aunty who is not really family, not blood family anyway. And it's not like she's someone who'd understand Salma's current dilemma about kissing her lesbian student, is she? Depressed, Salma does an inventory of family and friends and realizes that after two years in Canada, she hardly knows anyone.

And the two years here have drifted her further away from the people she loves in India. There are her parents in Bandra, who she calls twice a month with hopeful, happy reports of their progress in Canada. And they reply with equally sanitized stories of their lives, not wanting to burden her with worries about their deteriorating health: the gall stone her father passed last month, the upcoming cataract surgery planned for her mother. She exchanges infrequent letters with her older brother, Rahim, who entertains her with gossip and news about the people they know, which only leaves her feeling more nostalgic for home. His last letter promised a visit, perhaps next year, which both excited and dismayed her. Maybe things will be better by then, she hopes: better jobs, a nicer apartment, a pull out couch on which he can sleep?

She wishes she could have confided in Rahim about the times she spent with Raj. That was how she labelled her relationship so many years ago. *We spent time together.* Maybe Nas would call it dating, or being lovers. At the time, she barely knew what was happening and she had no words to describe it. She briefly considered telling Rahim, so wanted to be able to share her feelings with someone, to tell someone that she was exploding with love and happiness. To say that she felt confused, and scared too.

Not for the first time, she wonders if Rahim knew all along the nature of her relationship with Raj. She's often wondered if Rahim was that way too. *That way, deviant, unnatural, not normal.* The evidence stacked up, although being the private person he is, Rahim had never left many clues for Salma to find. Somehow he expertly avoided all pressures to be married, but then being male, he was never pressured the way Salma was. But still, there are his unmasculine habits – being unskilled at sports, but gifted in the kitchen and good with children – that made him awkward as a teenager but now regarded as a devoted son and uncle. Salma has never asked Rahim about his romantic life because despite their closeness, their relationship has never included talking about heady feelings like love. There has been no precedent for talking about such a thing as kissing a student or once being in love with a woman.

Salma longs for a confidante. But who is there? And how can she make friends in this cold, unfriendly place? How does anybody? In India, she was not very social or popular, but at least there was Ritu to keep her company. She thinks that perhaps she will write to her old friend. But what would she say? *Dear Ritu, do you remember that girl we used to see way back at the café? The one you called mannish? Well Ritu, I don't know how to tell you this, but she and I, well, we were more than just friends.* Salma shakes her head, admonishing herself for her stupidity. It would feel too silly to write to Ritu about that affair after all these years. Perhaps she should have tried to tell Ritu back then. Ritu would not have understood, but at least she could have been able to unload the secret. Salma is tired from the weight of it.

But she has told one person. She told Nas. Salma rubs her temples. Her head hurts from all this madness! She thinks about taking some pain medication but feels too tired to get up and look for it. More than ever in her life, Salma is exhausted. She is tired of being alone. She is weary from the grief of what she has given up. She is worn out from the choices she has made and the choices she has not been able to make.

She flips open the latest issue of *Ladies World* and throws back the pages to the advice column. She scours the plaintive questions written by Indian housewives and answered by Ms. Madhuri, who dispenses her wisdom to hordes of middle-class Indian women who read the glossy magazine. One by one, she reads the letters, searching for one which matches her situation. There are none. The closest one is signed by Guilty in Goa. It reads:

Dear Ms. Madhuri. Many years ago I had a brief affair with a man who was of the wrong religion. He Muslim, I Hindu. I loved him very much. He was my first love. No one knew about our relations. At the same time my family was pressing me to marry my husband. What could I do? I knew they would not understand. So I left him and get married. Now I love my husband too. But everyday I think about my first love, and sometimes when I am intimate with my husband, I sometimes see his face in my husband's, and one time I almost called my husband by my old love's name! I cannot stop thinking about my old sweetheart, no matter what I do. I feel very guilty. What should I do?

Salma, a teacher always, can't stop herself from penciling in Guilty in Goa's grammar corrections before continuing on to Ms. Madhuri's reply:

You must find a way to finish that first relationship. It is finished in real life but you are still hanging on mentally. Try to understand what makes you hold on. Do you have regrets, either about the relationship or how you broke it off? Only when you do this soul searching will you be able to stop obsessing about the old relationship and then you can truly devote yourself to your husband. Think about him. Does he not deserve to be the one and only object of you love?

Salma considers Guilty in Goa's problem for a moment. As usual, Ms. Madhuri's advice offers common sense thinking, with a little judgmental slap. Is there anything really wrong with thinking about a first love while being with a second, Salma wonders. Somehow Salma has been able to do what Guilty in Goa has not. She has buried Raj in the past. Until now.

Salma re-reads Ms. Madhuri's advice. Does she have regrets about the way things ended with Raj? Certainly. But she was young, and inexperienced. She wishes she had been more sensitive to Raj. She could have been more sensible by not letting things go so far.

By December, having grown dissatisfied with their semi-private bench in Jogger's Park, Salma and Raj strategized new ways to see be alone with one another. With her parents away in Pune visiting family for the weekend, she and Raj took the opportunity to meet at Salma's family's flat. There, they had three precious hours before Rahim returned home from work. Salma remembers how nervous she was that day, aware of the possibilities that an empty apartment could offer them. They ate a quick lunch of *daal*, rice, and *kheema* and then Salma timidly showed Raj around the flat. When they arrived in Salma's room, they lingered there for a moment and Salma awkwardly averted her gaze, studying Raj's toes poking through her leather sandals. She watched as Raj's foot took a step towards her, and felt Raj's arms encircle her. Salma raised up her chin and met Raj's mouth for the first time, their first real kiss on the lips. She noticed Raj's chapped lips and how they felt good against hers. There was a warm buzzing from her knees to her chest, and over-whelmed by the unfamiliar feeling, she sat down of the bed, and pulled Raj's hand in invitation to follow her. Without the need for the vigilance required in the park, they allowed their bodies and imaginations to travel to new, but still fairly chaste places: fingers unbuttoning blouses, palms cupping breasts, hands squeezing thighs. And with the recklessness of a first romance, Salma wasn't terribly worried about being careful and almost didn't hear Rahim's key in the lock.

"Rahim, meet my friend, Raj," Salma said breathlessly as they emerged from her bedroom.

"Nice to meet you. Are you two colleagues at the school?" asked Rahim, his eyes narrowing at Raj.

"No, Raj works at her family's computer store. You know Patel's?" Salma smoothed her mussed hair, straightened her blouse, tried to look casual.

"Oh, yes, off Turner Road? So how did you meet?" His face was smiling, but Salma knew that he silently appraising Raj and methodically gathering information.

"Well, it was at the café, wasn't it?" Salma said, her eyes darting between Rahim and Raj.

"Yes, that's right. And you see, I am just returning to school and since it's been awhile, I asked Salma to help me with some of my assignments. I have a paper due next week, and Salma's helping me." Salma admired Raj's quick thinking. She nodded vigourously at Rahim, studying his expression.

"Ah, I see, Salma's tutoring you." His face relaxed and Salma breathed for the first time since his arrival.

The lie provided the women a convenient excuse to meet from that point on. Raj arrived for her "tutoring" at the flat two evenings each week, carrying with her an old English textbook and binder as props. While Salma's family sat watching TV in the livingroom, Salma and Raj "worked" for two hours behind Salma's closed bedroom door. At the end of the evening, they would emerge flushed and happy, and Salma would say something like, "You should do very well on that test" or "I'm sure that essay will earn you top marks!" Her parents would distractedly look up from watching the evening news and trill, "Good luck to you!" as Salma saw Raj to the door.

Even the weather assisted their cause, allowing them to spend their first night together. One December evening, an unexpected storm drenched the city, and the forecasters warned of dangerous winds and a possible tornado. Of course, the couple barely noticed what was happening outside Salma's bedroom window, being so entranced with one another. Just as Raj readied herself to leave, Salma's father refused to let her go outside into the downpour and Salma's mother instructed Rahim to place a mattress on the floor beside Salma's bed so that she could stay the night.

While Salma's parents retired next door, Salma and Raj undressed. Salma looked away from Raj, feeling self-conscious, the way she did the first time she had to change out of her school uniform and into gym clothes in front of others at school. She wondered what Raj would think about her body. Sure, they had groped and slithered their hands up and under one another's tops and skirts and pants already, but what if after seeing her body for the first time, Raj didn't like it? She barely had enough time to worry about this before Raj guided her to her bed and helped her remove the last of her clothing.

Salma will always remember every detail of that first night with Raj. At least she thinks she remembers it exactly as it was, without too much creative embellishment that a memory of a first sexual encounter tends to have. She remembers the full body sensation of her bare skin sliding under Raj's. With the rain pelting down, they kept the windows shut and the room grew hot and stuffy. She memorized the taste and smell of Raj's salty sweat. She remembers feeling shy when Raj touched her inner thigh, can still call up the tickle of Raj's fingers slipping between her legs. She's committed to memory the feel of Raj's tongue against hers.

She surrendered to the experience while remaining vigilant to the sounds outside her room. She monitored Rahim's springy steps to the bathroom around midnight, her father's light snoring mixed with the howls of the wind outside, her mother's tired padding to the kitchen at first light to start breakfast preparations. She knew that if her family had opened her unlocked door, and saw the scandalous adventure that was happening inside, the tempest within the apartment would have been far angrier than the one raging outside. But perhaps it would not have been so dramatic. Salma's father might have yelled and threatened them, while her mother stood by and cried. Rahim would have had to step in and try to mediate the conflict while being disappointed himself. Her parents would have wondered what had become of their shameful daughter, questioned where they had gone wrong, and ultimately they would have blamed Raj, forbade Salma to see her ever again and forced a marriage upon her. But no one opened her bedroom door that night, and the storm passed over Bombay, the sun breaking through the clouds by daybreak.

Would Salma have blamed them for their judgements? She rarely thought about it at the time, moving through the world in love's first embrace, her mind possessed by thoughts of Raj: daydreams in the middle of Standard Five punctuation lessons, fantasies during school meetings, gleeful reveries while on the bus home. But there were moments during which her private thoughts were interrupted by worries that she was somehow abnormal, if not immoral. She wondered if she was experimenting with something that was beginning to feel dangerous, something that she should not have allowed to go on so long or so far.

Through the rest of December, Salma and Raj continued to be obsessed with devising ways to spend time together. They cursed the clear skies and settled weather for not providing them another easy excuse to sleep together. Twice they pretended that Raj needed to stay late to prepare for an exam, with the hope that they could easily extend the visit overnight. On one of those occasions, Salma's mother suggested inhospitably that Raj should leave before it got too late. Another time, Rahim offered to drive Raj home, rather than allow their meeting to extend past bedtime. Raj felt sure that Salma's family had begun to harbour suspicions about their relationship, but if they had, no one said anything directly to Salma.

In January, Raj told Salma that she and two friends were planning a trip out of town and urged her to join them.

"This is our chance to spend time together and overnight too! And my friends have been wanting to meet you," Raj pleaded.

"What will I tell my family?" Salma so badly wanted another night with Raj and this time without the threat of being caught by her parents. Together, they considered the excuses she could use to fool her parents.

In the end Salma's parents did not protest when she told them that she was going to a hill station with a group of women friends from school. Perhaps they were relieved that she was finally spending time with her other friends.

Salma and Raj waited for Maya and Anjali at the train station. Salma was surprised when two very feminine women appeared and were introduced to her. Both had long hair and wore make-up even! She had never met another woman-woman couple, so she just assumed that Maya and Anjali would more closely resemble Raj and herself.

They boarded a train to Lanavala, and Salma began to relax a little as the foursome chatted and joked during their journey. Salma looked around to see if any of the other passengers were staring or suspected the four women of being two couples. Once or twice she noticed an old lady across the aisle glancing over at Raj, but she could not tell whether she was listening in on the lively conversation, or noticing Raj's masculine style. She did not want to be given away by Raj and made sure to remain a safe physical distance from her during the three-hour trip.

Salma peppered Maya and Anjali with questions while they ate dinner at a local restaurant; she was curious about their feelings for one another, their secret arrangements, whether they were being pressured to marry, if they knew others like them. Although she had heard of homosexual men before, she hadn't thought that women could be this way. Anjali said that she called herself gay. Salma tried to fit this label onto herself. Wasn't it possible that she was just a normal woman who happened to like Raj? While they walked back to the inn after dinner, Maya spoke privately to Salma, while Anjali and Raj walked a few feet ahead of them.

"You know, it is very hard, and it is dangerous sometimes. But you can make it work if you really want it. You have to decide if you are ready for the struggle that is involved. Raj has been hurt by women who have stuck with her only for the fun and then left when the pressure got to be too much. I hope you've thought about what you want out of this," she cautioned. Just then, they arrived at the inn, and Raj and Anjali turned so that she and Maya could catch up with them. Salma pushed away Maya's words and focused on Raj, who was eyeing her flirtatiously. Why did Maya have to be so serious? They were there to have fun, weren't they? The couples parted ways and headed to their separate rooms.

Alone with Raj, Salma could finally let her guard down. For the first time they did not have to worry about sounds outside their room or someone walking in; the only person in one another's secluded locked-door universe was the other. Salma brazenly stripped out of her jeans and blouse and stood before Raj in her bra and underwear.

"You're not shy tonight," Raj said, the desire in her eyes making goose-bumps prickle across Salma's skin.

Raj stepped towards her and turned Salma around to face the dresser mirror. "Look at you, how beautiful you are." No one had ever told Salma that before. "And look," Raj said, pinching Salma's right nipple through her bra, "You seem a little cold."

"So warm me up," Salma said, embarrassing herself with her own lustful words. She saw Raj's smile in the mirror's reflection. She watched as she cupped both her breasts, kissed her neck and then ran her hands across her belly. She saw Raj's right hand push past and under her underwear's elastic and in the mirror Raj's eyes stayed on Salma's, willing her to meet them in the mirror. Salma felt her knees buckle and she closed her eyes, keeping them closed while Raj led her to the bed. She felt Raj's hands on her back and her bra falling away. She opened her eyes and watched Raj slowly unbutton her shirt and pull down her jeans.

"Close your eyes." Salma felt the scratchiness of the wool blanket as she was pushed back on the bed. "Keep them closed."

She did as she was told, feeling cool air against her skin and her underwear being peeled off. At first she was startled by the moist heat of Raj's mouth, and the kneading pressure of her tongue inside her. She had never imagined this was part of making love. *What is she doing down there?* She opened her eyes just a little, and they widened in surprise as she saw one finger, two fingers, maybe more, slid deep within her, pushing inside, pressing up against her, filling her up. She looked to the ceiling, noticed that the overhead lights were still on.

Feeling breathless, lightheaded, she closed her eyes again. She felt prickly heat across her chest, her stomach, down through her thighs. Her heart thundered in her chest and then everything was vibrating, humming – even parts of her she didn't know she had. When she opened her eyes again, she saw Raj smiling down at her and Salma laughed out loud, giddy with love. Then inexplicably, instantaneously, her mood shifted and her eyes filled with tears. Shame and confusion clouded her head, keeping her up the rest of the night. Had she done something sinful? But it had felt good. Could she be in love with a woman? She felt like she was going mad.

Later, in the long night that followed, Salma tried to push way Maya's warnings. But she was right, like the foolish girl she was, she had allowed things to go too far. She felt too much for Raj and she knew she would end up hurting her, despite those feelings. While she watched the dark sky outside begin to brighten, she deliberated about how impossible it was to maintain a secret relationship. The initial scheming and concealment of their relationship, the way they had managed to fool her family, had seemed thrilling at first. Now, in the dim motel room, with her lover sleeping beside her, their secrecy exposed itself for what it was; childish, selfish, irresponsible. The effort involved turned from exciting to confining and oppressive. Could they continue to live this way for three years, the way Anjali and Maya had? How had their families not found out? How many lies had they told?

Not wanting to ruin the weekend, Salma kept her worries to herself and with the skills of an actress, numbly smiled her way through the next day. On their second night in Lanavala, Raj reached for her and Salma rebuffed her with an excuse that she was too tired to make love. Raj looked disappointed, then confused. Salma did not know what to say, or how to reconcile her conflicted feelings. How could she explain that she loved Raj and also knew she could not continue loving her? Instead, she said nothing. She tossed and turned the night away while Raj, too, stayed awake, wondering what she had done wrong.

Salma avoided Raj that following week. "I'm sorry, Raj, I'm not feeling well, I must have caught a cold at the hill station," she said when Raj called her days later. Meanwhile, she began writing a letter. Her fourth draft seemed terribly insufficient and but she finally had to send it:

Dear Raj, I realize that I love you very much, but I also realize that I cannot go on seeing you like this. When I saw how Maya and Anjali have maintained their relationship, I was impressed at their devotion and tenacity. But I was also very aware of how difficult this must be for them. I cannot live my life with secrets, and we both know that is not possible to be open. Although I love you, I don't think I am enough like you or Maya or Anjali to make this my life. I am so sorry to hurt you like this. I hope you can forgive me. I will always love you. Salma.

After receiving the letter, Raj called a few times, pleading with Salma to meet her. She tearfully asked Salma to reconsider and tempted her with possibilities of staying together without secrets. She told Salma that she had created a plan to leave India but Salma refused to meet, refused to listen. She did not want to hurt Raj any more than she already had and she could not risk anyone knowing about their relationship. She firmly believed that it would be best for them to not meet for a long time and she kept to her decision despite Raj's calls and letters.

Now, Salma wonders if she was wrong to be so stubborn. What if she had hurt Raj even more by not meeting her? If she had to do it all over, Salma thinks that she would have seen Raj again, and certainly would not have sent that awful letter. At least she would have said goodbye properly. But she was younger then, and heartbroken herself.

Her family noticed that something was wrong. They witnessed a sudden weight gain, saw her sulking around the flat and not leaving except to go to work. She cried easily and often. When this continued through March, her mother suggested she see a doctor to see if anything was wrong. Her father told her it was time to think seriously about marriage. Ritu counselled her to take a few days off from work to rest. She complied with their suggestions, not knowing what else to do. Rahim was the only one who asked her about Raj. "Aren't you tutoring her anymore?" He wanted to know.

"No she did really well in her course and I thought she could go it alone." She longed to tell him about her despair. She wanted to tell him how pointless life felt without Raj, how unfair it was that she was in love with a woman. She wanted to have one person who would understand the new and constant pain that distracted her while she taught, gave her headaches during teachers' meetings, and made her cry on the bus ride home.

Now, so many years later, Salma still wishes she could have told someone. Impulsively, she decides to write a letter to Ms. Madhuri. But what to say? What to tell? It doesn't matter. It really doesn't matter. She decides to tell all, only editing out the names and place in case her letter gets published. She fills an entire nine pages, starting with how she first met Raj, and how she ended the relationship two-and-a-half months later. She tells Ms. Madhuri of the memories that won't seem to let go. She admits that she had wanted to see Raj after some time had passed, when the sorrow finally dissipated, perhaps even meeting her at Baldev's, to tell her that she was truly sorry. But the right time never seemed to come. And then months passed. She got married, entered a new life with Shaffiq, one so different from the universe she shared with Raj. And then she simply forgot. She pushed Raj so completely from her mind that it was like she had never been there in the first place.

She signs off the letter, "Goodbye from Canada," addresses an envelope, and licks the glue strip twice to seal it well. Despite the sour taste in her mouth, her relief is sweet. Later that day, on her way to work, Salma drops a very fat airmail envelope into a red Canada Post mailbox. It pushes through the yawning mouth of the box and hurtles down to the waiting mailbag at the bottom. It patiently sits with all the other letters and parcels, waiting for deliverance. Salma walks to work and the sidewalk before her is gloriously clean and white, leading the way.

Chapter 24

A WEEK LATER, Nasreen is just about to step out of her office when the phone rings, the indicator light blinking red. She hesitates, but on the fourth ring, leans across her desk and answers.

"Hi Nasreen, this is Miranda."

"Miranda! Oh hello! How are you?" She says, trying to tame the enthusiasm in her voice.

"Well, pretty well, but also not so good. I mean, I'm still not drinking –"

"That's fantastic, good for you," Nasreen gushes.

"Yes, it is an accomplishment. But I think I may have ended our sessions prematurely. There are some more things I'd like to discuss with you if you can still see me."

"Yes, no problem, Miranda."

"I understand I may have to go back on the waiting list."

"Yes, that's a consideration, but let me see what I can do to shorten the time. Can I call you back tomorrow? I was just on my way out and I will need to check with our administrator about the wait list."

"Yes, fine, that's OK. I'm booked up for the next month anyway, so I wouldn't want to start until after that." Nasreen hangs up the phone, makes a notation in her agenda and locks her door. To new beginnings, she thinks.

She heads off to dinner with Asha and Mona, who, except when Nasreen brings them together, don't tend to see one another. There seems to be a tacit understanding that since Mona and Asha met through Nasreen they should continue to convene with her as their link. Nasreen sometimes wonders about this, especially because her two friends get along famously.

As Nasreen walks south on Spadina, she sees Mona stepping down from the northbound streetcar.

"Wow, I thought I'd be late. I was at a housing squat in the west end," Mona says breathlessly, as she hugs Nasreen. Mona's organization has been taking over vacant buildings all over the city by rallying people to squat in them. So far the city has agreed to convert some of those buildings into low-cost housing.

"Think you'll get this one?"

"We think so. Octavia Morales, the councillor for the neighbourhood, is pretty sympathetic." They join Asha inside and Nasreen notices Asha surreptitiously checking her watch as they approach. Asha is always the first to arrive, and punctuality is her hallmark. If she is irritated by their ten-minute tardiness, she doesn't show it. She gives each woman a Montreal-style kiss on both cheeks.

This busy Chinatown restaurant has been their regular meeting spot for the last couple of years. "Cheap and cheerful" is how Mona likes to describe it, and it has enough "real Chinese food" to suit her second-generation Canadian-Taiwanese tastes. Even better is that it's popular with many of the lesbians of colour around town. Nasreen surveys the room and waves to a couple at one of the back tables. As she sits down, she whispers to her friends, "Don't tell me they are back together again!"

"I know, it is masochistic, isn't it?" Mona whispers, "They keep going back and forth, splitting up with a dramatic flourish and then moving back in together. Simone should go and find somebody else and stop settling for that two-timer. Simone is the marrying type."

"And Lucy is definitely not," say Asha with a smirk. She and Lucy were classmates and then lovers for a short period last year. "And by the way, she isn't a two-timer. She is non-monogamous and Simone has always known that. Do you know she's even doing her dissertation on the politics of polyamory? If Simone can't deal with that, she should stop taking Lucy back."

"Yeah, they really seem incompatible. I mean, Simone is one of the lead organizers of that whole gay marriage fight. Did you see her on the news last week? She's quite articulate," adds Nasreen.

"Yup, she's smart, and beautiful and butch. She'd be just right for me," sighs Mona.

"Or me," says Nasreen, reading the menu.

"I'm not so sure," says Asha, "Her politics are pretty conservative compared to yours. Come on, there have to be more important struggles out there than gay marriage. As if we all want to be like suburban straight people!"

"It's not an issue high on my own personal agenda. But I'm glad someone finds it important. It's a right we should have, even if we don't want to get married ourselves, isn't it?" Nasreen asks while trying to make eye contact with the waiter.

"Whatever her politics, she is cute. And you have to agree that there is a real shortage of single butches in this town," Mona says, trying to make eye contact with Simone.

They drink tea and chat while they wait for the food to arrive. They talk about Asha's professors, homelessness in Canada, and Mona's recent fling with a woman in her late-fifties. There is a pause in the conversation and Asha gestures mischievously to Nasreen with raised eyebrows.

"So, don't you have some news to share with us, Nas?" Nasreen was hoping that Mona's affair would be titillating enough to carry them through the meal, but unfortunately Mona tends toward brevity in her descriptions about her love life.

"So how did the meeting go with our so-called straight Gujarati teacher? Did she kiss you again, Nas?"

"Huh, who's kissing you?" says Mona, sipping her tea.

"We met at a coffee shop. Of course she didn't kiss me again," says Nasreen. "And speaking of coffee shops, did I tell you both that Connie is now working for Coffee Love? Mona, isn't there still a boycott on them for their labour practices?"

"Don't try to change the subject, Nas. So what happened between you and our lecherous Gujarati teacher?"

"What? I'm missing something. What's going on? Someone fill me in. And yes you already told us about Connie and Coffee Love. That's old news. Tell me about the Gujarati teacher," Mona says excitedly.

"May I?" Asha asks. Nasreen nods miserably. Asha tells Mona the backstory, with a few exaggerated descriptions that Nasreen corrects. "So what happened when you met up with her afterwards?"

"Well, she apologized, and said that it wouldn't happen again and we both agreed to move on and return to the way things were before it happened."

"That's it?" Mona looks disappointed.

"She did admit that she has been attracted to me for a while," Nasreen concedes.

"Shall I say I told you so?" Asha teases.

"No, that's OK. Anyway, when Asha and I told her that we're lesbians, or 'that way', as she puts it, she got triggered to thinking about her younger days when she had a girlfriend in India."

"That way? I haven't heard anyone say that for a long time," mutters Mona.

"Yeah, well, she just dated that one woman. Then she went on to do what was expected of her and got married and so on and so on. You've heard the story before. And when she told me it all, she started to cry. I held her hand to comfort her and then all of a sudden she was kissing me."

"Wow. Your Gujarati teacher kissed you," says Mona. "And you weren't there to see it, Ash?"

"Of all nights to be sick in bed, huh?" Asha says, laughing.

"Hey, there's one more thing. Did I tell you that her husband works where I do? He works as a janitor there. But he's really an underemployed accountant who can't find a job because he doesn't have Canadian experience."

"Wow. So Salma is really a lesbian and compulsory heterosexuality forced her to get married to an accountant who is now a janitor because of racism in Canada," deduces Asha.

"And now your stunning beauty is breaking through the bonds of her oppression," adds Mona dramatically. "It's so like that movie, what's it called? *Wind? Earth?* No, it's *Fire*. You know the Deepa Mehta film?"

"Ah yes, I see it!" Asha says excitedly, "Nas is the younger woman just married into the family and Salma is like the older, unhappy sister-in-law –"

"It's not like that at all!" Nasreen protests, holding her hands up in the universal sign for "stop." Smirking, she adds, "Come on, please, let's not get overdramatic about this. I can't take any more drama in my life. It was just a kiss. But I would generally agree with your point about my stunning beauty having an effect on her."

"Of course, that goes without saying," says Asha.

"But that effect doesn't include breaking through any bonds of oppression. Things are going to go pretty much back to normal," Nasreen insists.

"And you are just going to forget about that kiss? Asha said you liked it," Mona asks, eyebrows raised.

"She is a good kisser," Nasreen says, sitting up in her chair, trying to shake off the memory of Salma's warm lips on her own, "I suppose it felt good to be kissed. You know, to have someone be interested? I've been feeling a little, well, undesired since the break-up with Connie." Her friends go quiet and nod in understanding. With their full attention, she continues, "But there is a difference between desire and acting on desire when it is not appropriate. There is no way that I would take this any further with a woman who is essentially unavailable to me."

"Hah! You're such a therapist! I hope your therapy-speak reasoning goes for Connie too, girlfriend," Mona says as she helps herself to the tofu that has just arrived, "Sorry to be so rough on you, but don't you think she is essentially unavailable to you too?"

"Uh huh, that's very true, Nas. You have to take that extremely wise sentiment and transfer it over to that fabulous ex of yours. No more processing and doing closure while shagging her on the couch."

"Good point, Asha. I second that!" Laughs Mona.

"Thanks very much for that wonderful advice," Nasreen says wryly. "Let's eat before this gets cold."

Chapter 25

"SHAFFIQ, THERE YOU ARE." Ravi comes around the corner, his vacuum cleaner in tow, relief written all over his round brown face.

"What? What's wrong?"

"Nothing is wrong. Things are very right! Very, very right! But I need a favour from you. It's very last minute, I know, but if you could do this one thing for me, I will owe you forever, man." Ravi says, bouncing from one foot to another.

"OK, OK, just tell me what you need."

"Angie's parents went to Detroit for a funeral today, and they will be away for a few days. Angie wants me to take tonight off so I can have some time with her. You know, time alone, overnight?" he says, elbowing Shaffiq in the ribs. "Can you do my floors? Work the extra hours? I don't want to ask James unless I am already covered. I'll tell him I've suddenly got a migraine or something. You know how he gets if you ask for time off at the last minute." Ravi looks at Shaffiq, desperation in his eyes.

"My goodness, my friend. You do have it bad for this Angie! Giving up a day's wage to spend time with the girl! This must really be serious!" Shaffiq teases, prolonging Ravi's agony.

"It's just that, well, I'd like to spend a whole night with her. You know what I mean? She is always having to sneak back upstairs when it gets late so that her parents won't suspect anything. Or, it's me who is leaving to come in here for the night shift. We just want a night or two together."

"When are you going to tell her parents so that you don't have to keep sneaking around like that?"

"Soon, soon. It will happen. Can you do the shift?" Ravi asks, his brows furrowed, his eyes wide.

"Of course, Ravi. It's no problem. But be careful! Don't get caught!"

Ravi's plump face widens with his smile. "I'll be careful! Thanks! Thanks so much! I'll go tell James right now!"

Shaffiq watches Ravi walk away, the rush of love in his gait. He smiles at his friend's youthful joy. Then, for the very first time in his marriage, he calculates the frequency of his lovemaking with Salma.

On the fourth floor, Nasreen hears the squeak of Shaffiq's cleaning cart coming to rest in the hallway outside her office door. She looks up from her computer and sees him in the corridor, struggling with a black garbage bag. For a brief moment, she considers pretending she doesn't see him. After all, he is the husband of the woman who kissed her. Has Salma said anything to him?

"Hi Nasreen. How are you tonight? Still here I see. You want me to come back later? Am I disturbing you?" Nasreen looks at the janitor, wondering which question to answer first.

"No, that's alright. You aren't bothering me. Hey, Shaffiq, I haven't seen you for a while."

"Yes, I only come up here to cover the shift for Ravi. He is off tonight." Nasreen looks at Shaffiq's tired face, tries to interpret his expression. Does he know? She takes a deep breath.

"Hey you know what? I forgot to tell you that I met your wife."

"Yes? My wife. You met Salma?" He feels his jaw tighten slightly and sends a message to his brain to calm down.

"Yes, she is my Gujarati teacher."

"Oh my, you have been to my home? What a coincidence. She is your teacher?" Shaffiq tries to maintain a neutral expression, the way detectives do on the cop shows he watches.

"Yes, we were talking some time ago and she mentioned that her husband works here and I guessed it was you. I saw your photo in the bedroom, you know the wedding picture?" Nasreen wonders if she has revealed too much already. Will he wonder why she has been in his bedroom?

"So strange how things are. Such a small world. You told her that you knew me?" Shaffiq wonders why Nasreen was in his bedroom.

"Yes, I said that I had met you a few times. She didn't tell you?" Shaffiq shakes his head. Nasreen has her answer. Does that make her complicit in the secret? "Well, anyway, she's a good teacher."

"Oh yes, she taught English literature in Bombay, you know. She is probably better in English than her mother tongue. But she likes teaching Gujarati. I think she likes teaching anything." Shaffiq racks his brain to think up a way to ask Nasreen about the green blouse, about her telephone call to his wife.

"She is a good teacher," Nasreen says again brightly.

"Yes, she is." Not finding the words he's looking for, he searches Nasreen's expression for guilt and sees none. No, I shouldn't ask her about all that, he decides.

"She should try to get a job at a school here."

"Well, we looked into it. She has her accreditation now, but she needs more courses to get a job in Toronto. There is no time for that with the children. And it will be expensive. Perhaps in a few years."

"Well," Nasreen rolls her chair backward towards her computer, "I guess I should finish up here so I can go home."

"Yes, well, I will see you next time. Bye then."

Shaffiq walks away, reflecting on his wife's omission. Why would she not tell him that her favourite student works in the same place as he? But he can't really question her, can he? He has known for some time that Nasreen is Salma's student. He has kept the fragile secret to himself all this time just as Salma has. The only one not hiding anything is Nasreen. Or perhaps she is and she just has a crafty way of appearing innocent?

Shaffiq wishes he could dislodge the sense of suspicion and conspiracy teasing his mind. He wonders if these secrets mean anything or are just trifling distractions. The truth must be that they are all innocent: Nasreen, Salma, and himself. After all, he's done nothing wrong by not telling Salma that he already knew. Likewise, maybe Salma just forgot to tell him and there must be some kind of misunderstanding about the mystery of the phone call Nasreen made to Salma the other night. Shaffiq resolves to watch less TV on his time off, especially those crime shows. He should be using his time for job searches, for upgrading. He has to keep looking for a better job. He can't stay in this place forever.

Chapter 26

THREE DAYS LATER, within the yellow-grey walls of the Institute, a pair of Indian janitors laugh over tea and *pav bhajji*. Ravi is entertaining Shaffiq with his girlfriend troubles.

"You laugh now, Shaffiq, but it was a little tense there for awhile. You know, Angie and I thought her parents were going to be in Detroit longer than that. Then they came home, two bloody days early, and of course the first thing that bastard does, before even unpacking, he wants to come and collect the rent. Right away Angie hid in the closet and stayed there until I could write a cheque."

"He didn't suspect anything?"

"I don't think so. She went home a little later and told them she had been out at the store. She even took an unopened carton of milk from my fridge to make it look good. But I drink homo, not two-percent like them. I'll have to ask her how she explained that!"

"You were lucky! So did you have a good time while they were away?" Shaffiq winks at Ravi.

"Oh, boy, it was the best. We didn't worry about anyone hearing us. She even cooked me dinner upstairs, in their house. It almost felt like we were a married couple."

"Imagine if they'd come home to see you, their basement tenant, sitting at their kitchen table seducing their daughter!"

"We were just having supper. She made me *cannelloni*. I've never had that before. It's good! You ever tried it?" Shaffiq shakes his head. "It's this tube-like pasta dish with tomato and meat sauce, but she made it vegetarian for me and so –"

"*Arré*, continue with the story, I don't need the recipe, man!"

"OK, OK. Anyway, we are lucky that the parents didn't find out. But you're right, there would have been trouble. You know, Shaffiq, since almost being caught, Angie and I have gotten more serious. She wants to hurry up and tell her parents the truth so we don't have to hide our relationship anymore."

"So the day is finally coming. No more sneaking around for you."

"Well, what I'm thinking is that we could do it … if we were engaged first. You know, they might accept me better if I am not the boyfriend, but the fiancé."

"Has she said yes?"

"I haven't officially asked. I want to. But first I feel I should tell my Ma. I want to do things in the proper order." He shakes his head miserably, "I'm afraid of what she is going to do, when she finds out."

"Yes, yes," Shaffiq commiserates, considering Ravi's dilemma. He doesn't need to ask what her reaction will be. "But maybe it won't be so bad? Maybe she'll understand with time." Shaffiq doesn't really believe the false optimism, but doesn't know what else to say.

"Well, maybe," Ravi says, sighing heavily. "I guess we should get back to work, then. Our break must be over by now."

"Well, try not to worry too much. Worrying won't help you." Ravi nods, and the two men gather up their thermoses, throw away their garbage, and return to work.

The following Monday, Salma wakes her husband from a deep sleep, "Shaffiq, your boss is on the phone. He wants you to go in early and do a shift for Ravi again. You want it? Should I tell him yes?" Shaffiq remembers that last week Ravi mentioned that he might try to take a day off this week. Angie was going to arrange a meeting with his in-laws-to-be. These youngsters, always having to rush-rush into things, he thinks.

"Yes, tell him I'll do it." Salma disappears and then returns again, just as Shaffiq is drifting back to sleep.

"Is something wrong with Ravi? He takes a lot of time off work these days."

"Let's hope not." Shaffiq groggily tells his wife Ravi's plans.

"Maybe we should invite the two of them over again some time, you know, show them some support."

"Good idea," he says, remembering Salma's good mood after Ravi and Angie's last visit. "Let's see how tonight goes for him. Who knows, maybe we can throw them an engagement dinner, if he is lucky. Poor fellow. His mother is really against it. She sent his uncle over for a 'talk' with him. His mother wants to arrange a match with a Hindu girl."

"Maybe he'll be able to weather his mother's disapproval so far away from home. Things are different here. No one cares if you marry in the same religion or culture, or even if you marry at all. Just look at my two students. Independent women in their thirties. They can do anything they want. That's how it will be for our girls."

"He still has to pass Angie's parents' examination." Shaffiq looks up at Salma's distracted expression, "are your students coming today? You haven't mentioned them for a couple of weeks."

"We took a break. They were both very busy. But they are starting up again – they are coming over at six tonight."

"It's too bad I have to work today. I could have met them." Shaffiq pushes himself out of bed and into the bathroom. He watches for something recognizable in Salma's expression and seeing nothing there his own voice becomes muted. He so badly wants to tell her that he met Nasreen and knows that she is the same Nas as Salma's student. He yearns to ask her about the earring he found behind the painting. He aches to explain to her that *he* knows that *she* knows or thinks he knows what she knows. But as he studies Salma's closed face, he is afraid and so he remains silent.

Salma fries some *pakoras* for her students. The chick-pea snacks are a peace offering, a symbol of her desire to get back to normal and to acknowledge her wrong-doing to her students. She submerges a *pakora* in oil, waits for it to turn brown, expertly turns it over, and then raises it out of the pan and onto a paper towel. Not a drop of oil spatters on her clothing or the countertop. When she is finished, she turns off the stove and surveys the small pile of fried snacks. Will this be enough? she wonders. Will Nas trust her again? She feels so foolish and ridiculous. She brings the *pakoras* to the table and checks the clock on the stove console. How she admired this clock when she first arrived at this apartment. Never before had she cooked at a stove with an embedded clock. She polishes its already clean face with a wet cloth.

Her students should be here any minute now. She looks at herself in the hallway mirror, frowning at her untidy mess of hair. She pins some loose strands back into place and then, changing her mind, pulls out all the hairpins and shakes her hair loose. She runs her fingers through her mane, smoothing down some unruly waves, trying to achieve a casual look. There, that looks better. Her red *shalwaar* is a little wrinkled from wearing it all day. Should she change now? The intercom buzzes, startling her and she reaches over to press the white square button that permits her students' entry to the building.

She watches Asha follow Nas into the living room, and feels herself flush under Asha's gaze. She wonders what Nas has told Asha. Is Nas a gossip? She hopes not. When she considered this uncomfortable Gujarati class, she had not considered Asha's reactions. But of course Asha probably knows everything, and Salma realizes she will have to face her shame in front of both students.

To Salma's relief, Nas, too, is self-conscious and compensates for this by what Salma interprets as good-mannered cordiality. Asha, on the other hand, is uncharacteristically quiet, and this makes Salma nervous.

"Are the kids out at the neighbours again tonight, Salma?" Nasreen asks, trying to make conversation.

"Yes, they are playing again with their friends down the hallway. Here," she says awkwardly, not knowing what to say or how to conduct herself, "Try these, I fried them just a few minutes ago." She passes the women the plate of *pakoras*.

"Mmm, Salma, these *pakoras* are really yummy. You really didn't have to go to all this trouble, really." Nasreen says.

"Yes, they are good," Asha nods.

"Yes, really very good," Nasreen repeats.

"No trouble at all. They are very easy to make. Shall we get started? Asha, did Nas fill you in on the last class, or do you need a review?" Salma appreciates her poor choice of words when she sees the look of amusement on Asha's face. Nas intercedes, "Oh, sorry. I forgot to go over it with her. But that's OK, I could use a review too."

"Yeah, I'm sorry I missed the last class. A few weeks without Gujarati class has made me rusty. Tell me what you did last time," Asha says, smiling at Nas. Nasreen glances over at Salma and then shoots her friend a look of warning.

A strange sensation in Shaffiq's throat tells him that he should go home. Right away. He feels it first at five-fifteen, just a smallish tickle behind his Adam's apple. It feels a little like how a cold might start out; an infection crawling its way along mucous-lubricated pink flesh. It makes him cough a little, but he continues his work, spraying aquamarine cleaning fluid on a white sink, a rusty toilet, wiping away the day's dirt. Perhaps it is just the chemical fumes irritating him more than usual, he thinks.

Futilely, he attempts to ignore it. He starts to wonder if he has the flu. Soon, the soreness spreads further north and south in his throat, and then there is a soft whispering in his head that tells him "Go home. Leave here now, you must go home." He divines that what is paining him is not a bacteria or a virus, but something else. A warning perhaps. Unspoken words, itching at him, spreading down through his esophagus, tightening around his vocal chords.

He has the urge to vomit, and sits down again, holding his stomach, willing the feeling back, downward. A woman walks by. He keeps his eyes averted so that she will pass without noticing his discomfort. He takes a few sips from his water bottle, hoping to soothe the pain, but it just makes him feel more nauseous.

Across the city and deep into the suburbs, a newspaper carrier walks along a sidewalk, speaking angry words to his wife over his cell phone. He doesn't know why it's happened, but his relationship has gone to hell over the past few months. He hangs up on her, triumphant to have had the last word in their argument.

He approaches a house on his route. It's his third visit, this guy hasn't been home, and that combined with his low wages and recent squabble with his wife make him annoyed with the customer at 638 Meadowgrove Road. The Passat is in the driveway, idleing, and so he bounds up the driveway to demand his overdue payment before the car disappears into the garage.

It's there that he finds his middle-aged Indian customer lying unconscious on the oil-stained floor of his garage.

By six forty-five, the ache in Shaffiq's throat, esophagus, and stomach is so terrible he can no longer work. He puts away his cleaning cart and leaves a barely audible, hoarse-voiced message for James, his supervisor. For a moment, he wonders if James will be angry with him for leaving given that he was supposed to be covering for Ravi. He allows the thought to pass; he doesn't have the energy for it. He boards the number 27 bus from the subway, flops down, and rests his head against the dirty window, feeling the welcome cool against his forehead. When the bus starts to move his head thunks against the glass but he cannot summon up the energy to sit up straight and steady his wobbling head. Although there is standing room only, no one claims the seat next to his.

The landscape outside soon changes from two-story brick single family dwellings with green front yards, to cramped looking duplexes with adjoining walls and then to turn-of-the-century three-story brownstones. He is still blocks away from his neighbourhood, the old growth forest of tall, grey highrises.

The ride feels interminable to him, each red-light intersection, each passenger stop an excruciating torture that brings with it a new wave of nausea as the bus slows and then lurches forward again. He is grateful when the bus finally nears his street. He pulls the cord, but the bell doesn't ring. Using all his energy, he yanks it again and again and then realizes that it is broken and that he hasn't heard it ring once since he boarded. He panics and stumbles toward the back doors.

"Please, driver, stop! I want to get off!" He manages only a barely audible whisper and the bus careens past his building. Further back in the bus, a young Somali woman wearing a red and purple headscarf looks up from her newspaper, and notices Shaffiq's difficulty. Her reaction is spontaneous and swift and she is moved to shout louder than she has ever shouted in her entire twenty-one year existence. Her booming yell startles the driver, who slams on the brakes. The young woman is slightly embarrassed for the noise she has made, but also glad for its result. Later, she will tell her friends that it was not her own voice that called out to the bus driver, but that of her long-dead grandmother. They will laugh at her other-worldly imaginations and the incident will be forgotten. But in this moment, the young Somali believes in the guidance of her grandmother from beyond the grave.

The bus finally opens its doors and releases Shaffiq to the street. It is almost seven-thirty when he arrives at his apartment door.

The three women sit in the living room, awkwardly speaking rudimentary Gujarati broken with heavy silences and English.

A moment later, Shaffiq turns his key in the lock and opens the door. Salma, Nasreen, and Asha turn their heads and stare at the very sallow looking man standing before them. Shaffiq staggers forward into the apartment without closing the door, and lands limply on the couch, beside Asha.

"Shaffiq, what are you doing home? Are you sick? What's wrong?" Salma asks him, alarmed at his countenance. She gets up and closes the door. Asha shifts away from him, closer to Nasreen.

"I think I'm coming down with something," he croaks.

"What did he say?" Asha whispers to Nas.

"Shaffiq, you don't look well at all," says Nasreen.

"Shaffiq, I think you've met Nas before? And this is Asha. Let me help you to bed."

"Yes, I've met Nasreen before. But then, you knew that. We both did." Shaffiq rubs his hand over his throat, relieved that he can now speak. His voice feels stronger, his throat less sore. Nevertheless, he allows his wife to escort him to their bedroom. The two students watch, confused.

Just after being tucked into his bed, Shaffiq feels a strengthening in his body, a second wind and soon he jumps out from under the covers, and rushes to the living room, Salma following quickly behind.

"Nasreen, I think I found something of yours, an earring of yours."

"What? So it is hers!" Salma exclaims, indignant.

"Why did you hide it behind the painting?" Shaffiq jabs his finger in the air towards the *raani*. Nas follows Shaffiq's pointing finger, and studies the painting, as though seeing it for the first time.

"Why did you move it from behind her heart?" Salma says, pained, her hand over her chest, resembling a tragic heroine.

"What's going on here, Nas? I don't get it," Asha whispers loudly.

"Shhh, I dunno." She turns to Shaffiq, "yes, I lost an earring several weeks ago. I've missed it. That was a gift from my mother." The painting attracts her eye again. She thinks she sees movement from behind the glass. "You mean the silver one? A teardrop?"

"Yes, Nas. He found it. I have it here." Salma lifts the painting from the wall and rests it across Asha's legs. Asha, still confused, holds it steady for her.

"Yes, there it is. In the little packet. Salma, I don't understand, why did you put it there? Why did you keep this from me?" Shaffiq asks.

"It seemed safe there. I'm sorry," she looks at Nasreen, "I don't know why I didn't just give it back to you. I know it has sentimental meaning. I just saw it in his pants pocket," she says, gesturing toward her husband, who looks away, ashamed, "and I felt like I needed to take it away from him, and keep it safe," she says, handing the earring to Nasreen.

"Keep it safe? From what?" Nasreen asks, looking at the earring in her palm, a confused expression on her face.

"OK, this is really weird," Asha says, this time not bothering to whisper.

"Yes, I agree with you, Asha, it is very weird. He has been taking things from Nas's office, I don't know why and –"

"No, no, it's not like that! I found the earring. It was in the hallway," Shaffiq says, emphatically, his throat no longer sore, his head no longer cloudy, "I picked it up while I was cleaning. Near the elevators."

"But I asked you about it, and you said you hadn't seen it."

"Yes, well, by that time, I thought I'd lost it. She –" he says pointing accusingly at Salma, "she had already stolen it. Really, I wouldn't take something from your office Nasreen –"

"Well, there was the itinerary! Explain that then! That was from her office, wasn't it?" Salma is almost shouting.

"Salma, don't bring that into this," he say, whispering to her, "That was in the recycling bin. I barely knew who she was then."

"What itinerary?" Asha whispers to Nasreen. "These people are nuts!"

"I'll tell you what itinerary." Salma disappears down the hallway. The others watch her scurry away.

"Please, Nasreen, you must not be concerned by this. These are all just coincidences. I'm just like that, you see, I was a little homesick that day and then I was emptying your recycling bin it's just something silly I like to do and well, the job is so boring that I like to collect interesting things, sentimental things. It wasn't about you personally, you see –" Shaffiq, says in a pleading tone, his hands outstretched to Nasreen as he nervously watches his wife return from the bedroom.

"Really, Shaffiq. You might as well start being honest. You've been strange these last months. Not about her? This is her handwriting. You found it in her office." She passes the slip of paper to Nasreen, who takes it hesitantly.

"Bombay, Air India Flight 360, December 3, 17:40 (5:40 p.m.)," Asha reads aloud over Nasreen's shoulder, "Hey, that's your flight! Geez, Nas, it's like this guy's been stalking you or something."

"No. Please! No need for alarm," Shaffiq says, his voice rising in pitch, "this is all so silly. I'm not a stalker." He paces the living room, holding his head. Nasreen watches his distress, and feels some sympathy for him.

"Well, I guess he's right that he didn't steal anything from my office. I do remember throwing this away after I transferred the information to my daytimer. And it is possible my earring fell off in the hallway at work. I guess these two things could be a coincidence." Nasreen bites her bottom lip and frowns at her handwriting.

"Yes, exactly! Just coincidence! I know it might seem strange when you put it together, but when you look at the whole thing sensibly –"

"I'm not sure that I believe in coincidences," Salma looks at him with stern eyes.

Shaffiq is beside himself. With his voice rising to a contralto's he says, "Why did you lie to me about meeting Nasreen in the coffee shop? Why did you lie about the green blouse? Maybe you too could be honest for just a moment!" Salma looks guiltily at Nasreen.

"Uh oh," says Nasreen.

"Uh oh is right," says Asha.

"How, how did you find out about that?" Salma asks quietly.

"I heard Nasreen talking to you from her office. I was outside in the hallway cleaning."

"You were spying on her! Listening to our conversation!" Salma is quick to turn the tables on him.

"Shaffiq, you were in the hallway listening to my conversation?"

"I wasn't spying. I just happened to be there and was about to come empty your garbage when –"

"When you spied on her?" Salma challenges.

"Don't try to put this back on me. Answer my question. Why did you keep the meeting secret? What exactly are you two up to?" Shaffiq demands.

"Maybe we should go, and let them hash this out," Asha whispers.

"No, I am a part of this too. Whatever is going on here, I am somehow in this."

The four sit silently for a moment, looking at each other, cautiously.

"How about this then. How about I try to mediate," Asha suggests brightly. She passes the painting onto Nasreen's lap and then, standing up and facing the others, she says, "It seems to me that all three of you have been keeping secrets against each other. Why don't we go around and let each of you explain yourselves," she holds her hands up to stop Salma and Shaffiq, both of whom look as though they are about to restart their accusations, "without interrupting anyone. How about that?"

"Ah, what good it that? Look Salma, let's do this privately, between the two of us. This is a family matter." Shaffiq's says this quietly, self-consciously, as though just realizing that they have guests.

"I don't know. Maybe it's too late for privacy, Shaffiq. And what Nas says is right. She is in this too and you should hear her side of things also. I'm tired of the lies. Yes, Asha, good idea. You can mediate. Go ahead."

"You OK with this too, Nas?"

"Yeah, why not. Things can't get any stranger, can they?"

"Good! But first, I think we need to all sit down and have some tea. Shaffiq, please go into the kitchen and put on the kettle," Asha instructs Shaffiq. He obediently retreats to the kitchen where, with trembling hands, he boils water, chooses four fancy-guest-only cups from the cupboard, and steeps four bags of Red Rose in Salma's favourite teapot.

Chapter 27

MINUTES LATER, THE TEA is poured and Salma, Nasreen, and Shaffiq sit on the couch across from Asha, who is seated in a vinyl-covered chair pulled in from the kitchen. The painting of the *raani* and her servant is returned to its rightful place on the wall. Salma's eyes travel up to it and she imagines they are presiding over the proceedings, perhaps making their own judgements. Shaffiq, too, looks up at the painting and thinks he sees the *raani's* smile turn smug.

Starting from the left and working right, Asha listens to each unique point of view, periodically shushing someone who tries to interrupt, challenge or contradict the other. She takes meticulous notes in her spiral bound Gujarati notebook. When each couch-defendant has had their turn, Asha says, "Now I will summarize what each of you has just shared. Again, no interrupting!" She glares at the Paperwalas. "First, we'll start with you, Salma." All eyes turn toward Salma, who shifts an inch or two to the edge of the couch, away from Nasreen.

"Why me first? Didn't all of this start with Shaffiq?"

"Let's just move left to right. Everyone OK with that?" Asha doesn't wait for them to answer. "Salma. You've admitted to having a crush on Nasreen. But, you believe it was really not about Nasreen exactly, but some kind of internal struggle you were having with yourself about a relationship from your past. Yeah, right! As though things work like that!"

Salma flashes her a look of exasperation. "I didn't call it a crush, Asha. Those are your words. I said an attraction. And I repeat, it was somewhat confused with my memories about Raj."

"Clarification noted. Whatever." Asha consults her notes. "Anyway, you began to feel a bit jealous that Shaffiq had been bringing home items you were able to deduce belonged to Nas. Your crush also resulted in you losing control one day, and you kissed Nas out of the blue at a Gujarati class. I might add, for your benefit, Shaffiq," she says, turning to him, "that I was sick in bed that day and was not a witness to the kiss." She turns back to Salma to complete her monologue, "You deliberately chose not to tell Shaffiq about that day or the subsequent meeting you had with Nas at the coffee shop where the two of you talked about the kiss." Her audience shifts uncomfortably: Salma looks at the floor, Nasreen holds her head in her hands, and Shaffiq stares off into space.

Asha reviews her notes, and then her demeanour softens.

"Oh yes. You've also been very homesick and lonely here. Is that right?" Salma nods, looking down into her lap, and Shaffiq leans behind Nasreen to touch his wife's shoulder. Asha continues, "Gosh I'm good at this, eh, Nas? I should be a therapist too, huh?"

"Let's continue, Asha," Nasreen says impatiently.

"All right, already. OK, now moving to you, Nas. No, I think we should jump to Shaffiq." He opens his mouth to protest and Asha holds up her palm to silence him. "Nas has had the smallest role in this mess, and has really ended up, literally and figuratively, in between the two of you. I've changed my mind and so I'm doing her summary last," she says definitively.

"You are her friend and more than a little biased," says Shaffiq, pushing himself up and off the couch.

"Sit down, Shaffiq. Let's finish this thing. I'm not the only one who is going to be subjected to this," orders Salma. After a moment of him standing, arms crossed over his chest with the three women staring at him, he eventually complies and takes his seat again.

"You admit that you've had a strange interest in Nas all along, but you say it's not sexual or romantic. Like Salma, you want us to believe that Nas represents something bigger than that to you. Your theory is that as the child of immigrants, she represents something about settling in Canada? You have a list of worries. Worry Numero Uno: you did the wrong thing by bringing your family here. Worry Number Two: will your family ever be as at home here as in Bombay? Finally, Worry Number Three: will your children turn out to be as westernized as Nas? Is that it?" She pauses until he looks up and grudgingly nods.

"That's quite a simplistic summary of my worries, but I suppose you got the gist of it," Shaffiq admits.

"You know, your daughters could do worse than end up being like me!" Nasreen grumbles.

"I didn't mean it like that!" Shaffiq says.

"Yeah. But you know, Nas, I didn't believe him before, but now his theory is sort of making sense," Asha responds pensively. "I read something about this kind of thing once. I don't think it's personal. It is more like you embody what is so familiar and foreign at the same time to him, you know?"

"Hello, hello! Can we get back to what we were talking about?" says Salma.

"Yes, you haven't finished my summary," Shaffiq complains.

"Sorry, I digress. I just find this so interesting. There's a dissertation topic in this. Anyway. Now, the itinerary, you said you picked that up innocently, because you were feeling homesick. At the same time you knew it was Nas's and you didn't tell your wife that. You say that it was not relevant at the time. The earring you found, you thought might be Nas's but you weren't sure. But when you lost it, then later found it hidden behind that," she says, pointing to the painting above them, "and you heard from Salma that she had a student with the same name, you figured it out. So it wasn't quite a coincidence, then, but you maintain that it was all innocent. You knew that both you and Salma were in contact with Nas, but you didn't reveal that you'd met her, as didn't Salma. You both kept that a secret," she says, looking accusingly at Salma. Then she turns back to Shaffiq.

"This secret seemed to build on itself, didn't it? Then, you overheard the half of the conversation between Nas and Salma when you were skulking around outside her office." She holds her hand up again to silence his protests. "Come on, Shaffiq, you admitted to being a bit of a nosey man. You are actually a little bit of a stalker. You could have walked away when you heard her on the phone, but you didn't, and so you overheard the call and began to wonder what your wife was up to with Nas here. Did I get that right?"

"I am not a stalker!" He turns to Salma, "But really Salma, this has blown up into something huge. A mountain out of an ant hill. I would forgive you for kissing her, I think, if you'd told me when it happened ... I mean ... ," he blusters, trying to think of the right words, "I mean, I don't blame you, in fact. It's obvious, at least now, anyway, that you are susceptible to the influences of women who are like that and after all, she's a very pretty girl, not that I think of her in that way –"

"Shaffiq, you'd better stop while you're ahead. And by the way, you might as well accept that Salma here has her own role in being attracted to women. She's probably a lesbian too, for all we know," says Asha.

"What? No! I'll have you know my Salma is not a lesbian!"

"Does having two attractions to women in my lifetime make me a lesbian? Maybe it does, I don't know. But I do love my husband. I'm not sure what any of this means."

"Asha, move along please. I don't think we need to define anybody's sexual orientation tonight," Nasreen says tiredly.

"All right, let's move to your side of the story, then. You've just come out of a break-up and have been dealing with some heartbreak there. When you began to sense that Salma might have crushy feelings for you, which by the way, I told you so!" She looks at Salma, "I could tell from that very first class!" She spots Salma's look of ire and continues, "you didn't do anything to dissuade her because, face it, Nas, it was good for your ego after what Connie did to you."

"Who's Connie?" Salma asks.

"Her lying, cheating, good for nothing ex-girlfriend."

"Oh," Shaffiq says quietly.

"Anyway, do I have your story right, Nas?"

"Yeah, I guess so."

"And then we come to the night of the kiss. You did pull away from Salma and realized that things had gone too far. You later called her because you thought it was a good idea to talk about the kiss, or 'process its meanings', as you called it. You both decided to put it all behind you and continue with the Guju classes, which is why we're here tonight. Oh, and yes, you never knew that Shaffiq was married to Salma until the night of the kiss." She takes a breath. "So, that summarizes everyone's part in this whole deal. Did I miss anything important? Anything anyone wants to add at this point?"

"No, I think you got it all, sort of, in all its complete full craziness, Ash." Nasreen concedes.

Salma looks at the ceiling. Shaffiq shrugs. Asha continues, "Good. Here is what I suggest then –

"Wait," Shaffiq says, rising from the couch, "There's just one thing more. I might be stupid for doing this, but I don't want to ignore this detail." He walks toward the shelf holding the Gandhi book and the photo of Nasreen and the scribbled out woman he retrieved from the

Institute's trash bins. I just want to –"

He is interrupted by a cellphone ringing the medley to Let it Be. All eyes turn to Nasreen's singing purse. She rifles through it and after a moment, answers the phone.

"Hello? What? Omigod … Oh no. Where is he? I'll be right there, thanks."

"Who was it, Nas? What's wrong?" asks Salma.

"I have to go. My father is at Mississauga General." Nasreen hastily gathers her belongings together.

"What! *Su tayuu?*" Shaffiq says, turning away from the couch.

"He had a heart attack."

"I'll drive you," Asha says without hesitation. The two students pull on their coats and while Salma and Shaffiq see them to the door.

"*Kuddafiz,*" murmurs Shaffiq, wishing them to go into the company of God. Nasreen hears him and turns to acknowledge the farewell while Asha pulls her into the waiting elevator.

"Now what?" asks Salma, sitting heavily on the brown couch.

"Well, I guess it depends on how serious the heart attack was. It is good he's at the hospital. Hopefully he got help in time."

"Yes, let's hope so. But that's not what I meant. I meant about us. This evening. All that was said."

"Well, I think I have to find another job. I am obviously so bored there that I have become too involved in my detective-hobby. It ultimately went a little too far," Shaffiq says, joining Salma on the couch.

"Come on, that's not what I was talking about. I never knew that you had mixed feelings about being here, Shaffiq. You never shared your doubts with me, your doubts about us making our home here, about the girls growing up here. Why didn't you tell me?"

"How could I? I pressured you into moving. You haven't been happy from the beginning. I know that. Look what you sacrificed to come here. The most important thing in your life when we first met was your teaching. I took that away from you. I had to try to make things right here. The very least I could do was be positive. I had to be the one who was hopeful," he says, his eyes hesitantly probing hers.

"I don't need you to be hopeful. I need you to be honest with me. I need to know that we are together in this."

"Are we? What about those crushes? What about what's her name, Raj, is it?" Salma nods. "Are you still in love with her? Do you really want to be with me, or are you like Nas and Asha?"

"We are –" She takes his hand, "we are together, Shaffiq." She inhales deeply, "And I don't know if I am like those two, Asha and Nas. I suppose in some ways I am, otherwise I would not have loved Raj, or had that little attraction to Nas. But I do love you. The rest I don't know right now." He searches her face, trying to understand her words.

"OK," he says, tiredly, not sure what else to say. His mind and eyes wander back to the Gandhi book still on the shelf hiding the photo.

"I'm relieved that you and I could finally be honest with each other. We haven't talked properly in a long time."

"Yes, you are right. Maybe we just need to spend more time together." He guiltily turns his attention away from his hidden treasure.

"Maybe that's what it is," she says, noncommittally.

Shaffiq strokes her cheek and guides her face to his, kissing her softly, cautiously. After a moment, she pulls away, distracted by the *raani*. Shaffiq follows her eyes.

"This painting, it kind of tricks the eye, don't you think?" she says.

"Yes, have you noticed that sometimes it seems the *raani's* expression appears to change? Sometimes when I've looked at her for a long time, it is like her eyes get smaller or bigger, or her mouth turns up or down."

"And sometimes that half-naked servant also does it. It's got to be some kind of optical illusion, or maybe it's our imagination."

"Or our own insanity," Shaffiq says, laughing nervously and looking up at the *raani*. "Well," Shaffiq says, "I meant to tell you about that. But, I kind of like the painting now. It's grown on me."

Chapter 28

"YOU GO AHEAD, NAS. I'll park and then come and find you."

Nasreen slams the car door, runs up the sidewalk, and steps inside the automatic revolving door. It moves slowly and she pushes against the glass pane in a futile attempt to hurry it. Once inside, she rushes past the coffee vendor and restaurants to the information kiosk. She gives her father's name to a bored looking receptionist. After what feels like an interminable wait, the woman provides Nasreen with directions to the Emergency Department.

"Wait, hold on just a minute, honey. Looks like he's been moved to the Cardiac Care unit on the second floor. Room 212," she says, and Nasreen hurries away without thanking her. She stands at the bank of elevators, anxiously pressing the button several times. Cursing under her breath, she sees a stairwell and decides to jog up the stairs, taking them two at a time. After asking for directions once more, she finds her father's silent room.

Inside, Bashir lies sleeping, a myriad of tubes connecting his nose to oxygen, his bruised arm to a slow dripping clear liquid, and his wrist to a softly beeping monitor. She moves to his side and sits on the hard plastic chair beside the bed, watching him sleep. She ineffectually tries to decipher the red flickering lights on the monitor. There is movement under his closed eyelids, his eyes roving jerkily in his sleep. She wishes that she had some lip balm to rub on his parched lips.

She takes his cool dry hand gingerly in hers and waits. She waits for him to stir or wake, or show some sign of life. She studies his still figure, his appearance of vulnerability. She can't stand this reversal of roles, the way she is instantaneously shifted into the stronger one, the one watching over. She felt the same way during her mother's illness. Then, she resisted being her mother's caregiver, avoiding as much as possible the embarrassing moments of feeding, bathing, and dressing. Her father didn't seem to mind the role, which he seemed to grow into so naturally. She tries not to think about what it might have been like for him to change her mother's diaper, a husband becoming a nursemaid.

She inhales the hospital room's odour of disease and dying and hopes that it is not her father giving off that smell but the institution's cleaning solutions, or the wheezing man in the next bed over from her father. She leans close to her father, sniffs his neck near where a thick artery pulses listlessly. There is a faint odor of rubbing alcohol, but that is all. She sighs in relief. Death is not coating his skin yet.

She turns her attention to the room, surveying the bare whiteness of its walls. This place is much too familiar to her, reminding her of her mother's old room three floors up from here, in the Oncology unit. Zainab's sick room had an ironic cheer to it, the result of her father's ministrations, his attempts to infuse hope into her mother's three-month hospital stay. Vases of roses and lilies crowded every available surface and Nasreen soon started distributing the overflow to other patients on the floor.

Nasreen now wonders how many hours her father has been here, alone, before someone called her. Her eyes well with tears as she realizes that no one else would know about his heart attack. She is his emergency contact. His next of kin. She will have to call his friends if any are to come. She begins a mental list of who to call first, remembering the friends who visited her mother, those people who looked at her, and him, with pitying eyes.

"Dad, I'm here," she whispers. She thinks she sees his eyelids flutter, acknowledging her words.

"Nas, how is he?" Asha walks in, her eyes scanning Bashir, "Is he going to be OK?"

"I don't know yet. I haven't had a chance to ask. I haven't even seen a nurse since I arrived."

"It's these damn cut-backs, you know. The staff are probably too busy. I'll go see if I can find someone."

"Yeah, can you go get a nurse? Oh, and I need you to make some calls for me too."

"No problem. I'll be back in a minute."

Later, after visiting hours are over, Nasreen sits with her father through the night, her mind aimlessly shifting between her father, right here, right now, lying in his hospital bed, and the memories pulling her three floors up, and two years into the past, back to her mother.

Chapter 29

NASREEN SITS ON HER couch, Id purring beside her. She unwraps the crinkly wrap from a new photo album. Its pages are blank, plastic, expectant. From her knapsack, she finds the photos she has just picked up from the drugstore, new and old photos from an undeveloped roll she had almost forgotten inside her camera some time ago.

A week earlier, she and Asha brought Bashir home from the hospital. Nasreen had a bag ready so that she could stay with him a few days and at the last minute, decided to pack her camera. Her father's departure from the hospital seemed like a strangely appropriate time for picture-taking, a Kodak-worthy moment. With no extra rolls of film, she was relieved to find that there were still a few exposures left in the camera.

Her father smiled obligingly for her. Perhaps he also felt that his return home after two weeks in the cardiac unit was a celebratory event, or maybe he was too tired to argue with the girls' insistence that he pose for them. Asha took two photos of Bashir and Nasreen in his room and a friendly nurse took a picture of all three of them in the hospital lobby. The camera signalled the end of the roll when Asha snapped father and daughter at the front doors of their house in Mississauga. Nasreen hopes that this last photo got developed.

Nasreen opens the photofinishing paper envelope and studies the first few shots. They are of Nasreen's last birthday, taken at a restaurant in the neighbourhood. Mona, Asha, and a few other friends sit around Nasreen, waving wine glasses or forks at the photographer, who must have been Connie. Then there is a photo of Nasreen with her mouth open, as though she is yelling something to Connie. Nasreen tries to recall what she might have been trying to say. What had she been feeling that evening? Were they getting along that night, or was there tension? She can't remember. She flips hurriedly through the rest of the birthday photos and then she finds her father's homecoming pictures.

She opens a photo album and places her birthday pictures carefully inside, four to a page, in the order in which she guesses they were taken. Even though she doesn't like looking at them, she feels that they deserve a place within the album; they are a part of her history. She even keeps one of Connie.

Then, turning the page, she arranges the most recent photos in the album. She likes that all four fit on the same page. First are the two from the hospital room, then the lobby photo and last, there she is, standing with her father in front of the Mississauga bungalow. Her arm is linked in his, supporting some of his weight as they stand in the cold December wind waiting for Asha to push the button and the shutter to fall.

Shaffiq is alone in the apartment, the television on, a talk show blaring in the background. He barely notices the jeering and cheering studio audience. His attentions are focused on Salma's old photo album, the one she recently relocated from her trunk in the bedroom to a place on the living room bookshelf, right beside his mirrored elephant. He wondered about this album for years, saw glimpses of it at the bottom of her trunk when she opened it to search for something else. Despite his curiousity, he never invaded Salma's privacy to look inside.

But today he takes it off the bookshelf, carrying it to the couch and setting it upon his lap. With a deep inhale of expectation, he flips through its pages, traveling through Salma's younger days and then lingering long on the photo he has both hoped and dreaded to find. He peers closely at the snapshot, then turns on a lamp to have a better look. There she is, his Salma, looking younger but really very much the same as now, standing with three other women in Lonavala. She showed him the photo years ago, but its meaning evaded him back then. She told him that they were a few friends on vacation at a hill station. Now he knows the truth.

He stares at the photo until his brain begins to feel foggy. And then his detective-mind returns, focused, mindful, and observant. He steps toward the bookshelf and retrieves the photo of Nasreen and Connie from the Gandhi book. He places them side by side, studying first the picture of Salma and Raj, then the shot of Nasreen and Connie. And then he looks at Raj again. And then he sees it: his Salma, held by the devoted, adoring gaze of her first love. For the first time in well over two years, he cries, fat teardrops pooling on the plastic covered pages of Salma's old photo album.

Chapter 30

"HULLO, NASREEN? It's your father."

"Hi Dad, you know, you don't have to say that. I know your voice by now."

"Yes, I suppose so," he chuckles, "Force of habit. Look, I have something to tell you. I hope it doesn't upset you too much, but I've made quite a big decision." There is silence, the sound of her listening and waiting. He continues, "Nasreen, I've decided to sell the house. It's much too big for me now. It is meant for a family to live in, not just an old guy like me."

"Oh," she replies, considering his words, thinking that they don't sound unreasonable, or surprising, or upsetting at all, "Of course, that makes sense to me, Dad."

"You know, I'll wait a little while. The doctor says that I should hold off on anything strenuous for another month or so," he pauses and then says proudly, "Dr. Stokes says that I already am doing too much walking, but I can't help it. I'm so bored. At least I have the computer. What would I do without that?"

"You'd go crazy, I'm sure," she says, laughing with him.

"I just bought a new digital camera. Did I tell you?"

"No, you didn't. I guess you need a new toy, being so housebound."

"Yes, I do. I'll send you some photos I took this week. I snapped some of the icicles forming on the side of the house. They turned out very well. Almost artistic," he says laughing, self-consciously. "So then, this decision – selling the house – it doesn't upset you?"

"No, not really. I mean, I have some sentimentality about it, after all, it's where I grew up, but you know, it's not really my home anymore. And anyway, it actually seems like a good idea for you to let it go."

"I'm thinking that I will buy something smaller, I only need two bedrooms at the most, one for sleeping and one for my office. I was thinking, if you were interested in this," he hesitates, then, as though choosing his words gingerly, he says, "perhaps we could buy a duplex together, or something like that, you know, in the city near your work, with separate units so we could be near each other, but still have our privacy. Investing in real estate would be good for you, Nasreen." He starts to speak faster and she imagines his pulse quickening with his words, "you've been paying your landlord's mortgage for too long, in my opinion. And well, it would be good for me to see you more often, not that I would bother you too much, I would respect your privacy and all that –" He doesn't hear her at first when she cuts in. "Sorry, what did you say?"

"I said maybe, Dad. That might be a good idea. We'd have to talk more about it for me to decide for sure, but I think maybe it wouldn't be a bad idea. I could use a move too."

"Oh, well, that's great. Let's think about that then. I'd really like that." There is an awkward pause that Nasreen can't bear to leave uninterrupted.

"And what about our trip to India? Did you find out if the cancellation insurance covered us?"

"Yes, they did honour it. We can still go. But maybe not until next fall. You probably have used up most of your vacation time anyway for this year, right?" He says this with an apologetic tone.

"Mostly. I think I used up about three week's worth in total," she says, calculating the time in her head.

"I appreciate you taking so much time off to stay with me in the hospital and then at home. I hope you know that."

"I do…. You know, the time off work was good for me too. With the exception of the first couple of days at the hospital, it was almost a nice change of pace for me. You aren't very hard to look after," she says, her voice light. "But I probably can't go to India until I've built up some more vacation time."

"I want to fully recover and then move first, anyway. Home can wait … I mean, India can wait…. Funny how I still call it home. I don't know if it's really accurate to call India my home anymore."

"Yeah, I never understood how you called it home. It's been so long since you left there."

"I suppose my generation will always be immigrants, will always long for the mother land. Your generation is a different story all together. You schooled here. Grew up here."

"Well, we'll always be seen as immigrants in this country, won't we? Where's home then, Dad? Mississauga? The house?"

"Maybe. I never really thought about it. If your mother were still alive, I would say so. I am not really sure because, when she was alive, she also thought of India as her home." He inhales, exhales. "Nasreen, where's home for you? Do you still think of this house that way?"

"No, not the house. Not for a long time, I guess since I moved out. But my apartment isn't really so homey either. I mean, it's where I live, and I like it, but home? I haven't really thought about it."

"How about when Connie was there, was your apartment home to you?"

"Yeah, for a while. Yes, I suppose so. Geez, Dad, this is a deep conversation."

"Yes, well, I guess the heart attack has turned me into a bit of a philosopher."

"I suppose illness will do that to you."

"More than illness. That was a brush with death. If the paper guy hadn't come just then, if I hadn't been late with my payment, if he hadn't had a cell phone with him –"

"Yeah, I don't like to think about that, Dad. It was a close call. I don't like to think of you all alone having a heart attack. I hope you gave him a really good tip," she says, breaking the tension.

"Are you kidding? I'm thinking about including him in my will! But getting back to philosophical matters, I believe we make home with the people we love. That's why this place isn't home anymore. You don't live here and your mother is gone. And your apartment isn't home anymore either now that Connie is gone. And that's why I think the two of us should find a house together."

"Yes, I guess that makes sense. Does that mean we are both emotionally homeless, Dad?" she says, wanting to deflect his lobbying.

"Well, yes. Hey, that is a very good way to put it. That's why you are the psychologist and I am the amateur philosopher. We both have places to live, but no real home."

"Hmmm. You might be right."

"So maybe then we can sit down together and talk about where we'd like to live, and then if we come to some agreement, I can contact a realtor," Bashir says, his voice hopeful.

Nasreen holds the phone tightly in her right hand, and takes in a deep breath while her father charges on, gushing out his ideas for housebuying. She thinks about the past few weeks she's spent with him after the heart attack, the surgery, and his recovery at home. While his body has been recuperating, his arteries unblocking, and his tissues regenerating, her heart has been mending itself too. There has been time for herself, for letting go of Connie, for missing her mother.

She considers what her decision might be, that she may say yes, or possibly turn him down, but for once, her Daughter Guilt is noticeably absent.

Chapter 31

SALMA COUNTS OUT CHANGE to a middle-aged woman and says mechanically, without looking up, "thanks, see you again." Her mood is not up for the superficial friendliness required for the job. She watches the woman's back as she exits and is grateful for the quiet of the empty store.

When she and Shaffiq heard the news that Asima's husband's cousin was able to hire Shaffiq as a bookkeeper, she was a little surprised at her reaction. She was not immediately thrilled. Yes, she celebrated with her husband and her daughters at a restaurant in Little India, eating *dhai puri* and *gulab jamuns*. She raised a toast of mango *lassi* for him, all the while really wanting to disappear, to go somewhere, be alone, and cry. *But you can't always do what you want when you have a husband and children, can you?*

The new job, this job that Shaffiq finally found after two long years in Toronto, holds the promise of permanent life in Canada. Now they can stay, will stay, have everything they need to stay. A part of her has always hoped that Shaffiq's terrible night shift job and her boring dry cleaner work would lead them to the only possible, rational conclusion about their big adventure in Canada; it would be a failure and they would have to return home. She held on tightly to this belief, even while she kept busy decorating their apartment, settling her children into school, acquiring the necessary ID, and finding work. But now things are working out for them and they will stay. Now they will be successful immigrants.

Shaffiq's new job has also allowed her to hatch a plan, one that she hadn't before really carefully considered, believing she would soon return to Bombay. The plan, worked out on the back of a drycleaning receipt and precise enough to satisfy an accountant, will allow her to go back to school to complete the courses she needs to compete for teaching jobs. In her mind she has temporarily converted The Girls' University Fund to the Salma University Fund, and in two years there should be enough saved to pay for it all. In two years. Something to wait for, something to hope for, but still two years away.

A young executive-type strolls into the store, the electronic door chime signaling his arrival. Salma takes his barely dirty shirts, writes out a receipt and sorts the laundry into appropriate bins to be taken away for cleaning. The customer leaves and she sighs. What's next for her? She spends the rest of the quiet afternoon remembering her life as a teacher in Bombay and thinking about first loves. Her mind lifts above Blue Dove Cleaners, drifts to Shaffiq's new nine-to-five job, flits to her first day back at teacher's college, and calculates a repayment plan to the Girls' University Fund.

For the last time in his life, Shaffiq loads his cleaning cart with matching bottles of aquamarine cleaning solvents. He checks whether he has enough large and small garbage bags and then locks the janitors' supply closet behind him. He pushes the cart to the elevators and then once inside, presses the second floor button. He steps out and heads for the men's washroom, begins his work. He discards two styrofoam cups left on the floor and a cigarette butted out in the sink. He notices an empty pill bottle that once belonged to Luis Lopez. He tosses it into the trash.

He then sprays the toilets, letting the harsh chemicals do most of the cleaning for him. He remembers when Ravi gave him that advice during his first week here, recalling how grateful he felt for the assistance, and later, for his friendship. As he flushes each toilet, he utters a little prayer for his friend, for the nervous son greeting a worried mother at Lester B. Pearson Airport tonight.

Shaffiq moves on to the women's washroom. He insisted on giving two weeks' notice before starting his new bookkeeping job because he wants to leave this place well. And, to Shaffiq, two weeks isn't so long to wait. After all, it took years to immigrate to Canada, an eternity to secure his janitor's job at the Institute, and then many more months to be considered at Quaid's cousin's factory. However, he is a little surprised to be feeling sentimental about his last night at the Institute. As he wipes down faucets and empties the garbage, he wonders how this evening will go: will it be a normal shift with an anti-climactic ending? Will anyone remember to say goodbye or miss him after he is gone?

He shakes his head at his foolishness. Surely this should be a night of unbridled celebration? Finally, he will have daytime employment in his field. He will share the same schedule with his family, joining them for breakfast and dinner, being able to read his girls bedtime stories. Perhaps now he and Salma will be able to grow close again, the way they were before they left India, before all the confusion happened with Nasreen Bastawala. As he leaves the women's washroom, he once again says a prayer, this time for his marriage.

As Shaffiq passes the second floor elevators, he hesitates a moment and then presses the "up" button. The elevator arrives, empty, waiting for him to board, but he doesn't move. The chimes ring and the doors close again.

Nasreen waits patiently for Shaffiq to round the corner and walk past her office, as he has done many times before. She knows that it's Shaffiq's last day at the hospital. He told her two weeks ago and she penned the date in red in her agenda book. Will he come to say goodbye? She hopes he won't intentionally avoid her tonight, allow this last day on the job, this ending, to happen without her. She checks her watch and waits a little longer.

As she works on her files, she is distracted by every little movement and sound in the hallway. She looks up each time and unsatisfied, returns to her work. She absentmindedly thinks about Salma and their last Gujarati class, when she got the call about her father's heart attack.

Of course, she hasn't seen Salma since then. With her father's poor health, the trip to India was cancelled and there was no immediate need for more Gujarati classes. And Nasreen has been too busy helping out her father anyway.

She considers going to find Shaffiq tonight, in case he doesn't come to say goodbye to her. She has a gift for him, something that she has wanted to give him since the last time they saw each other two weeks ago, something that would admit at least to them, that the shape of their relationship has altered. She nervously picks at her cuticles, and then smooths them down again. She peers out into the hallway, sees no one. But then after a few more minutes, he is there, with his cleaning cart, a plastic garbage bag in his hands, and a slight smile on his face.

"Hullo, Nasreen. Working late again I see. How are you?" He asks and she smiles back at him with a matching, tightly-contained smile.

"I'm good."

"And your father? Recovering well?"

"Still moving around slowly, but going to be fine. So how do you feel? This is your last night here. It's too bad that you're going so soon."

"Yes, well, it was time to go. I found a better job you know, and it is at least in the daytime and in my field."

"Yeah, that's good. I'll bet Salma will be pleased about that."

"Yes, it will be good for all of us."

"Well, I'm glad for you. But it's too bad that you won't be here anymore. I've enjoyed," she pauses, trying to find the right words, "meeting you."

"Yes. Me too. Maybe we will meet somewhere again. Who knows? The world is not so big. Maybe you and your father will rebook your trip and you'll take classes with Salma again?" She knows that he is saying this to be kind, to smooth away the layer of tension they both know lies beneath their words. She knows that Salma will likely never offer classes to her or Asha again. Maybe it's better that way, she thinks.

"We did have cancellation insurance. My father must've had a premonition about that. Maybe we'll go next year. I don't know. I do still need to learn Gujarati," she says, participating in his kindness.

Shaffiq bends down to reach for her garbage can. She gets to it first and hands it over to him. He tips it out into his bag. He notices that inside is an empty coffee cup and the crusts from what looks like a tuna sandwich.

"Thanks. Look, before you go. I have something to give you. Something I want you to have."

She reaches across the desk and grabs the small gold box. She fingers the glossy surface a moment and then thrusts it at him, feeling shy now. "Here, please take this. I want you to have it. It's a good-bye gift." He hesitates a moment, wondering about her intention. Then, he regards how she holds the box out to him, sees her brown fingers clutching the sides tightly. He looks into her eyes and sees within them a secret shared between them. Her eyes are kind, friendly, understanding.

"I thought you might like it. I saw you looking it at a few weeks ago when you were in here cleaning. My parents bought it for me years ago when we last were in Bombay and I wondered it might remind you of India." She smiles warmly at him.

"Thanks," he says, "it is very nice." He could say more, but decides against it.

There is a twinkle in her eye and so Shaffiq allows his own eyes to rest a moment on hers. He takes the box from her as though it is the most precious thing that he could ever own and sets it on top of his cleaning cart. Nasreen watches as he moves down the long hallway, rounds a corner, and then disappears out of sight.

Acknowledgements

No book is ever written alone. I feel incredibly lucky to be surrounded by a community of family and friends who have nurtured me and this novel over the last few years.

Thanks to my first readers who I (very tentatively) passed these pages to and who gave me critical feedback and encouragement: Maria Gould, Samantha Haywood, Amina Ally, Esther Vise and Silvana Bazet. I'm also very grateful to my editor, Luciana Ricciutelli, who offered significant insights and helped me with final revisions.

To all of my family and communities who root me in the world, and who inspire my characters—a big thanks. Special appreciation goes to my father, Shamoon, my sister Fariya and my Aunty Rashida (for honouring my creativity), and to my Aunty Roshan (who helped me choose names).

To the past and present members of my writing group—Teenah Edan, Saira Suberi, Nuzhat Abbas, Leah Piepzna-Samarasinha, Julia Gonsalvez—I owe you a debt of gratitude for helping me grow as a writer.

A huge thank-you to the "circle of agents" who support me in various ways: Nupur Gogia, Kristyn Wong-Tam, Shoshana Pollack, Anke Alspach, Anju Gogia, Michael Pastore, Jake Pyne, Ginny Santos, and Hershel Russell.

And finally, to my partner, Judith Nicholson, who has been a constant support since the beginning of this project—this is for you.